OKAY DAYS

Jenny Mustard

sceptre

First published in Great Britain in 2023 by Sceptre
An imprint of Hodder & Stoughton
An Hachette UK company

1

Copyright © Mustard Stories Ltd 2023

A CIP catalogue record for this title is available from the British Library

Hardback ISBN 9781399713467
Trade Paperback ISBN 9781399713474
eBook ISBN 9781399713498

Typeset in Sabon Mt Std by Manipal Technologies Limited

Printed and bound in Great Britain by Clays Ltd, Elcograf S.p.A.

Hodder & Stoughton policy is to use papers that are natural, renewable
and recyclable products and made from wood grown in sustainable forests.
The logging and manufacturing processes are expected to conform
to the environmental regulations of the country of origin.

Hodder & Stoughton Ltd
Carmelite House
50 Victoria Embankment
London EC4Y 0DZ

www.sceptrebooks.co.uk

For Mormis
and for David

PART I

180 DAYS LEFT

Sam

We are in the bathtub. I lie on top of Luc with my back on his stomach. The water is too hot so I ask him to close his knees together, push me upwards. He does. Now I am only half covered by the water, my stomach and breasts and thighs slowly cooling. This scorched back, chilled front should be manageable, an overall equilibrium. Still I am on edge. I hum while he thinks.

'The Fifth Element,' he says. I want to turn around and interpret his face because today he sounds off.

'Looper,' I say instead.

We are playing the Bruce Willis game. His turn, and he is taking it seriously. I will likely lose, only having one more movie in stock before I run out. *12 Monkeys.* One of the two hundred VHS tapes my cousin Diwa recorded from the TV when she was a kid. Some of them starting five minutes into the film or with ad breaks every twenty minutes. Sugar Puffs, Head & Shoulders, Chiquita Banana. Each videotape with a neat title written on the spine. Each in alphabetical order.

Halfway submerged and I am still too hot. I feel my cheeks flush, a pulse in my temples. I am wearing yesterday's makeup and I don't think it is covering my feverish face. The foundation is only meant to last twelve hours and I am pushing twenty-four. I want to look in the mirror.

It is midday soon and we are both hungover. This morning his eyes were droopy and mine puffed up.

'Sin City,' Luc says. I let him win even though I have *12 Monkeys* because I want to get out of the tub now.

Dried and dressed, I sit at the kitchen table. A small round antique piece by the window, maybe mahogany, I'm no expert. This is Diwa's North London flat and I am only staying for the summer. The sofa, kitchen table, large furniture, are all hers. The bed is my own. I dragged her hard mattress and cast-iron bed frame to the narrow walk-in closet. Flipped on their sides, they just fit. Then I bought a memory foam mattress, my most adult purchase ever, even if on sale. It is on the floor, no frame, and this changes the whole mood of the room. I worry about mould so I flip it over every two weeks. When she comes back in September I will let Diwa keep it.

Luc opens the fridge and grips a bottle of chilled coffee. Ice cubes. Glass straws from the third drawer. Whisking thick soy milk in a bowl, his wrists tense. There are fine hairs on his forearms. He sticks his tongue out a bit when he concentrates, moves it around. I find this charming so I don't mention it because I don't want him to stop. He pours the froth over the ice cubes, then cold coffee on top, then cinnamon.

We have only been sleeping together for eight nights but this is already a routine. We wake up and shower, or take a bath on days off, then iced coffee and videos of sea animals at the kitchen table. I like the manta rays best. He is more a seahorse type of person.

He is beautiful. I like his body. It is medium, not short or tall, not hairy or naked. Slim, defined, but not overly muscular, like a person who looks after himself. His face I like the best. Unfitting his supervised body, he has a rascal's face, asymmetrical with mischief written across it. He looks at me and I feel naughty without any reason to, like we share a perpetual in-joke whatever the scene, whoever our target. I often don't know what exactly we are smiling at.

We flip through yesterday's tube station newspaper and agree the world is doomed. And today his rascal smile is absent. He rubs his eyes. 'Let's skip forward to the personals yeah?'

We read them aloud, first him then me. We try to amuse each other with silly voices, which isn't even that funny, it's more to have a thing that's exclusively ours. One lady is looking for a young tall man to babysit her cat during her quarterly golf trips. Why young and tall, she doesn't say. Maybe the cat has a type.

Today his personal ad read seems half-hearted, like an AI customer-service bot programmed to sound friendly. Just slightly off. I tell myself I am imagining his lukewarm performance, but my nerves have been present since wake-up because he slept with his back turned and didn't touch me before rising. We seem off-kilter.

My stomach rumbles.

'Let's go for lunch,' I say.

'Yeah, sure. What do you fancy?'

'Bibimbap?'

'The place by the canal?'

'Yes, and then we could stop by that shop you like on the way home.'

He looks up. I regret using the word home. It is my home, I don't want him thinking I refer to it as our home. And really it is Diwa's home anyway. Semantics are too delicate at this early stage. I constantly mess up because I am a messy person and sometimes when he falls asleep I lie awake next to him wondering how he feels about my faux pas. I much prefer falling asleep first.

Out of eight nights since that first time, we have spent six together. Twice he has gone back to his place in Hackney, to do I don't know what. Both times I asked and both times he grinned and said, 'I have to sleep at some point don't I.' Both times I took it as a vague but irrefutable insult. He needs to change his clothes I guess, or water his plant if he has any. But spending the night away to water plants feels like a sexual slight any way you turn it.

I am running out of nice underwear. Next time he waters his plant, I will go buy some. I have to call Diwa to borrow some money, two hundred at least. All this eating out and drinking out and going dancing is hurting my already quasi-depleted bank account.

Diwa has money. She is not rich, but comfortable. Six years my senior, she is very time efficient and also good-looking, like a fifty-something ballet teacher who used to be a prima ballerina before a tragic knee injury. All tight hair knots and sharp elbows and soft knitted dresses over small breasts. She looks stern but she's not. Diwa has a large, disproportionate laugh. She booms. And she likes worthless nineties high school comedies about pot and house parties and the ugly geek winning the gorgeous girl in the end. Or the ugly geek becoming the gorgeous girl if it's that type of movie. Films so politically dated I can't enjoy them and it's times like these I can tell she is older.

Diwa is spending the summer at her girlfriend Milly's house in Greece. It is early July and I can stay until September twelfth, when I will go back to Stockholm. I have my flat and my job waiting, although autumn in Sweden is not my favourite.

Luc and I have not yet discussed tonight's sleeping arrangement and there is a turmoil like a lump of uncooked pasta high up in my stomach that I know won't go away before this has been decided. But I don't bring it up.

It feels strange, being this careful. Usually I am too blunt if anything, shooing the boy home after a night together, not willing to exhaust myself with the myriad dating rules. Balancing tone of voice, choice of words, body language. Showcasing my unique personality while staying on the cute side of eccentric. It is too much for me, all this calculation. Instead I houdini, sneak out, and call things off before they start. But Luc, I don't want to shoo him off. I don't balance tone with him. Yet today he is making me anxious. And here I am balancing.

Across the kitchen table, Luc looks clean in a heavy white t-shirt. With his moist hair back like this, his cheekbones are high enough to cause vertigo. He likes clothes and he dresses well so I make an effort, alternating boyish blazers with revealing outfits and lots of lipstick. I want to figure out what he prefers but so far he seems pleased either way.

'You're so cool,' he told me on night number four, walking home drunk after a quick club visit. A patch of grass on our right, the canal on our left, my heels click-clacking on the tarmac. Fresh cut grass and pungent canal water mixed in a curious aroma cocktail.

The sky was black, but summer had arrived so I wasn't cold in my camisole. It was so low-cut I worried my nipples had slipped out on the dance floor, but if they had, Luc didn't mention it.

'I'm cool?' I said.

'Yeah I don't know, you're good at like, presenting yourself.'

'That's a strange compliment.' I laughed a little, took his hand in mine and swung it back and forth.

'Yeah it is, I guess. I mean.'

'Go on then.'

'So, you dance nice and you dress well, and you're good at small talk. You're like the least awkward person I know.'

'You're drunk.'

'So are you.'

'But thank you, never heard that one before. Points for originality.'

He would sometimes give these unorthodox compliments, mirroring me back to myself. This innocent generosity caught me off guard, made me unable to mask my delight. I was soaring all the way to the flat, sashaying, making bold jokes. He laughed and said, oh you're cocky now. When we got home, we had intense sex. I wanted to live up to the hype. Not sure of his opinion, but to me it set a new standard. The conscious awareness of my body faded and I didn't make sexy faces or sounds. Instead I kind of overtook him, like the sex version of eating without chewing. We pushed ourselves until we'd had enough, on our backs, staring at the ceiling, panting. His hand burning my ribcage. My thighs heavy on the mattress. Too tired to talk.

Later I put on a short waffle robe and went to the kitchen. He was browsing films while I cut strawberries into squares to eat with ice cream. Early July and warm weather finally. I put ice cream bowls and strawberries and teacups on a round tray and carried it through to the living room. My naked feet made creaky noises tipping on the parquet, the wood cool and yielding. I was still drunk and a bit lightheaded. It was like the phantom waves through your body hours after you disembark a boat. I felt the waves of Luc. Phantom sex.

We started watching *The Handmaiden* at 4am. Once finished, the sky was eyeshadow blue outside the open windows and seagulls shrieked on the rooftop. We liked the film so much we watched it again.

Then I went straight to work smelling like Luc and tasting like alcohol.

•

But today it will be our ninth night and I still don't know if he will spend it with me. I don't bring it up and I get annoyed with myself, timidity not being my modus operandi.

We eat Korean food outside, the murmur of voices from the restaurants bouncing off the canal water makes for perfect white noise. I record it on my phone for later when back in Stockholm but then I remember I don't want to go back to Stockholm so I abort the recording and delete it.

We are lazy, the sun benign and easy-going. Sunday early afternoon and we are nursing a pint each, neither of us having any responsibilities. My real job is at an attitudey Stockholm PR firm but for the summer I am doing a placement at one of the largest marketing agencies in London, the workplace of my uni friend Tabatha who got me the job by talking me up. My Stockholm manager generously agreed to my leave of absence, both for the added value to my credentials but also because it won't cost them a krona. The agency placement is earning me an intern's salary. It is not enough for both life and rent so Diwa says I can pay her retrospectively. I doubt she will reinforce this payment plan but I will as soon as I am reinstated to my Stockholm cubicle.

I studied marketing just like most preoccupied twenty-somethings too distracted to make career decisions, a why-not box-ticking following two restless gap years. But why I also did the masters I can't really say. I guess I got a taste for the topic, the intellectually challenging puzzle-solving aspect. Also that the programme was at a London uni didn't hurt. Two whole glorious years of walking the streets up and down, of speaking English, of East London clubs and South London food. Hours of smoking with Finn and pestering Tabatha and not once thinking about what will come next. What actually did come next was moving home to my first employment in Stockholm, which was fine but not interest-ing so I transferred to my current firm within a year. I've been there a year and some months now but once I am back this September I might start eyeing the ads because my cubi-cle does seem somewhat lacklustre after a summer at the London agency.

It is strange thinking that another two years have passed since my masters graduation because being back in London this summer, working with Tabatha, smoking with Finn, it feels like the years in Stockholm were just a blip. A glitch in the space-time continuum. And suddenly I am somehow twenty-eight.

Luc works in a boutique with thirty-two pieces of cloth-ing on the racks. The shop is called Darling. Ironically I assume, but in exactly what way I'm not sure. He fits in there with his modern monochrome way of dressing. It is his old part-time job from his student years and being back is highly temporary he tells me. When not working, he is applying for mechanical engineering jobs, for which he has a bunch of degrees, the latest finished mere weeks ago. He doesn't look it. Although what do I know about the appearance markers of a mechanical engineer.

He wants to up the odds of the planet by refining sophis-ticated eco solutions, like the unmanned solar aeroplanes bringing free internet to the world's entire population. In a hectic voice he talks about the education provided by the internet as a human right, a necessity for achieving informa-tion equality. He likes the win-wins, where green engineering intersects with politics beyond environmental sustainability. I find all this extremely hot.

Condensation runs down the outside of the beer glass and hits my finger deliciously cold. I kick off my sandal and pinch Luc's calf with my toes. It is meant to be sweet but he doesn't reciprocate and he is wearing sunglasses so I can't see his eyes. Still no rascal smile.

I feel too full now. Nauseous.

'You ready to go?' he asks.

'We haven't finished our drinks,' I say, thinking of the dent this lunch is making in the two hundred I haven't even borrowed from Diwa yet. But I can tell he is done so I wave for the bill.

'Should we go to the shop?' I ask. He says sure and stands up, fishes for his wallet in his pocket. I say this one's on me, as if paying for bibimbap means he owes me staying the night.

'You sure?' he says. I pay the bill.

The shop is actually a café. A bar in the middle where you order. Around the walls are books, magazines, DVDs, records. Curtained windows creating a perpetual dusk. It is frou-frou but we like it. They have a good selection and I find the analogue content romantic. There is an old listening booth in the corner, like a phone booth but with headphones instead of a telephone. On night five, a Wednesday, we crammed both of us in there and listened to Dinah Washington and Da Brat and Dolly Parton. We kissed in the booth for a long time, until a member of staff knocked on the glass and told us to cut it out. We laughed at that, cut it out, and sometimes now say it to each other.

That night, night five, before going to sleep, we talked about bad dates we'd been on and I told him that my relationship history was about quantity not quality. Short and sweet, nothing too serious. He didn't seem that surprised, which I wasn't sure how to unpack, and the next morning he went to work and then straight home to water his plant and didn't text me until late. I wondered if this had somehow changed his opinion of me. Like he was thinking oh she's one of those people, whatever a relationship-inexperienced person was supposed to be like. Night six he spent in his flat but night seven we went dancing and got silly drunk. Neither of us mentioned previous relationships so maybe it was not that important.

I get drunk most nights now and I like the sensation, it's very close to feeling free. And we have got a good setup, Luc and I. Two months before I leave London for Stockholm, many days together with no acute responsibilities and one empty flat. But today Luc is not smiling so maybe we won't have many days in the empty flat. I am likely being paranoid. I very much hope I am.

After Luc has looked at the menu and asked about ingredients, I order us both takeaway bubble tea which is the right thing to order at a place this frou-frou. Black bubbles for me, green for Luc. They are four fifty each and although ridiculous this is a good sum to add to the symbolic debt he owes me. He browses the DVDs but I know he won't buy any because he has nothing to play them on. He just looks at the covers and notes what to watch later.

He slurps his bubble tea. 'Cut it out,' I say a bit too loudly and nudge him with my hip. He smiles but has no clever retort. I wonder for a second if anything could be achieved by shaking him hard.

I go over to the book section and pretend-read blurbs. I glance over at him. His back is turned with his head tilted forward over the American New Wave section, the strain in his neck making the tendons visible from where I stand. His arms are pale, his neck-hair soft. Today is only night number nine and already I know what his skin will smell like if I walk over and kiss it. But I don't. I pretend-read blurbs and chew bubble tea tapioca.

Now my back is turned to him and he asks if I am ready to go. He doesn't sneak up. He doesn't slide his arms around my ribcage.

At the tube station near my street, he stops.

'Think I'll get the tube home probably,' he says.

'Water the plant?'

'Sorry?'

'Nothing.' I look away. The uncooked pasta turmoil in my stomach is pressing its way upwards. Now in my throat, I worry it will reach my eyes.

'So might not see you for a few days,' he says. 'Got to work and wash some clothes and go see Dad and that.'

'I don't mind you in dirty clothes,' I say and pull his t-shirt. 'Or you could borrow mine if you want.'

'That's a nice offer. But have to decline this time probably. Maybe meet up at the weekend. Saturday or something?'

The weekend. Five nights from now. This is Luc dumping me.

Night nine will not be spent with Luc. Night nine, I will be in bed analysing, every text up for scrutiny. This is not something I am proud of.

He moves closer and kisses me. Closed mouth, too quick to enjoy. Our last kiss and I didn't enjoy it.

He turns away and skips down the stairs to the station. And that back, that head, those tiny soft neck-hairs disappear underground.

I walk home, stunned. Tiptoe barefoot on the parquet. Sit at the kitchen table with a glass of water in front of me that I don't drink. Absentmindedly flip through yesterday's newspaper. Then I go to the bedroom, remove the bed linen, and flip the mattress over. It lands with a bang. And I get over myself.

I text him.

12 Monkeys.

He replies.

The Whole Nine Yards.

164 DAYS LEFT

Lucas

She sits down next to me and hands me an earbud. I push it in and she scrolls through her playlists looking for a song. It is hot in the tube, I hope my armpits don't have sweat stains but since there isn't anything I could do about it anyway I don't look.

Our tube rides have become a thing, just like many things have lately become a thing, maximising our short time together into lots of memories and special she-and-me traditions. Although not so smart to get involved with someone you know will leave, we talked about it and decided to not be smart. We sit skin-close, her thigh warm through the layers of fabric, my hand on her leg. When she touches my neck the hairs on my head stand up and I close my eyes, dazed.

The song starts. Upbeat drums, busy piano. I recognise the intro but can't place it even though it's a famous song and really I should know this one. I smile knowingly at Sam as if to say, ah this one, good choice.

Then Nina Simone starts singing o-o-h child and I'm thankful for her recognisable voice.

This is our special tube thing. We sit down or lean against each other, she gives me an earbud and plays me a song from her various playlists. Sam calls these rides my musical education, which is made no less embarrassing by being a joke because it is also accurate. She knows a lot. And she is flippant about it, doesn't seem bothered by my sometimes shocking gaps in knowledge. But it bothers me. It makes me feel like I am on the outside of a colourful aquarium looking in, and even if invited I wouldn't know how to breathe water anyway.

I dress as if I know about music in a synthy kind of way, trousers cut above the ankles and shoes with tractor soles. This confuses people into talking to me about fringe sub-genres I know nothing about.

Sam asked me a music question, the first time I saw her after all those years apart. We had only met once before when we were seventeen eighteen and I had no idea if she remembered. The night I saw her again, Sam's friend Tabatha had a party in her substantial South London flat. I was looking in the fridge for something without sugar to drink, when a voice asked what I thought of the song.

'Should be your type of thing by the looks of it,' she said.

I closed the fridge door and there she was. Impossible yes, but definitely her. Years later, older, leaner, but her. Arms folded, raised eyebrow, sexy. Her amused expression made the overall effect inviting despite the crossed arms. Her black hair was thick and messy.

'Actually I'm not sure I've heard this one before,' I said, searching her face for signs of recognition.

She raised her other eyebrow too. 'You don't know it? Seriously?'

'Can I get you a drink?' I said, opening the fridge again.

'I'm Sam,' she said.

So, okay, she didn't recognise me.

Holding my hand out for her to shake, I said, 'Luc.'

She ignored my hand and moved in for a cheek kiss. I wasn't ready for it, didn't get her intention, so I pulled my head back, then realised my mistake, pushed my head forward again and kissed the air, our cheeks smacking together hard. She laughed. 'Easy there.'

'Yeah let me try that again,' I said and placed my cheek on hers, softly, moved my hand to the back of her arm. She kissed the air and I let go.

'I'll have a beer,' she said.

We went into the large living room where Tabatha and other people from their group talked loudly about something. Sam clinked my beer bottle with her beer bottle and went over to them. I found my friends Henry and Patti in another corner, discussing work things. Henry stood stiff as if wearing a spine brace like always, noodle thin and posture oblivious. Patti was his polar opposite. Round, dark, slouchy.

'Mum asked if you're coming on Sunday?' Henry said.

'Yeah, I'll come over.' I was invited to lunch. His family lived close to my dad in Edgware and Henry and I grew up together. The Perlmans were tucked in a small semi-detached, his many family members a loud contrast to my own diminished bloodline.

Patti and Henry started comparing flat deposits and their associated anxieties and although I wasn't drunk I couldn't focus on the conversation. I kept looking over at Sam and sometimes she looked back.

My initial overwhelm of joy started changing into lowkey dismay at her not recognising me until finally there was almost no joy left at all. I ached for her to come over, talk to me more. But she was the one who had approached me by the fridge. If I wanted something to happen, I had to do the something, it was my turn. I drew a hand through my hair and rolled up the sleeves of my sweater. It was made of navy cotton, tucked into navy chinos. I had thought this a good look at home but now I had doubts, hoping she didn't think I'd tried to look French or whatever. She was wearing a dark brown shirt, unbuttoned low. It looked satiny like chocolate. The music changed, a slow lofi beat. I walked over.

Before I changed my mind I said, 'Do you want to dance?' and held out my hand, even though it was so not the thing to ask at a party like this. She stared at me as if not understanding, leaving my hand awkward mid-air. It was mortifying really. 'Yeah I was asking if you like, want to dance with me?' I saw a moment of recognition in her face but maybe I imagined it.

'No but thanks for the offer.' She grinned. 'This is Tabatha and Finn,' she said and nodded at her friends in turn.

'Yeah, we know each other from before don't we Finn, but nice to meet you Tabatha,' I said, surprised to already sound recovered from the rejection. I was sure they would make fun of me later, though maybe it was worth it because now here I was, talking to her.

Finn was a graphic designer who sometimes did work for Henry and Patti's office, and the few times we'd met, he'd only been friendly. He talked with hands flying in Cockney spiced with Hongkongese and his face was animated as if made of stretchy clay. Tabatha seemed another brand altogether, her face clay dried stiff. Sam looked at me and her eyes were magnets and I stopped noticing things about Tabatha and Finn.

An hour later I was searching the fridge for another drink when she took my hand and I followed her outside. She lit a cigarette. I declined when she offered me the pack.

'Can't bring myself to roll my own,' she said, holding the smoke in. 'I know it's the economic thing to do but back home no one does. And I'm too impatient anyway.'

'Back in Stockholm?' I asked and bit my tongue, not supposed to know this about her.

'My accent that thick?' She snorted. 'Do. you think. I talk. a lot. like. a Scandi. navian?' she said in a shocking exaggeration of the staccato Nordic lilt.

'Wow.'

'You find it sexy? Surprised I'm not all blonde and blue-eyed?'

'Yes. And no.' I nudged my head upwards. 'Do it again.'

She laughed. 'I'm leaving now I think. Do you want to come with? I've got wine at home.' Her face was so straight you'd never guess she'd just made me an indecent invitation. This was about to become my favourite trait of hers, her deadpan treatment of feelings. Even hard-to-talk-about feelings. As if to her, honesty wasn't difficult at all. Unlike me who sometimes couldn't even tell myself if I was lying or telling the truth. The chronic genetic ambiguity of the English.

She chattered non-stop on the bus. I took her hand when we got off. She looked for her keys in her bag outside her apartment building and unlocked the door. Before going inside, she turned back to me.

'You sure about this, mister?' she asked, that amused eyebrow again.

'Yes, definitely. Why?'

'Just checking if we know each other well enough yet. Or if you'd find it, you know, Off-Putting.'

And with that, I knew that she knew. I took two steps and kissed her. Her shoulders shook from laughter.

'I didn't think you recognised me,' I said.

'I didn't know if you recognised me.'

'I did. At once.' And with my left hand I smoothed her messy hair.

•

I graduated again last month. This time a one-year course in environmental engineering. I had decided to go back to university after my masters because although there were decent jobs for mechanical engineers, the decent green jobs were few and the competition extreme.

Before, when my money worries had made me over-refresh my bank balance and my job applications rarely moved past the thank-you-but emails, I had caved and taken a position at a pharmaceutical company. It was soul-ripping working there, walking the hushed corridors before going home to google the tax scandals and unethical practices. Illegal testing, animal abuse, exploitation of third-world communities. I couldn't afford another uni stint but Dad used some of the inheritance to put me through the environmental engineering course and now I was back sending applications for the green jobs. So far only thank-you-buts. I would just keep at it until I found something, hopefully by autumn. One more summer spent in the clothes shop, Darling. I could handle it probably.

Nowhere else had I reached the level of boredom as when tending that shop, stocking so few items I had nothing to tidy or fold or hang. Hours went by without a single customer. I wasn't allowed to use my phone.

I suspected the severe boredom had unhinged my brain chemicals somehow, making me care more about things than other people would. Like waking up hungover bothered me, the self-abuse aspect of it. Some of my friends would still sleep away most of the weekend, waking up late and eating fried things, only to go out again. I have never been into fried food but even staying out late had at this point lost its appeal because sleeping in ruined the whole flow of the day, making me stress to catch up on whatever I had missed.

Though somehow I didn't worry about hangovers with Sam, and it didn't seem to worry her at all. Our first week together had been thrilling but borderline alarming, how willing I was to abandon my routine. So I tried slowing down, not sleeping at hers every night. But spending time on my own hadn't cooled my feelings even slightly. It just made me feel isolated, like turning off an analogue TV, the broadcast continuing whether I watched it or not. So I embraced it, two more months with Sam in London and I would spend as much of it with her as she'd let me. Soon we would get real jobs and real partners and own furniture.

I wasn't unhappy with my flatmates. Still, what I wanted was a place of my own. It felt done, this living like a student, but I had spent so much time studying there wasn't even an early-stage deposit in my account. If I got a decent job this autumn I would give it half a year's stinginess and then rent my own place, whatever my savings got me. It could be tiny in zone four I didn't even care. And then I would start growing that mortgage deposit. These two months with Sam were final orders. Our last irresponsible summer, the deep breath before the plunge.

It still hadn't sunk in that two years ago Sam and I did our masters at the same time, in the same city, graduating the same week. Though not allowed, when bored at Darling I would often stand behind the till and look at photos of Sam. Her instagram was chaotic but with a frantic sort of aesthetic. Half-emptied pasta plates and smoking with friends. I thought of the randomness of us meeting. She had been studying in London for two years, her friend Finn knowing Henry, and yet we had not met once until a couple of weeks ago. This was hard to grasp. I imagined alternative scenarios where we met year one, year two. And I wondered about near misses. Brushing shoulders in coffee shops. Reading the same news article on the same day and reacting the same way to it. Both invited to a party and then one of us not going. Synchronised retweeting. Kissing other people at the same time. I distracted myself coming up with scenarios like these until 7pm when I could close the shop and in real life go see her and hear about her day.

My masters graduation had been two days before Sam's. It was exactly as expected. July weather, sunny since dawn. The gown and hat ill-fitting. My dad proud, but unable to express it. My mum, still dead.

Dad was okay, we were fine. As a single parent, he had never given me a hard time or shouted at me or been strict. But we didn't know each other that well. I was lucky to have found my way into Henry's family. Although it was something you shouldn't have to find. It's something you're supposed to be born with, isn't it.

Sometimes I wished Dad had been more strict. With Mum around my life had structure, always tea at six, always homecooked and talk about the day. No TV or mates before homework. I was a kid way more desensitised to broccoli than my peers. But after she died, neither Dad nor I could stomach sitting down at the kitchen table at six. Anything reminding us of her was off the menu. Instead Dad would heat something frozen, the beiger the better, to eat in front of the TV. Talking about the day became anecdotal, perfunctory, and it seemed like he didn't have the heart to enforce the homework-before-friends protocol. For more than a year, I lived off fish fingers and potato wedges and pan pizza. Our everyday became liquid, lost its shape without Mum there as anchor.

Dad was at the graduation ceremony, my only guest. I saw him in the audience and my chest cramped and he gave me an encouraging nod and clutched the programme tight. It would be crumpled when he let go. We went to dinner afterwards at the same Italian we always go to. He ordered a glass of Prosecco each before we even looked at the menu.

'Cheers to you, Lucas.' We raised our glasses but didn't clink them together. 'This is quite a special day. And Mum, I know she would've loved to be there, at the ceremony.' He exhaled. 'So what I want to say is, well done. I'm proud of you.' We tasted the Prosecco, both quiet. It was stiff but the best we could do, and though I tried not to let it, this made me somewhat sad. I just wanted to order our food and eat and pay and leave and go get pissed with Henry.

'Know what Mum would have done this morning?' Dad said. 'Baked a marble cake.'

'Marble cake?'

'Don't you remember, you used to love marble cake,' he said and I searched each brain crevice for the memory.

What I did remember was how relaxed he'd been around her, sort of unlaced. If she had been at the ceremony, Dad wouldn't have gripped the programme so tight. I wondered how I would have been. At the ceremony, but also you know, as a person.

'What about her yellow dress, the one with the white flowers, her favourite, remember that?'

I did.

'I do.'

'I think she would have worn that. And her perfume.'

I smiled and finished my Prosecco, trying to recall the smell of that perfume. I wondered if Dad still had a bottle somewhere. If he allowed himself to spray.

•

Now, my thigh against Sam's on the tube seat, the Nina Simone song is finished. A new song intro starts, one I don't recognise. I fret as she looks at me expectantly and pinches my leg.

'Shirley Bassey?' she says, like a question.

'Oh yeah, what's she famous for?'

'Ah mate. Diamonds are forever, the love story song, big spender, goldfinger.'

'Right. Doesn't compare to Nina Simone though.'

'Agreed. Hey, want to hear a new obsession of mine?'

I really don't. I want to stop this game now, worried she will one of these tube rides realise I am just an impersonator and quite standard and not so hot as my clothes imply. She likes parties. I know the calorie count of everything in her fridge.

Sam finds the song and it starts. I take the earbud out and stand to walk towards the tube doors. My stop is coming up but also I don't want to listen to any more songs. She follows and takes the bud out of my palm and pushes it back into my ear.

'Hey,' she says. Her smile is so natural and so free of judgement I feel my worry is condemnable. She is fairly transparent in her intention to be with me and since materialising behind that fridge door she has not once been coy. Still I'm so eager to impress her. Honestly she deserves me to be more trusting.

I stop trying to hide that I am a musical illiterate and also not so hot. I relax and listen to the song. She takes my hand and moves her thumb up and down, smoothing my palm-reading lines. The song is slow and scatty.

'Flora Purim,' she says. I ask her to turn it up and I lick my lips because they are dry and tight, the underground air dusty. Sam reaches into her pocket and takes out a lip balm and smears it on her lips. A thick, waxy layer. Then she places her hands on my cheeks to adjust my head tilt and puts her lips exactly on top of mine. The breath from her nose tickles my skin. She moves her lips from side to side, playing a tiny harmonica.

She pulls back and gives me a smack kiss. 'There. Better?'

'Do it again,' I say and kiss her hard and she laughs through her nose.

My lips now taste of grapefruit and oil, and her lip balm is added to the smells my brain will associate with her.

Another day, wanting to be transported back to this tube ride, I will only have to buy a grapefruit.

We approach the station. I am switching trains, she is not.

'Will I see you tonight?' I ask.

'I want to go to the cinema.'

'Okay I'll check what's on.'

I need to get off now so I slip out just as the doors close, nudging my shoulder. I turn on my heel and she kisses the air and I wave my hand and start walking. Flora Purim is singing about butterflies. I match my pace to the beat.

Then the music stops. The silence abrupt.

Sam's earbud, it has lost connection to her phone. I turn back to the tube door. She is holding up an earbud to me. I hold up the other. She shrugs. I mime sorry.

The train moves and disappears down the tunnel. Sounds from the station take Flora Purim's place. And I feel stranded, disconnected. Like a cord has been cut.

153 DAYS LEFT

Sam

I breathe in deep and hold it. The smoke burns my lungs. I let it out slowly and as it passes my lips, intermingles with the air, I feel in a way sensual. It is Saturday afternoon on the first of August and I am having coffee with Tabatha and Finn. We are sitting outside.

I am the only one currently smoking and I have this urge to grab the table and exclaim something to make them laugh or applaud but I don't. Instead I lean back and hold the cigarette close to my mouth and watch the smoke drizzle upwards, free of gravity.

So far, this summer has been constant clear skies with the saturation turned up. Blue in daytime, pink at night. Sometimes purple like a new bruise. But today it is raining, a lazy big-drop type of rain. The outdoor area is covered by white-and-blue striped marquees and the raindrops make pleasurable noises, as if hundreds of small frogs are jumping across the fabric.

Normally I only smoke when drinking as I'm not a fan of the taste. It is more something to do when you are bored with the party and your fingers start searching for an occupation.

But today I feel sort of luxurious and smoking seems an appropriate illustration of this.

It is unusual for me to be this still. I am not in a rush to go anywhere, do anything. My legs motionless under the table, feet heavy on the gravel. But deep in my chest there is a tightness, the anguish of knowing this moment will end. Six weeks till Stockholm.

Though the chest tightness could also just be the smoking so I decide to ignore it.

'So? How is Lucas?' Tabatha asks with innuendo intonation. Her red lipstick is skilfully applied.

'He's good. He'll come by after work.'

'Come on, share with the group,' Finn says. 'Talking about your sex life is the only sex I'm getting at the moment.'

'Not sure that's how it works.'

'Yes, by proxy.' Finn, real name Finley, actual real name Shun. He told me once Shun means pure in Cantonese. We both laughed at this. Tabatha and I studied marketing together but how Finn fits in, I don't remember. He was sort of just incorporated. Despite my two years in Stockholm with only the occasional video call nightcap, when I landed in London we returned to our old ways. Cigarettes on Tabatha's balcony, involvement in each other's business.

'Well I like Luc obviously,' I say. 'He is smart and we talk a lot.'

'And?' Finn's smile-wrinkles create paths across his face when relaxed, like rivers on a map. Deltas and fjords carved by past happinesses.

He unbuttons his shirt collar, picks up his coffee cup, and looks at me intently. He often says outrageous things but gets away with it clean. And he vulgar-flirts with both of us, which I enjoy the indecency of, although going along with it makes me feel vaguely unfeminist.

'The sex is good, I've told you as much already,' I say. Finn flicks his finger at my pack of cigarettes and I light him one and hand it over. 'He is very attentive. Likes to ask me things, if I enjoy what he's doing and that.'

'A talker. I've had one of those,' Tabatha says. 'He'd tell me about other girls, what they looked like, different locations, you know, in the car or in a pool or once on a squash court.' She cocks her head and her hair shines like stretched toffee as she gathers it on one shoulder.

'During sex? A bit rude,' I say.

'And who are you, exactly?' Finn says. We laugh.

'It was fit though, I got into it,' Tabatha says and smirks and looks lovely. Somehow you can tell she is wealthy just by her face. She can afford the good skincare that comes in medical-looking glass bottles with pipettes. Her hair doesn't frizz. And her clothes, it's like my own clothes don't belong to the same species as Tabatha's. Her pieces heavy, rich in colour, fitting her curves just so.

She treated me to a facial once. Confined to the bench with the hands of a stranger kneading my tissue on and on, my legs started trembling. I endured forty minutes then apologised and sat out the remaining twenty in the lobby, waiting for Tabatha's treatment to finish. I pretended I had enjoyed myself since it was expensive and she was paying. But I would never go again. I cut my hair myself and I haven't been to the dentist in four years.

'Luc doesn't talk about other girls though,' I say. 'More about things he's noticed about my body or teasing me about random things.'

'And you're into that?' Finn asks and places a hand on Tabatha's shoulder and massages it. I like looking at this. I think for a moment. Sex used to be such a serious thing but with Luc it is cheeky, the opposite of staged. 'At first maybe I was surprised. But now I am into it. It adds a dimension.'

'You fancy him so hard,' Finn says.

'I think we all fancy Lucas just a little bit don't we,' Tabatha says and licks her lips. Although Luc's appeal is not my doing I still take pride. His eyes will zone in on you like he is actually listening instead of waiting for the moment to cut you off. The type who refills your glass before it is even emptied.

My phone pings on the table. A text from Diwa. *How are things? Burned down the flat yet? Invited questionable people over?*

After a moment's consideration I reply, *Just Luc.*

Finn is telling Tabatha about a tiresome colleague and I have heard this story before. 'Sorry,' I mime to Finn and point at my phone. He can be strict with device etiquette.

Who the hell is Luc? Diwa asks.

Don't you remember? Lucas?

No? And then, *Oh wait.* And then, *You mean the Lucas?*

Indeed.

Call me.

I'm out with friends. Tomorrow? I sip cold coffee and don't even mind, already drafting the story I will tell Diwa. Which details to leave in, in what order. She will like the part when he asked me to dance and I knew that he knew who I was.

Tomorrow early.

Sure early. How is Greece? And Milly? How's the house?

It's not a house it's a villa. You should come. Bring Lucas. You're so funny I'm laughing. Talk tomorrow.

•

It was because of Diwa I met Luc in the first place. She was my favourite family member and I would rather hang out with her parents than my own, although admitting this made me feel despicable. She was born in London. I, in Stockholm. My pappa came to Sweden from Bucharest to study, and met Mamma at a midsommarfest. Diwa's mum, my aunt, left Bucharest for London and soon married a student from Beirut, my uncle. Diwa is an only child. I have two younger brothers. But Diwa feels more like a sibling than either of them.

Every school break I would ask my parents to go to London. Diwa and her parents, Sofia and Abdel, seemed fine with this and I never felt like a nuisance.

I was eighteen. February, my school's annual winter-sport break. Ten days in London and by then Diwa was twenty-four and living by herself so I could stay in her

35

flat. She thought I should socialise with people my own age and set up dates with the baby sister of a friend. The baby sister was nice and invited me to go shopping with the girls.

There were three of them and they reminded me of the Powerpuff Girls. Like triplets in appearance but with widely varied personalities, which I told them the second time we met. They were delighted by this and seriously deliberated who was the red girl, who was the green girl, and who was more blue. They made fun of my poor English and my cute-boy Swedish clothes but in an inclusive way, like they had this new exotic addition to their crew to show off.

Two days before going home to Stockholm, they were waiting outside the flat when Diwa and I came back from dinner with her parents.

'Hurry, we're late,' the red girl said as Diwa opened the door.

'To what?' I asked.

'A dinner party afterparty.' She pushed me inside.

Green girl ransacked my suitcase in the bedroom. They decided to let me keep the trousers I was wearing but changed my sweater for a boxy button-up shirt. Diwa poured us each a glass of white wine mixed with orange juice. Two ice cubes, cocktail umbrella. They were all sitting on the bedroom floor except blue girl who was straightening my hair in front of the mirror. I had thick wide bangs back then, which was on trend in Stockholm but not here. The girls had complimented me on this style and I thought maybe one or two of them would cut their own after I left.

I was wearing long johns under my trousers because it was freezing outside, and my legs had not been shaved for more than a week. I considered removing the long johns and shaving quickly before the party but the Powerpuffs were rushing and there was not much point since I had trousers on anyway. I wasn't wearing enough makeup but they said to put on lots of lipstick and it would cover the fact. Even in the midst of all that flurry, I felt extremely content. Diwa and the girls drinking juicy wine on the floor, gnawing on their umbrella cocktail sticks. Blue girl working brush and hair straightener on me while I applied many layers of crimson lipstick.

In the hallway mirror, lacing up my boots, I saw I looked good. Possibly too Swedish with angsty bangs and boyish clothes but I felt confident despite hairy legs under the long johns. Likely it was the wine.

Diwa gave us taxi money and told us to stick to beer or cider or wine. No spirits. Definitely no weed.

Green girl's friend's mate in East Finchley hosted the party at his house. Not far from Diwa's Kentish Town flat geographically, but very much so financially. Used to Sweden's standard one-storey villas and decent apartments, the wild differences between London streets made me queasy. It seemed as though in London, you were either shuffling to pay rent or earning more than what's reasonably spendable. Green girl's friend's mate belonged to a family of the second category. Judging by his house anyway.

We rang the bell and the friend's mate opened the black lacquered door, air kissing each of us on both cheeks which took an awkward long while. Through the long dark hallway, we entered a stainless-steel kitchen and red girl put our bottles of beer in one of the two fridges. The kitchen looked box-fresh and smelled of artificial lemons.

The friend's mate had already ventured back to the dining room and we followed. On a long table were empty plates and dirty cutlery. Roses in vases and an ice bucket with wine bottles. They were our age, seventeen eighteen. I found this dinner party strange, adult, linen napkinned. I wondered who had cooked the food.

The girls sat down in whatever empty chairs. I lingered in the doorway. Maybe twenty dinner guests, already tipsy or drunk. The guys wore clothes I couldn't interpret. Either prissy dinner jackets or sweatshirts with big logos. The girls all wore minidresses that looked designer. I wished I had stayed at home with Diwa, eating rice pudding in front of bad TV. I took a swig from my beer bottle, thinking this was probably a place where you poured your beer in a glass.

On the far end of the table a boy was talking to a girl in a sequined dress. It looked like he was trying to keep up conversation. Leaned back with an arm on the backrest, polite smile, foot tapping the floor. He might have been British but also he might not. A face like someone was gently pulling the skin backwards, all features slightly elongated. Slanted eyes. High cheekbones. Smooth, wide mouth. Very good lips. To me he stood out as if his stage spotlight was slightly turned up. I sipped my beer and decided that this boy, he was mine.

I dragged a chair over and sat down next to him. 'Hi,' I said.

He turned to me. 'Hi.' The girl in the sequined dress stood up and left. 'And thanks,' he said.

'Looked like you needed a rescue,' I said, conscious of my halting English.

'I did. Observant of you.' He held out his hand. 'I'm Lucas.'

'Sam.'

'I like your outfit Sam.'

I died.

We talked for a bit. Just normal small talk, which was manageable on my language level. Where I was from, who I knew at the party, etcetera. I had been nervous walking up, but needlessly because our chat was easy. He didn't seem bored when I took a long time finding a word. His eyes didn't start searching the room. It emboldened me to the point of even attempting some wit, which mostly landed well.

He said he was there with a friend from school, only knew a few people. He was a year younger than me, seventeen, and said he was as shocked as me by the size of the place. I asked about his house. He said he lived in a decent area, that he grew up in London, the cheapest house on the nicest street. He said chatting to the sequined girl was fairly hard work but that he had tried his best to be a good dinner partner.

'You sat next to her all through dinner?'

'She only wanted to talk about sex and gossip and kept asking if I have drugs.'

'Do you?'

And that was the first time he slipped me his rascal smile.

It felt like we were keeping a secret from the others but I wasn't sure just what. Red girl soon came and dragged me outside for a smoke and a briefing. She handed me a shot of something clear and I took it although I had promised Diwa no spirits, too high-strung to care. It warmed everything between my teeth and my stomach. Red refilled my glass and we downed another one, giddy. She had already kissed one of the jackets. But she was eyeing a sweatshirt.

Green was nowhere to be seen, Blue was dancing with some other girls in the living room. I wanted to find Lucas. I searched the sofas but didn't see him. Tipsy, I leaned against the wall and looked at Blue swaying to the music, drunk and happy and kind of hot.

'Do you want to dance?'

I turned and there was Lucas. Several seconds of me frenzying over what type of dance he would initiate and whether I had the rhythmic machinery to pull it off.

He smiled, leaning closer. 'So I was asking if you like, want to dance with me?' I felt his breath on my ear.

'Sure.' I took his hand and stepped towards the makeshift dance floor.

I didn't have to worry about my rhythm because mostly we just moved our arms a bit while chatting. We talked about the house, neither of us ever being in a kitchen with two fridges before.

'Hey,' he said. 'Let's explore.' I grinned and felt in sync with the universe.

We found a staircase leading to a subterranean floor with a number of closed doors. We stood in the corridor, the music soft down here, beats dropping down the stairs but no audible lyrics. He pulled me close and placed his hands low on my back. I put one arm around his neck and with my fingers in his hair, I kissed him. A straightforward kiss. Natural. Wet. Shockingly intimate.

I took his hand and opened the door to a guest room. Someone was already there on the bed. We closed the door and snickered, our hands over our mouths. Behind another door, the cleaning cabinet. Third door, the gym. The floor was padded. We sat down and kissed again surrounded by glistening barbells ordered by size. Soon lying on the floor and he smelled like clean skin, the absence of scent. His tongue was slow and slippy. I could feel his heart through his chest.

Our lips and bodies moved naturally around each other, like we were having an easy time. This wasn't the first time I met someone at a party but it usually felt clumsy and unsynchronised. As if you needed practice to learn the choreography. And it made this feel like not a first practice at all. More like dress rehearsal.

'Do you mind if we take some of this off?' I asked, waving at our clothes. I wasn't sure how far this would go but had no wish to stop.

'Sure,' he said and pulled his t-shirt over his head. A pale, firm body. Protruding belly button. Maybe a football player, some sport where you run a lot.

I unbuttoned my shirt and started on my trousers, then remembered my hairy legs and long johns. My face felt hot. He pulled my trousers down and looked at the long johns, then up at me.

'It was cold today,' I said, stupid.

'Don't think I've seen anyone wear these before.'

'I'm Swedish. Oh and, I didn't have time to shave my legs.'

I thought of the girls upstairs. Threaded eyebrows, waxed armpits. I felt childish. The cousin from the country, literally. Embarrassing to have thought the Powerpuffs would ever cut their hair like mine. I was charity.

Lucas rolled my long johns from the foot up to my knee. He slid a hand up my calf. 'Stubble,' he said. His hand moving up my shin, I got goosebumps. And hardly felt like charity at all anymore.

He lay on top of me and we kissed again, pressing against each other with thin cotton the only barrier. Me in my bra and long johns, him bare-chested in trousers. It felt like a strike of luck, me getting him, this warm pale boy on top of me. A statistical fluke. When I started on his belt, he sat up.

'Do you mind if we don't?'

'You don't want to?' I withdrew my hands reflexively.

'Yeah, I do. Very much.'

'Me too.'

'It's just that, whatever, I never sleep with someone before I like, get to know them.'

'Oh.'

'I don't know, I just find it kind of off-putting?'

'What does Off-Putting mean?' I asked, trying out the word. I got up on my elbows.

'Oh. It's like, gross?'

'Wow. Harsh.'

'No, jesus, I don't mean you being gross, obviously. More like the thing itself, having sex with someone you've only just met or whatever. I'd feel a bit grimy doing that.'

'Okay, sure,' I said, pretending to know what grimy meant. 'I mean, I definitely wouldn't find it Off-Putting. But we don't have to. Kissing is good.'

And it was.

When our lips throbbed from overuse, we went back upstairs. Blue and Red were on one of the sofas, joking about Green. We joined them. Green reappeared and I suspected she had been one of the two bodies on the guest room bed. They talked and talked and I tried to stay with it but I was drunk and they used many slang words. It didn't matter because the girls seemed to like Lucas a lot and I was proud his arm was around me and not them.

It was late and Diwa had called three times and texted angry emojis twice. I sent her a taxi emoji back.

'So maybe I could have your number?' Lucas said outside waiting for the car. It was so cold his exhalation looked like cigarette smoke.

'Yes, let's do that.'

He took his hands out of his pockets and we swapped phones. While adding his number he said, 'And maybe I could show you some London spots before you go?'

The cold had sobered me somewhat and now my nerves woke up. 'I'm leaving the day after tomorrow though,' I said.

'Oh. So maybe tomorrow?'

Seeing Lucas alone with blood free of alcohol seemed like a blueprint for certain humiliation. Tomorrow, I probably wouldn't want the current me to have said yes to this so I told him I was spending the day with my aunt and uncle.

'Right. Next time then.' He gave me my phone back and kissed me one more time, both hands on my face, before I got into the taxi.

I checked my phone contacts. A British number. Under the name Luc. I pictured telling my Stockholm friends, 'Luc, short for Lucas.'

I turned around to look at him when we drove off. So did the girls. His hands deep in his pockets, just standing there.

'Fuck you guys look hot together,' Green said and the girls shrieked and the taxi driver laughed and shook her head.

•

But today I am having coffee under a marquee in the rain. Across the café table, Finn finishes his troubling colleague anecdote and Tabatha makes a comment about

London-centrism. She lifts her spoon and stirs her cup. I shiver at the noise of metal on ceramic.

'Why are we drinking coffee anyway?' I ask. 'Let's order wine.'

Soon Tabatha pours three glasses of rosé and places the bottle back in its cooler. It looks delicious, cold and crisp and strawberry pink. We raise our glasses and I take a sip and taste peaches and vanilla. It is too sweet but today that's fitting. I light another cigarette and listen to the tiny rain frogs on the marquee and this moment is flawless.

Finn is parodying British people. In BBC English, he imitates Tabatha trying to get out of a date with her school friends, coming up with a dozen euphemisms for I don't want to. His taunts are fearless and this is why I get along famously with Finn. It is a relief to untie my frankness with him after holding my corseted breath around the Brits. Even with Luc I sometimes worry he'd prefer me less blunt.

None of my London friends are Swedish, so there is this substantial part of my identity they can't relate to. Sometimes my jokes are interpreted as earnest. Some of my observations fly over their heads. A lot of their pop-culture references mean nothing to me.

Paradoxically, I never feel truly Swedish in Stockholm. I am half Romanian sure, but I think the feeling stems from a lack of Swedish reservation rather than genetic makeup. I am crude and blunt and say too much. Swedish culture is saying what you mean, but never too much. A restrained type of honesty. I never learned the restrained part. On the other hand, even though Pappa is an immigrant, his instinctual reserve makes him a prototypical Swede. I wonder if he feels more Romanian or Swedish. If he tells jokes I sometimes interpret as earnest.

I get extremely lax, the first shy buzz of alcohol reaching my head. Luc is not even here yet but in a way this is preferable, the waiting. Only six weeks left in London so anticipating him before I experience him seems somehow time efficient, as if enjoying him in absentia before even being on the clock yet.

After the night nine scare, he has not caused me any more anxiety or uncooked pasta turmoil. He slept at his place the four following nights but when he returned he attached himself like an appendix. I am so solidly myself with Luc it feels like I have known him a long time, which in a way I have, considering all the teenage daydreams I have scripted since meeting him at green girl's friend's mate's dinner party afterparty. The real Luc is well cast in the role of daydream Luc. Clever, metropolitan, fun.

Fun to kiss.

Maybe not as wild as expected. More Ella than Nina. Likes early mornings and ingredient listings and crease-free clothes. Dislikes anything with the prefix binge. Eating, drinking, watching. I'm more suspicious of the prefix moderate myself.

Our deadline has lately become a fixation. Sometimes when lying in bed solving a crossword puzzle or despairing about society together, I start panting. My stress about leaving London ruining the present, as if already living in future Stockholm misery. As if the current moment is just a memory for my future self. So I get frantic about noticing details to recollect later. In autumn, when we are over.

But now I am smoking and sipping cold pink wine and Luc is not even here yet. I forcefully push the deadline out of mind. Instead I think of the heat last night and the open windows and how he put ice cubes on me and told me don't move. I feel a pulse between my legs.

Maybe we will go out tonight. Get silly drunk and say things we tomorrow can pretend we didn't mean. Luc will likely want to stay in and talk and watch a film and have sex. He likes to plant me on a chair while he cooks. I find it extremely soothing to watch Luc cook and have cheeky sex and watch movies. At first this surprised me, it being years since I could watch a full film without twitching and repeatedly plucking at my phone. With other people, sex had become a sprint to orgasm before my mind went off to places and I lost the sense of touch. It could be his constant talking, as if our movies have a commentary track and our sex an intellect. It seems his speech speed keeps up with my thought frequency. There is no time for me to grow impatient. And my legs stop shaking and my finger fidgeting subsides.

But tonight I don't want talking. I have six more weeks. It is summer. This is London. I am not staying in.

That first night, the dinner party and my bad English and kissing on the home-gym floor, I had wanted nothing more than to stay in London. Stockholm felt like a bleak imitation of a city by comparison. It still does. The day after the party, I composed a text to Luc and made Diwa check for mistakes before sending. He replied. Nothing special, just it was nice to meet you, what are you doing today, that sort of thing. So wary of missteps we didn't express much. That night he called me. I panicked, didn't pick up, fretting my English and everything else. I thought maybe I should text in the morning at the airport saying sorry I couldn't talk I was having dinner with my aunt and uncle. But I didn't text. Neither did he. I just got on the plane and flew home.

136 DAYS LEFT

Lucas

Then I didn't see her for ten years. And I thought I never would, but now she is next to me and today, like every day, she is walking fast. I have grown used to it. My own steps lengthen and my thighs tense and relax, tense and relax.

We are searching the backstreets of Soho. There are cobblestones and tight alleys and sex shops with wide-eyed tourists. The sun is out and it smells of last night's depravity and waffles. It is late August but summer is holding on for Sam, giving her the best London possible. Three more weeks.

She wants to find a concept store she has read about and later we will meet up with Tabatha.

'Do you get annoyed with my accent?' she asks, in her abrupt fashion.

'No,' I say and think for a moment. 'I like it. It's kind of a trademark. Besides, you hardly have an accent anyway.'

'But when we first met, could you tell?' She stops and turns to me. She tries hard to mask her Swedish intonation asking this.

I stop too. She has a brown speck on her cheek, maybe makeup. 'I sort of gauged you were from one of the Nordic countries, yeah.'

'How?'

'It's something with the vowels. You say them so quickly, gives you like a drumbeat sound. Marching band.'

Her eyes open big at this. 'That's bad.'

I chuckle. 'As accents go, yours is fairly charming, promise.' I rub the makeup speck off her cheek with my thumb.

'You think I should keep it? Or work it off?'

'Definitely keep it. For charisma,' I say. 'Makes it easy for me to find you in a crowd.' Her messy hair blows around in the breeze and her shampoo smells like nuts. It makes me hungry. 'Also, being an immigrant has its perks,' I say.

'Oh it does now? And you would know.'

I can't tell if she is annoyed or amused. Probably a bit of both, judging by the raised eyebrow. She turns and starts walking back towards Piccadilly, not giving up on finding the shop.

'It gives you a certain mystique,' I say, catching up. 'You're fluent in English, just with a marginal accent, and your name makes sense in English, so no one knows exactly where you're from unless you want them to. And you have other traditions and food and things to impress people with. All in all, it makes you maybe fifteen percent more interesting I'd say.'

She stops and laughs at this. 'These are the kind of things you can't say when we're around other people or like my friends. They'd butcher you.'

'Sam, almost everything we talk about I wouldn't say around other people.' Which is true. Because whatever unattractive thought I say out loud, she doesn't look

50

uncomfortable. She only nods upwards encouragingly, like go on. Maybe she has a taste for deep humanity, wanting the most private out in the open. It is often mortifying hearing myself say these things, like sad things about Dad, but then she nods her 'go on' and the mortification fades and at times I do go on, but other times I feel it is plenty already and stop. Afterwards I will often feel lowkey exhilarated, like I have got away with something.

Sam starts walking again, the cobblestones making her sway in her sandals. 'Yeah, well, it's weird because here in London I look generic but have an accent, and in Stockholm I sound generic but look sort of foreign,' she says, too flippant.

'Which do you prefer?'

'Oh definitely here. Because you know here I actually am an immigrant. I'm not supposed to fit in completely. Not like in Sweden anyway.'

This makes me want to console her but before I can think of anything, she says, 'Besides, you forget the best part of my immigrantness.'

'Which is?'

'Being nine hundred miles from everyone who knew me when I had braces and bad skin.'

I laugh. 'You never had bad skin.'

'Okay that was for effect. But braces, I had those.'

And with that, she is the one administering consolation.

Despite her brusque demeanour she is surprisingly good at it, the thoughtful stuff. The other week she bought two books of Chekhov's short stories. One for me and one for her, to read simultaneously. Whenever we have the same thought at the same time, reading the same thing or discussing something we agree on, I feel kind of overwhelmed. We agree on almost everything, which is unexpected considering how dissimilar we are in all other aspects. Background, behaviour, personality. Our views on the world match, we just behave differently in it.

Sometimes she exhausts me. My normal day to day has vanished these weeks with Sam. I am used to sleeping well, circuit training four times weekly, eating fibrous food, drinking water and coffee mainly. My body feels different, waking up late, often too wrecked to work out. I am losing muscle and somehow feel both waterlogged and dehydrated at once. My stomach isn't flat. And mentally I am out of comfort. Not used to relationships this emotionally acute, I now don't have the space to worry as much about what will happen. Like with my finances. Lack of finances. It is intense, but since only for the summer I think it's probably fine to indulge. Once she leaves I can care about other things again and that is a relief although I don't like thinking this way.

The Chekhov stories are in chronological order and I am still on his early work making slow progress because I find them hard to concentrate on. But one called 'Verochka' I liked so much I later read it aloud to Sam. I told her I figured it was about longing for a connection so much you misread your feelings for someone as romantic when they're not, and the disappointment when realising your mistake. She said, 'Like reality killing your daydreams.' It is beautiful but mostly depressing that story and afterwards when we had sex, it wasn't our usual chatty sex, it was slow and quiet and close. Disorienting to breathe so hard from such small motions. Now I am thinking that this whole reading and then slow sex is good for Sunday mornings before we go out and eat lunch in the sun somewhere.

We have been up and down Berwick Street three times so maybe the concept store has closed down. She checks her phone again. 'I don't understand, it should be right over there.'

'Maybe it's in a courtyard or something. Yeah, there.' I point at a tight alley on our right.

She's off and I have to jog to catch up. Then she stops. 'Found it,' she says, beaming.

The store has an impressive array of items, considering its sparse shelves. Sam picks up a scented candle, smells it, puts it back. Touches a long-sleeved t-shirt, leafs through a large book of birds. She hums. It must be unconscious. She never hums a full song, only a few notes. Sometimes the same three notes over and over. Sometimes just one note in different lengths, creating more of a beat than a tune, like she is scared of silence.

Socks in grey. Soap bottles labelled simply 'soap'. Wall clocks like the ones in school, an East German strictness about the ticking, as if a constant reminder time is running out. Three weeks and change until she leaves.

I go over to the book table and pick up a paperback with quotes, zone out and think of our immigration conversation outside. To be honest, I envy her. She is a foreigner in this country, that means certain things. Like never fitting in completely, not knowing all the cultural references. She will always, in some ways, be an outsider looking in. But she will have a reason. Unlike me, British in Britain and still feeling alienated.

Envying Sam for her immigrant status is ungrateful and insensitive at best. She must have been through hard times because of it I reckon, but she is so self-assured she moves like she belongs everywhere, unbothered by social subtleties. Sometimes it stings to see that, though mostly I'm happy for her.

Home is where the heart is, the quote book tells me. I put it down.

Sam buys a pencil, a wooden label-less pencil for three fifty.

'Haven't seen one of these since middle school,' she says.

'Do you even have a notebook though?'

'Right,' she says, pleased for a reason to go into another concept store on another day. I smack my lips. Sam is bad with money, that's the truth. I pity the future partner she will join accounts with. But then again that's not my business so what do I care. My own balance is pitiable enough.

The three real girlfriends I've had before all had opposite personalities to Sam. Too careful, not too reckless. It is strange to me now, how I have always been the energetic one in the dynamic, getting restless, wanting more. Whichever part of my brain decides who to fall for must be in an experimental phase this time with Sam. I wonder if it would have been, in a scenario without a time limit.

Back in the alley outside, she calls Tabatha. They decide on a bar in Covent Garden specialising in caffeinated cocktails, in case you want two drugs collaborating in your bloodstream at once. While on the phone she stares at the mouth of the alley. She points. I turn and see a movement, a small flutter. It's a pigeon.

'What?' I mime at Sam.

She ends the call, then says, 'Is it hurt? Why is it moving like that?'

We go closer and yeah, it is hurt. Lying flat, one wing at its side, one flapping out on the ground. At the base of its neck, there's a horrible wound. It has been pecked. The bone is visible. I feel sick, clammy.

'That's grim. What do we do?' I ask. But Sam is already on her phone, googling.

'I'm calling someone. The RSPCA, is that right?' she asks. 'Or Wildlife Protection?'

I stare at the pigeon, blinking, as if something might happen to it the moment I look away.

'Luc! Which one?'

'I don't know, maybe RSPCA?'

She talks to someone and explains the situation calmly but her voice shakes a little. The longer the call goes on, the more exasperated she sounds. 'What do you mean if it was a fox?' And, 'I don't get it, what's the difference?' And, 'That's mad, what am I supposed to do then?' And, 'Okay fine, I'll give it a go.'

'What did they say, are they not coming?' I ask.

'No. They're not.'

'Oh.'

'We have to take care of it ourselves.'

'What, you mean, kill it?'

'I'm not going to kill it. Are you?' She looks me up and down like I am the least likely pigeon killer in the world. Which perhaps I am.

'So, let's take it to the vet?' I say.

'Do you want to watch the pigeon or do you want to find a box to put it in?'

I tell her I'll find the box. I need to move, do something pro-active, but also I don't want to be alone with the bird. 'There's a Tesco a couple of streets over,' I say. 'Will you be okay?'

She nods and I jog out the alley.

There is a pile of rubbish outside Tesco. Leaning against a lamppost are big discarded boxes folded flat. I flip through them in a frantic rush to find the smallest one, the whole situation slightly surreal, my hurry seeming futile but still imperative. Tesco Finest Colombian Coffee Beans, the size of a big shoe box.

'How will we get it inside without hurting it more?' I ask Sam once back in the alley.

'God, we will hurt it, won't we.'

I take her hand. 'We will do our best. We can't just leave it.'

She nods and grabs the box. I place my foot right next to the bird as support. It flaps one wing but doesn't get up. It looks exhausted, eyes darting to Sam, to me, back again.

She flips the box on its side and gently scoops the bird in there, my foot keeping it steady. It lands on its back with a thap. Struggles to roll onto its belly. Two blotches of blood soak into the cardboard. Sam closes the lid. A sour taste comes up my throat. I swallow.

I google where the nearest vet is and when we get on the bus, Sam points to the box and tells the driver to please drive smoothly. 'We've got an injured bird in here.'

The driver says, 'Just don't make a mess, okay.'

We sit in the back of the bus, the traffic so heavy it takes forever to move just a few streets. The bird rustles now and then. Even coos once. It breaks my heart, that sound.

Sam seems calm holding the box firmly in her lap with one hand, squeezing my thumb with the other. She looks so innocent, a few summer freckles on her nose.

'I can't believe we're doing this,' I say. 'We're like the bird rescuers.'

She laughs at that. A shrill, shocked sound. And suddenly I am giddy. We make some bad inappropriate bird jokes that are strangely comforting. Both our voices have that tremble you get when you're about to cry.

With Sam, almost anything can be funny, often without a clear reason. Stupid stuff mostly, we're not being very intelligent or anything. Now in this bus, telling bad bird jokes, I feel so insanely alive. Hypersensitive, my legs heavy on the seat, her hand holding mine. Around her, that driftiness dissipates. I had figured it to be universal, the crucible of my generation, jaded by 5G radiation. But now I wonder if it's maybe just me.

Sam often works late even though her payslip is that of a poorly paid intern. She doesn't seem to mind, not here to make money but to see the insides of an international mega agency. Although maybe even more so it's to be back in the city. I like tidying the kitchen and cooking before she gets home from work since I am spending most nights at hers rent free. I wish I could pay for more things. Dad would lend me money if I asked but I don't because his savings are mostly inherited from Mum and I wouldn't use her death money on nights out and takeaway. Letting him help with university was bad enough. But I like cooking for Sam anyway because I enjoy making her life a little easier or just like better. As if I have inserted myself into her routine and it would affect her negatively if I pulled out.

Before Sam, I ate almost every meal at home. I am lucky with flatmates. Henry I knew would be easy to live with, but Hitesh turned out to be unannoying too even though we found him randomly online. Sam has visited my place twice but her flat is much nicer, and also we are alone there.

We eat, we nap, watch tiktok, have sex, take showers. We read the paper, go out, come back, have sex, stream movies. I watch her do her makeup, we argue about small things. And it doesn't stop, the talking. Bored at work I continue in my head, thinking of things to tell her, then sometimes not sure if I have told her already or just planned to.

And increasingly I think about what will happen when she leaves.

•

'You'd be a great mum or like school teacher,' I say.

'Excuse me?'

'You're ace in a crisis.' I nod at the bird box in her lap.

She rolls her eyes. 'And you didn't think I would be?'

'Kind of expected you would, yeah. But there's the proof now.' I gently tap the box. 'And like, I'm born here and still you thought of the RSPCA before I did.'

'What, are you saying I'm out-Britishing you?'

'Something like that.' She is teasing but even so it stings. 'If not for your marching band accent so.'

She pinches my side. And I think although not as good in a crisis I have other skills useful for a parent but maybe Sam disagrees because she doesn't return the compliment.

At the vet, Sam places the box on the reception desk and explains to the woman behind it. The woman opens the lid and peeks inside. She makes a face which seems a bit unprofessional but also involuntary.

'I'm really sorry dear, but I don't think there's anything we can do besides put it to rest,' she says, her consolatory tone gaining her back some professionalism. I want to tell her to at least try, we'll pay. But Sam says, 'Of course. I mean, don't worry,' and gives an awkward little laugh. 'Not like we expected you to patch it up and nurse it back to health.'

But up until this point, I realise, this was exactly what I had expected.

'How much will it cost to, you know, put it to rest?' Sam asks, searching her bag for money. I hurry to place my wallet on the reception desk.

'That's alright,' the woman says. 'Don't worry about it.'

Back outside, I hug Sam and say, 'So not exactly bird rescuers after all.'

'Of course we are.' She looks straight at me. 'That pigeon is better off put down than flapping on the street I would think.'

I nod. It is sad but also I am happy we stopped instead of just walking on, leaving it flapping. I feel good about this.

'So. What do you fancy doing now then?' I ask.

'Shit, Tabatha.' Sam picks up her phone. 'Sorry we're running late, be right there. Can you order for us? Cheap Prosecco, on me.' I wonder if Prosecco is ever cheap in London, though at least the pigeon euthanasia was free. We walk towards Covent Garden, Sam still on the phone with Tabatha. 'I bought a pencil today. Yeah, a wooden one, like in school. Very nostalgic.' She takes my hand and swings it back and forth in big arcs. 'What's the best place to get a notebook? Like a classic one.'

The evening sun is low and hits my face, blinding me. Sam's hand is heavy in mine.

114 DAYS LEFT

Sam

There is no way this will all fit.

'You getting everything?' Luc asks.

'There's no way it will all fit.' I have a panic playing in my throat which I blame on the overfilled suitcases. But I know packing problems are not such a valid excuse.

My two identical bags are huge and soft-shelled and hard-edged. Flipped open, they take up most of the bedroom floor. I have paid for extra luggage but even with my rucksack, hand-bag, and these two colossi, I will have to leave things behind. I take everything out and make piles on the floor next to me. The parquet is hard on my ankle knuckles. My flimsy skirt rides up and my thighs look taut like two uncooked sausages.

Luc leans against the wall, arms crossed, blowing on a cup of coffee. He has put on our best playlist but it only makes things worse. It is not a good day.

I have to force myself to stay put and fold and pack and fold and pack and discard things because my limbs are all telling me to get out and get drunk or go smoke with Finn. But it is still morning. And if I finish this now I will have tomorrow and the day after with Luc without packing or other moving-abroad things. Two full days. Before Stansted, Stockholm, suburb, sorrow. Slit my wrists.

'Let's take a break, okay? Have some coffee,' says Luc.

'I'd rather get it over with,' I say. He gnaws his bottom lip. 'Why don't you go see Henry or Patti or something and we'll meet up after I've finished. This is no fun.'

'I want to keep you company though.'

'Yeah, no, I'd rather you didn't.'

'Right.' He gets this injured look and I can't bear it. Especially since I am the cause. Sometimes in moments that call for sadness, I instead react with flashes of anger. Then I feel guilty and overcompensate, until the next frustration flash. So capricious that I exhaust myself and whoever in my vicinity. This must be my least flattering trait, objectively. I don't want him experiencing me like this. It is better to be capricious alone, so as to skip the guilt phase.

'I'll make it up to you tonight,' I say. 'You can cook whatever you fancy.' I wonder if he knows me well enough to spot the overcompensation. By now I have learned it is a kindness to Luc to give him a job, let him take care of something, make me feel better. Today would be easier if I could just pretend it is working, but I am such a bad pretender.

'Right. Okay I'll be back later,' he says, 'will go buy some food and that.'

The door closes softer than usual. Like he is slinking out.

I hold up a shirt for inspection. Dark chocolate brown, silken on my fingertips. I wore this at Tabatha's party, that night Luc and I met again and he made a fool of himself by asking me to dance, twice. He had been so good-looking with his cheekbones. Sleeves rolled up, his sweater tucked into a belt I knew I would later unbuckle. The inevitability of sex not making the hours preceding the unbuckling any less thrilling.

Though the first time I met him he was seventeen and would only sleep with people he knew well. At Tabatha's party I had wondered if he still followed that rule. If so I would have attempted to get to know him with swiftness.

We had sex that night after all. He said ten years was a long time to know a person by anyone's standards. He undressed me, unbuttoned my shirt without rush. I was standing on my bedroom floor with a glass of wine in my hand. Soon I was wearing only trousers. They had a zipper at the back so he reached around me with both hands and the hairs of my neck stood up pleasurably when his arms brushed my ribs. My trousers dropped to the floor and I held his shoulder when stepping out of them. He put a hand on my hip. This simple thing, his hand on my hip keeping me steady, the muscles moving in his shoulder, his breath on my skin, was furiously sexy. I wanted to just stay there.

I lay on the bed and he pulled his sweater over his head and dropped it on the floor. His bellybutton protruded like I remembered. He sat on the bed, one knee between my knees. He put his hand on my neck and moved it downwards, between my breasts, over my stomach, down one thigh. He stroked my calf and said, 'No stubble today?'

We went slow, that first time. Both more concerned with the other's physical reactions than our own. I was curious to find out his rhythm and preferences. I remember thinking oh, he's into grabbing my hips, coming very close. This made our movements small, and I could feel him inside in acute detail. But then I didn't think much more because although he was moving slowly my fingers weren't and soon after I came.

Later, with him in the bathroom discarding the condom, I went to the kitchen for seltzer. I poured two tall glasses and the bubbles looked elegant and delicious. When I returned to the bedroom he was on his back, resting his head on his arm. He looked like he'd been kissed a lot but not recently hugged. I lay on my side and slung a leg across him.

This is my most revisited memory of Luc. I wonder how many times I will replay it, in total. I throw the chocolate shirt on the bed behind me. Better not keep it, only depressing to wear it in Stockholm, reminding me I'd rather be here. I should leave it for Diwa.

The moment I land in Sweden, I will calculate how much money I owe her. Rent, emergency money, party money, nice underwear money. I am not worried. I have a decent salaried job already. Besides, Stockholm firms salivate when hearing you've studied in London. And after this summer, I have real experience from one of the world's top agencies. I can likely cajole a raise or if not, book some interviews. And I will have a good Swedish job, with good Swedish money and paid Swedish vacation and every day walk out at 5pm sharp like any other Swede. And I will pay Diwa back and buy a small apartment and reconnect with old friends and date through apps.

Even with a Stockholm job, never working evenings or weekends, I will miss my placement. Tabatha's mum is a department manager and she put in good words for me. Landing this placement, I felt illicit. Nepotised. But I tell myself I deserve the position because of my impeccable work ethics.

My department is brand strategy. The team comes up with broad ideas for how to position a brand in the market, which then get turned over to the designers and copywriters and developers. The best moments have been the big concept meetings. Minds with healthy appetites tackling client identity and positioning, keen to impress each other and looking smart. During my placement I had many ideas, every meeting, but bit my tongue and knew my place which was a personal victory for me. Sometimes I'd tell the junior manager my ideas afterwards. Twice now she has repackaged them as her own. I don't mind. I find it flattering more than anything.

I fold a t-shirt to pack when I notice a tea stain. I throw the shirt in the discard pile which is steadily multiplying. It is stressful to part with things I associate with London, as if I won't remember without physical proof. Though what memories a tea-stained t-shirt would evoke, I couldn't say. Next I pick up my sweetest blouse. White, puffed shoulders, as cute as I can dress without feeling like in costume. I wore this to Henry's parents' twenty-fifth anniversary last week. I had thought I looked garden party appropriate but maybe I was wrong.

Luc had assured me I didn't have to come, to the point where I questioned him actually wanting me there. He then assured me he did want me there, only that I might be bored because I didn't know anyone except him and Henry. But I was ragingly curious, less so of the Edgware semi-detached than of the family that had soft-adopted Luc.

The house was cramped, full of small rooms and corridors, clean but cluttered with plants and pillows. After he kissed Henry's mum on the cheek and she had shaken my hand with both of hers, Luc led me through to the garden. It was much larger than expected, with two sets of dining tables, an outdoor brick kitchen, even an inflatable paddling pool. Maybe thirty people were milling. Henry's three siblings with partners and children, and the aunts and uncles and cousins with children. The adults dressed in light-coloured summer clothes they wouldn't wear to the office. Luc walked up to a group and said hello and hugged one man hard and introduced me to the rest. I shook their hands and said I'd go get us drinks because I saw Henry over there pouring Cava into flutes.

'Hey you, let me help,' I said. He squeezed my shoulder and gave me a cold bottle to pour. I looked over at Luc while trying not to spill and he was immersed in some conversation I couldn't overhear. He stood with his feet apart, pulled a hand through his hair, and looked not like the rascal but really quite adult. There was a little jolt to my stomach but I didn't spill a drop.

I walked around the grass and talked to all the people and tried to have natural charm and easy laughter. I made some jokes even. Later a girl of maybe seven or nine wanted to show me something and led me by the hand to the far end of the garden where there was a pile of wooden blocks and one more small girl. They showed me how it worked and it turned out to be an oversized game of Jenga. We played a few rounds and it was an okay game and the girls were funny without meaning to be. But in my pocket my phone was vibrating with Finn texting our plans for the night. It was only 4pm. I was marginally restless and wondered how many more rounds before the girls would let me refill my glass. A woman walked up who Luc had introduced as Henry's older sister, Jeannie. Almost his height but not as spindly. 'Having fun?' she asked.

I stood and brushed my knees. 'Well, I am winning so.'

She laughed a little and handed me a flute filled almost to the brim. 'You're good with them.' She nodded at the girls who were still playing but with that recklessness indicating they were soon to lose interest and abandon pursuit.

'Oh, well I have brothers. Younger.' We both took a sip. 'Any of these yours?' I waved a hand over the scattered children.

'Just the one, sleeping already. He's only two.'

'What's his name?'

'Albert.'

I didn't know what to say next or what the appropriate line of questioning was, but before I spoke she said, 'He's having a good time isn't he,' and nodded at Luc who was talking to Henry's mum and using his hands to emphasise a point.

'Yes. I mean, he loves you guys.'

'No, as in more than usual. He looks sort of, loose, I guess.' She winked. 'I think it's you.' Before I could politely object she said, 'No no, it's good for him probably. You're still young, you should enjoy yourselves while you have the chance, before you know, all this.' She swooped her arm non-committally, presumably meaning inflatable pool get-togethers.

'Well, we try,' I said. 'I am moving soon though.'

'He told me.' She nodded. 'But maybe for the best, in a way. You'll be like the fun chapter in his memoir, before all the boring bits.'

Unreasonably, this hurt like a punch to the chest. I said oh thank you that's nice, which was a stupid response to a punch. She smiled and we talked some more but soon she clinked my glass and walked off. I stayed where I was and looked at Luc and Henry trying to instigate some sort of pool-jumping activity among the older kids. I slid off my sandals and felt the cool grass between my toes. And god help me I wondered about the boring bits. At Henry's parents' thirty-fifth anniversary, who Luc would bring. I couldn't stomach picturing a partner or child, but I didn't mind picturing Luc. Thirty-seven, maybe less hair but still a stunning sense of style. A house that he owned with a garden and a kitchen, having people over, his natural hosting skills put to use. I was not in this picture because I didn't fit. Even in my sweetest blouse I stood out in this crowd like a spectacle.

Luc scanned the garden until he found me there in the corner. His face looked open. He lifted an eyebrow as a question, prompting me to communicate my emotional state by way of facial expression. My face muscles went lax for a moment, so entangled in conflicting emotions I was unable to convey just what I was feeling. In the end I decided for chipper. I smiled wide at him and he nodded me to come over. I gave myself a second to completely empty my lungs, after which I would cross the grass and help him score the athletic prowess of the pool children and drink two more glasses of Cava before we would say goodbye and kiss some cheeks and go meet up with Finn.

•

But now thinking of this, being the fun chapter in Luc's memoir, I can't say what had been so hurtful. Now I find it a rather excellent compliment, to be the fun girl. To be thought of fondly, causing nostalgia. The wild one that got away.

A text from Luc.

Thinking we could make sushi tonight but then I realised I don't know if you like daikon or not. How strange that I don't know that about you right. So this led me down this metaphysical route of listing things you dislike and wondering how many I need to prove I truly know you. I got maybe 20. What do you think, solid enough number? I'm at Sainsbury's by the way.

Then, *Oh, so do you like daikon?*

And then a photo of what I presume is a daikon.

I will miss his texts. But Luc and I won't do the long distance thing. Technically I am not even his girlfriend. It was just ten weeks.

Even without a time limit we couldn't keep this up, careless with money and abusing our health. Luc says he's lost muscle mass and his skin is sometimes slack in the morning like he is slowly imploding. I think he doesn't like it because he is not as sociable with mirrors as he used to be. Curiously I instead wake up inflated, my eyelids puffed and skin stretched. I have nurtured a seasonal alcoholism that needs tending once back in Stockholm. This carousel has run its course and though carousels are fun you wouldn't want to be on one perpetually I don't think. Anyway I know Luc wouldn't want to.

Even so, this morning he asked if he could visit me in Stockholm, his voice potent like the question had been percolating. 'I might even, you know, like it. Stay for a bit.'

This reality flashed me for a moment. Luc visiting for a week, then prolonging his stay, convincing himself he likes the place because I am there, quitting his job and living with me in a boring Stockholm flat in the suburb projects, not knowing a lick of Swedish. His only human contact my bleak Stockholm replica. Always tired, always rushing, collar turned up. I hated myself in Stockholm. He probably would too. Besides, nothing made Luc more electrified than talking about his engineering future. It was lovely to hear him, very fetching. Not speaking the language, he couldn't get a job like that in Stockholm. And I refused to be some sort of dream crusher. Better I leave and let him get on with things, getting a job, buying a house, hosting inflatable pool parties. Myself, I would try Stockholm one more time, maybe change jobs. If next summer I still hated my Stockholm self I could always move someplace new. That would be nice. Another country completely, one where summer was counted in months not days.

'Yeah maybe one day you could visit,' I said. 'Or you know I'll come back to London too now and then.' He took the hint and hasn't brought it up again.

·

Two weeks ago, I told Luc about my London bucket list. Touristy things, historical things, local things. We have been ticking some of them off. Luc has been a good sport but grunted in the queue to the London Eye.

'You really don't want to be here, do you?' I asked, poking his shoulder.

'This goes against my principles, as a Londoner.'

'Don't worry, your secret's safe with me.'

'I will know though. The man in the mirror.'

'Oh come off it.' I boxed his arm. He smiled like a scoundrel.

Once up in the air, his hesitance vaporised and we took in the blinking nighttime city together, his hand sweaty in mine. My breath was taken away but not literally because when I leaned close to the window the glass turned misty. Luc wore a black sweater loosely tied around his neck. The sight of him and the glittering city below, this could have been the twenties or the fifties. Timeless. A perennial panorama.

In the pod next to ours, a man in a suit proposed to a woman in a red gown. They had the whole pod to themselves, Champagne and strawberries in a basket. She said yes. Our pod started applauding. It was some time before the couple noticed but once they did, they took a little bow and laughed self-consciously. My throat clenched. Luc swallowed many times. He said, 'If you propose to me like that, I'll say no.'

'Ditto,' I said and we grinned.

Back on the ground, we strolled towards Chinatown. It was dark but still warm, humid and electric like before a storm. I was wearing a dress with a naked back, his hand hot on my skin. September already, Brit summer or Indian summer or what's it called. I cleared my throat often to snap me out of thinking about the approaching airport goodbye.

The most prominent feature of Chinatown isn't the lanterns or the neon signs or the gold and red. It's the smell, mouthwatering despite its heavy sweetness. Makes you think of fried spring rolls greasing your fingers and curly wheat noodles thick and glossy in paper boxes. We had dim sum in a tiny restaurant with different teas and rice wine. According to Finn it was a good place for Hongkongese food and therefore on my list.

The waitress showed us to a window table. The sky crackled with lightning. And then a downpour. Outside people ran to shelter, Chinese newspapers over their heads. The steam from the bamboo baskets clogged up the windows, condensation running down the glass in intricate patterns. Like worms digging through earth.

We ordered vegetable dumplings, steamed buns with soy mince, tofu skin rolls, and sweet red bean soup for dessert.

Luc closed his eyes when he tried a dumpling, chewing slowly, a drop of soy sauce on his bottom lip.

'Good?' I asked, knowing I would eat most of them.

He looked up, beaming, mouth full. His face obscured by the steam from the baskets on the table.

'Okay here's the thing,' I said, leaning forward. 'This obsession with food you have, I can't tell if it's love or hate.'

'You're joking right. Love of course,' he said, still chewing.

'So explain the oil-free stir-frys.'

He swallowed. 'Vanity?'

I puckered my mouth, not convinced vanity was really the crux. 'Go on,' I said.

'I mean sure but you'll be disappointed, it's not like a big thing.' He licked the soy drop off his lip. 'One day I just looked in the mirror and didn't like it so I started playing more football and stayed off fried things.' He placed his chopsticks on the wooden holder and wiped his hand on a napkin.

'What, you were a chubby kid?' I asked, unable to picture Luc as any type of plump.

'No not at all, like a very healthy kid. But after Mum died, me and Dad, we couldn't be bothered cooking for a while. And I was only twelve thirteen, I didn't exactly worry about it. Then my grades were going too, and we kind of lost it there for a bit. It wasn't the best of times obviously.'

His tone was still light. I thought about taking his hand across the table because my heart ached but he didn't seem to want the sympathy. He looked unfazed, a crinkle next to his eye.

'Then when Mum had been dead for maybe a year I was in gym class jumping plinths. I had on a white tank top for whatever reason, waiting my turn, and then I glimpsed a kid to my left I didn't recognise because we didn't have any chubby boys in my class so I turned my head and he had the same white tank top as me, and then I realised it was the reflection from the window and we did in fact have a chubby boy in my class and it was me. And no one had told me.'

'Bastard kids.'

'I know right. No one called me fat once.'

The rain smattering the windows was a strangely cheerful soundtrack. The restaurant was almost empty and the muffled steamy air created a cocoony atmosphere. It felt like this should be a horrible story but the way Luc told it made me

74

more giggly than anything. I slowly chewed my tofu skin roll to mask the mirth tickling my mouth.

'And when I showered after class,' he said, 'I thought about Ella Hutchinson turning me down when I'd asked her to the cinema. And I connected the dots.'

'Someone should give Ella Hutchinson a talking to.' I made a motion to crack my knuckles but no sound came because my knuckles weren't the crackling kind. Didn't matter, it being a symbolic gesture anyway.

'So I told Dad I wanted to go back to what Mum used to cook. Broccoli and brown pasta and that, orange wedges.'

'What did he say?'

'Oh he grumbled about it for sure but that was expected of him, you know? He had grown quite a stomach himself and I think he was a bit embarrassed by it too, so we took turns cooking dinner and lost the post-funeral weight like straight away. It was nice.'

'You were a good kid. Taking care of your dad.' I said this in a half-mocking tone and pulled a strand of his hair to take the edge off the sentiment. Though what I heard him say with all this, with his incessant reading of ingredient lists, wasn't vanity. Ella Hutchinson or not.

'I better see a token of it in his will.' Luc put another dumpling in his mouth.

'I mean, you're an only child,' I said. 'But maybe suck up to him a bit now when you have the chance.'

The waitress came with another bamboo basket. Two perfect white domes of shiny dough. When I bit into the steamed bun, too hot and so soft and salty and sweet at once, I questioned if I would ever feel at home in any other city.

·

I hold up the backless dress I wore that night and fold it again. This I will pack. Of all the days this summer, I wonder if suit-man-proposing-on-London-Eye-then-dim-sum-in-Chinatown wasn't the pinnacle.

I hear a key in the door.

'Hey you, I'm back,' Luc says and peers into the bedroom. I don't look up because I know he will have this inquisitive face, scanning my expression, and I hate that I cause his apprehension. He goes to the kitchen and puts groceries in the fridge. I push my earbuds in and listen to a podcast about people who are successful and how they became successful and why they are now feeling like money can't make you happy. I rub my eyes.

The episode is rounding off when Luc reappears.

'I've prepped dinner already, sushi rice is in the fridge. So.'

'So, what?'

'So maybe let's get you out of this flat and out of this funk, yeah? You're making me nervous.'

'Sure. And sorry, okay. I just hate this.' I stand up and dust off my hands and he looks optimistic, albeit cautiously.

We go on our usual walk by the canal. There is an old houseboat rebranded as a second-hand bookshop and we embark. Neither Luc nor I are big on literature but we sometimes read Russian classics aloud to each other, which makes us feel somewhat cultural.

Luc buys me a copy of *Virginia Woolf's London*. I find my new pencil in my bag and he signs the book. *Thanks for everything, I had a nice time. Luc.* We laugh at that to establish the inscription as humorous and I smell the book before I put it in my bag.

'Any last things to check off your bucket list?' he asks.

'Let's just hang out today if that's okay.'

He stops to tie his laces. I walk on slowly. In some ways I'd rather just leave today, not knowing how to stomach two more days of this before Saturday, it's too bleak. But I can't tell Luc to not see me. That would be hurtful. And I am hurting him already, being this on and off. He seems sentimental, wanting to wallow in memories and make our last days special. But to me it is slow-pulling a bandage best ripped. Still, I will try to act normal and finish this on a good page but I am volatile and I can't help it and I see it confuses him.

He catches up with me and slows his pace. My skirt ripples in the breeze.

'You want to get some bubble tea?' he asks, trying so hard.

'Yeah do you mind not being so nice to me, you're kind of making it worse.' I try a smile and achieve a grimace.

He looks at me apprehensively and I want to just leave.

'Look,' I say, 'I'm not handling this well and you seem to be doing really okay and I feel like I'm messing up our last days together. But like, this is all making me kind of miserable and now I guess I'm making you kind of miserable.'

'Jesus, relax will you. It's not such a huge deal.'

'It is though.'

'Okay sure I had pictured our last couple of days a bit more, you know, or whatever. But it's fine, it's a weird situation.' We're walking next to each other so I can't see his face and have to gauge his tone of voice which is sometimes hard even when I have his face in front of me for reference. I don't know if I am more upset by me handling this so poorly or by him handling it so well. As if unperturbed by the situation. A mere fly-in-your-face annoyance.

'But even if we are fairly miserable now,' he says, 'to be honest I'd rather have two more miserable days with you than two okay days without.'

This makes my heart warm but also excruciatingly brittle, one more push and it will shatter. We are so tense it's like a poor stage rendition of our love story. Bad casting, wrong director, wooden dialogue. Unrehearsed actors meandering across the stage. No standing ovations.

We go to the frou-frou café. My stomach is all wrong. He orders us takeaway bubble tea by the bar. Black bubbles for me, green for Luc. Four fifty each. We don't go into the music booth and Luc doesn't buy a DVD.

Outside, walking back, we pause to watch two border collies playing with a frisbee. One of them has a limp. I suck tapioca bubbles up the wide straw and try to swallow. It hurts all the way down, my throat too tight. I picture a bubble getting stuck on its way to my stomach, clogging up the oesophagus. I don't know whether it's only dangerous when food clogs your windpipe or if the oesophagus is also a bad deal. Luc films the border collies on his phone. I say the video should perform well on instagram. He says no, this is for his private collection, which is a joke so I laugh.

Back in the flat Luc picks up the chocolate shirt flung on the bed.

'You're not packing this?' he asks.

'Think I'll leave it for Diwa.'

'No, you should keep it, I like you in this.' He works the fabric between his fingers. 'You wore it that first night, right.'

'I did.'

'I remember you looking fairly sexy in this unbuttoned all low, showing that mark on your chest, like the one silent movie stars have on their face?'

'A mouche.'

'A mouche, yeah. And also I could see your nipples through the fabric a bit because you weren't wearing a bra, which was somewhat captivating.' He puts the shirt down on the bed.

'You weren't wearing a bra either as I recall,' I say and we snicker at that. 'But you did look hot.'

'I did? I worried you thought I was trying to look French or something.'

'Luc once and for all, you can stop worrying about your looks.'

He smiles and shrugs his shoulders. I ask for a few minutes alone to decide which shoes to keep, obeying my four-pair limit. After closing the bedroom door I play my Pharcyde playlist loudly and place seven pairs of shoes in a neat row in descending order based on size. I can't decide, my head too scattered. The afternoon sun creates slanted boxes on the floor. I scooch over and sit square in a sun box, the rays warming my sausage-taut thighs. On top of the clothes already in my suitcase, I put the signed Virginia Woolf book from Luc. He opens the door right then, two large tumblers in his hands, filled with pale green sparkling liquid. Lime slice on the rim.

'What's that, some kind of mojito?' I ask and get up.

'No, my own invention. Be careful, it's sour.'

I take the glass he holds out to me. 'Here's to two more miserable days,' I say.

'To miserable days,' he echoes. We clink glasses and drink. It is sour. So cold it hurts my gums. I take another taste, the ice cubes chinking the glass because my hands have a tremble.

I sit on the floor, put the glass down, and close my eyes. Place one hand over my mouth so I won't say anything. My eyes fill up, my palm kind of slapping my thigh. Then the song changes and 'Runnin'' comes on. The bass hits my chest.

Luc stares at me, teeth tight, shoulders tense. His eyes slitted and his face completely smooth, the only thing moving is his jaw working. It's the first time I see it, this look on his face. Like he is searching for a physical outlet for an extreme, overbearing emotion. Shouting something or throwing my suitcase across the floor. 'Enough already,' he says, breathing hard. 'Get over yourself will you. If it's such torment to leave, then don't. Just, don't.'

I stand up and get over myself, grab Luc's arms, kiss him hard, push him back against the wall. The impact makes us bounce and I bite my tongue. He takes my head and pulls me closer, spins us around, my back to the wall now. I struggle with his trousers, get them off. We hurry like we're late. He gets a condom from the nightstand, rushes it on, then pulls my underwear down under my skirt and lifts me up. With him inside I arch back and close my eyes and allow myself the daydream. Staying in London, cancelling my flight. I could get a job, afford rent, pay council tax. Put vinegar on chips. Read the paper with Luc over iced coffee.

The position is impractical so I can't come. I don't mind, the sex so sexy I will come to it later. We are out of breath and the tension is released and lying on the bed I take a photo of the mouche on my naked breast with Luc's phone. 'For your private collection.'

If he asked me to again, I might have cancelled my flight. But he doesn't. This couldn't last anyway, if I stayed we would only ruin it, grating each other like ill-fitting machine parts.

We talk about useless things. We eat sushi, drink more cocktails. Late at night in bed I ask him, 'If I stayed, if I didn't go, how big a chance do you think we'd have?'

'Chance of what?'

'You know like girlfriend boyfriend.'

'Sixty forty,' he says.

'In which way?'

'Sixty in favour.'

Which is rather good odds but we will never know because two days from now I will go to the airport and he will kiss me goodbye and I will look at him as he walks off until I can't make him out in the crowd anymore. And he will be here. And I will be gone.

111 DAYS LEFT

Lucas

And I am on an airport shuttle back to the city. It feels like the things around me aren't actually here. The Italian women eating Pringles across the aisle, the hyper host on the radio. The low-hanging sky looks like a stage set. Flat, 2D. I touch my arm but it is definitely solid.

Today has been grim. We woke early, Sam with sour hangover breath and me with gravel in my eyes even after washing my face. She walked around the flat tidying, binning bottles, wiping surfaces, pausing as if taking mental photographs. I set the table.

Diwa was coming home from Greece and we would eat breakfast together before I took Sam to the airport around lunchtime. It was my first time meeting Diwa and I would have been nervous if not for the bigger event around noon.

We had cleaned the flat and Sam was all packed. While Sam made the memory foam mattress with clean sheets, I sliced fruit and bread and tomatoes. We had spent too much money on breakfast things. Tofu scramble was frying on the stove. The good bread from the bakery. Juice not made from concentrate. To thank Diwa for giving us a place this summer.

She arrived at half nine. I carried her luggage into the bedroom which gave me a thing to do but then I felt awkward knowing my way around her bedroom so well.

I heard them hug and chat in the hallway and their familiarity was so obvious it likely meant Sam told Diwa things about me that I would myself consider personal. Maybe even sex things. Or like, other things. But I had slept in Diwa's bedroom for weeks, used her shampoo. I owed her some private details for balance.

Diwa ate a lot and Sam did too but I couldn't taste much. Diwa tried to make me feel at home by asking lots of questions. Sam rubbed my leg under the table as if to tell me to snap out of it. So I tried my best, asking Diwa about Greece, about the villa, about her girlfriend.

'Milly is fine, she went straight home to sleep. We got up at like four this morning.'

'Wish I could've seen her,' Sam said.

'She as well. But, I've got some news sort of.' Diwa covered her face with her hands as if shy. 'We're moving in together,' she said through her fingers. Her hands were brown and her colours deeper than Sam's, and you could tell she was older. Otherwise they looked alike, as if Sam were a next-gen edition of Diwa. It was startling, their similar mannerisms and facial expressions and the way they both randomly chewed their lips for no reason. More like siblings than cousins, as close as sisters, although what did I know, never having had one myself. Again it struck me how connected Sam was. Unlike me, helium-filled, the only

84

thing right now between me and the sky being Sam's hand holding the string.

'What, really?' said Sam. 'Diwa, wow that's such a big step.'

'Yeah wow, congratulations,' I said, trying to convey that despite today, I was excited for her. We cheered in orange juice and I finished my whole glass, thirsty all of a sudden.

Diwa leaned back and held her collarbone as if bursting inside but trying to appear sombre because Sam's situation demanded it. I thought then that Diwa would make the best mum. Affectionate and reliable, but still pure fun. I had spent about an hour with her and already I felt I would trust her in a crisis or talk to her about stuff. Next to Diwa, Sam looked so young. She would make a great aunt. The type to teach you about flirting and take you to your first horror movie.

When we'd finished the coffee I cleared the table. The left-over scramble in the fridge, the good bread in a paper bag in the cupboard. It hit me then that Diwa would finish our scramble, our soy milk, the soap in the bathroom. This to me was devastating.

I took the bread out of the bag again and put scramble and tomatoes on two thick slices. I didn't cut the crust off because I knew Sam liked the crust. I got the paper wrap out of the third drawer because I knew that's where paper wrap was kept and I packed the sandwich for Sam to eat on her flight.

I washed the dishes while they took a tour of the flat. Sam owned up to the water stain on the parquet in the living room. I tipped a glass one night when drunkenly kissing on the floor, both of us too wrecked to mop it up properly. I've been stupid drunk more times this summer than the last two years combined.

Like last night. We threw a goodbye party in the flat. Some of Sam's friends I didn't know that well or at all so I talked mostly with Finn and Henry and Patti. It was my last night with Sam and wasting it on other people gave me a panic, but one I couldn't act upon.

The party had an air of celebration which I found vaguely offensive, but also I was happy Sam was having a good time. She darted here and there and talked to everyone and laughed slightly too loud. Wearing her backless dress, cut so low her underwear flashed when she bent. She was magnetic like a black hole.

She came up and gave me a light kiss. Her lips tasted like cigarettes and salt.

'Am I being dramatic or does Tabatha look a bit smitten with Patti?' she asked.

'I was thinking that too,' I said, suddenly excited about this prospect. 'So Tabatha is bi?'

'Or whatever. Unlabelled. What about Patti?'

'Haven't asked.'

For the remainder of the night, Sam and I resolved to matchmake the two of them. This is what I mean by stupid drunk. Four or five drinks in, we often get a shared fixed idea. It creates various mini dramas, only ever spanning one night, Sam and I always on the same team. Often I would regret our fairly obnoxious behaviour the morning after. But last night it seemed to us like Patti and Tabatha might actually hook up. Maybe start dating. Maybe become serious even. Another couple forming at Sam's and my breakup party, their relationship created by our ripples. One good solid thing coming out of our short summer. I got a twinge of envy, them just starting their thing while Sam and I were ending ours.

Later Henry came up and said, 'About to leave soon I think. How are you doing?'

'Ah, you know.'

'I'm surprised you lasted this long honestly.'

'Yeah, it's actually not that late?'

'No I mean this whole thing.' He nodded at Sam who was miming some ridiculous scene at Finn and others.

I stared squarely at Henry but didn't say anything because I didn't want him to go on.

'It's just, it surprised me you've been okay with spending your whole summer like this.'

I turned my head away from him and looked at Sam. 'I wasn't okay with it,' I said quietly. 'I was fucking thrilled.'

He sighed and patted me awkwardly on the shoulder blade. 'I'm sorry man. But maybe you needed to get it out of your system then.'

'Yeah.'

I checked the time. After 1am already. The noise grew louder and bottles emptied. Sam smoked through an open window. No one was going home.

Much more of this and our last night would be nothing but slurred words from exhausted brains. I wanted everyone to leave, was dying to be alone with her. I wanted a last falling asleep together that I would actually remember. Good sex. Chatting afterwards. But Sam was the loudest in the room.

'Having a good time?' I asked.

'I am not about to call it quits yet Luc. You look like you're ready to pull the speaker plugs.' She laughed to soften this remark but it still stung so I decided that this was her night and gave up the idea of chatting in bed until falling asleep.

Once the flat emptied around four we were too tired to talk, too exhausted to have sex even. Instead we watched octopus videos on her phone, Sam's head on my arm, the bubbly sound of the ocean so hypnotic we fell asleep.

•

The airport shuttle swelling up and down as if on water doesn't help my hangover. The Italian women's Pringles look good, I should have made myself a paper wrap sandwich. Head resting against the cool bus window, I try to sleep. But that drifty sensation is lingering, like I'm not attached to anything. I hold on to the seat and stare ahead.

We pass many cars on their way to the airport, all with their own version of Sam to say goodbye to or pick up. I think about that first night when I closed the fridge door and she was standing there, eyebrow raised, hair tangled. How it had felt like a reunion but stupidly since we'd only met once, as kids.

I am impressed by our teenage selves' instincts at that dinner party. They had chosen each other then and ten years later Sam and I still wanted each other just as much.

On the bus floor is my gym bag with the last few bits I kept at Diwa's. Toothbrush, razor, some clothes. Checking whether I forgot my grey sweatshirt, I put the bag on my lap and unzip it. My sweatshirt is there. And next to it, on the top, is another piece of clothing I recognise. Sam's chocolate shirt. I touch it. It is soft as water almost. I pick it up and put my face in it and inhale through my nose.

It smells like you, I text Sam.

I sprayed some perfume, she replies.

The bus stops and I get off and take another bus and then I close the door behind me to a quiet flat. I switch the overhead on and it illuminates the hallway with an electric whirr, the sound exaggerated by the flat's overall silence.

I go to my room and put my bag on the bed, then unzip and unpack and place each item on the duvet. I return the toilet things to the bathroom and hang clothes in the wardrobe, put Sam's shirt on a hanger and smooth it with my hand. The fabric is so thin the light from the window sieves through, creating like a sepia filter. I hang it in the wardrobe next to my own shirts.

I go to the kitchen. My movements are off, as if I am zapping forwards in stop motion. This makes me dizzy and I wonder if I might faint. But then I remember that people saying they will faint never do. If you pass out you tend to go ahead without warning.

By the sink I fill a glass of tap water which I drink staring at the drain before I fill another glass. I turn around and lean against the counter. It is a decent flat, in Hackney, albeit a still grimy pocket of Hackney. It has small windows but my room's an okay size. Though after a full summer at Diwa's it doesn't seem like this is where I live.

I habitually check my phone without deciding to. No notifications. Her flight is in twenty minutes. I set my alarm.

Back in the hallway, I stop outside Hitesh's room. Henry is for sure at the office but Hitesh sometimes works from home. Deep down I know he's not there but I knock anyway. There's no answer. I knock again. No answer. I go back to my room.

On my bed, I research random things for a while. Flight safety. Distance Stockholm to London. Engineer entry-level wages. Buy flat in East London. Buy flat in South London. Buy flat in Manchester. Setting up retirement fund. Feeling dizzy reasons. Movies set in Stockholm. Buy flat in Stockholm.

My alarm goes off. Sam's flight. I picture her in the aeroplane seat, reading things on her phone. Unpacking my sandwich and tying her hair up as she does before eating. I lie down, cry, and fall asleep.

•

I had followed her to the security check, after sour coffees in the airport café. I wish we had skipped the coffee, the taxing

90

morning and long bus ride had left us numb and we had nothing more to say and the café was too loud for talking anyway.

At the glass barriers she became fidgety. Her eyes darted from her phone to the information screen to the security guard to the exit. I took her face in my hands to slow her down. She exhaled deep and her shoulders fell.

'This is it huh,' she said.

'Looks like. It was good though. No regrets.'

'Me neither. Thanks for all the sex.'

'You liked that, did you?' I said and touched her neck. 'Text me when you land, okay.'

'Sure.'

But I sort of knew she wouldn't.

'So.' She picked up her rucksack and slung it on one shoulder.

'You got everything?' I asked.

'Yeah.'

'Sometimes the gate is really far from the terminal so make sure you have enough time.'

'Luc, seriously?'

'Sorry.'

'I'm jealous you get to see Taba and Patti's first kiss.'

'I'll film it.'

'Another one for your private collection.'

'Quiet you.'

She kissed me then, her mouth still sour from bad coffee. And then it ended and she spun around and skipped through the sliding barrier to the security check. Once through she turned and waved. She just stood there with her hand up like a ceremonial greeting so I reckoned I was the one to leave first. I waved and walked towards the exit, knowing I was supposed to turn around one more time, it was good manners. I walked a bit further, until she wouldn't be able to see if I was crying. So that she could decide for herself, in her version of the event, whether I was or not. Almost by the exit, I turned around. She was still there, bag slung across her shoulder. I couldn't make out if she was crying. In my version, she was not.

·

I wake up and take one relentless breath, rub my eyes hard and then open them. On my laptop, I create a plan to get my life back to normal. Work out four times weekly, cook food for me and Henry and Hitesh, stop getting hangovers. Update CV, find a job. Amass deposit. I figure I can manage one more month of stupefying boredom at Darling, but October twelfth will be my final day. I note this down in my calendar. And despite the sadness of today there is a shudder of anticipation, my future wide in front of me.

Between my ribs there is a wretched lump but I figure this is normal, it will go away. I can rely on my proactive streak to get me through whatever hard time, I have done it before. And tomorrow morning I will start building myself up on the gym floor. Sam still airborne and I am already moving forward. It's a relief of sorts because counting down to this day has been obsessive. Now finally here, the anxiety has an outlet, it's done. We knew this was temporary, the impermanence making the overdose safe. Without the deadline we would've had doubts from the start, being such opposites in nature. This is better. One sensational summer.

My phone rings. Patti.

'How are you feeling love?' she asks.

'Yeah, I'm good.'

'Really?'

'A bit weird obviously, but I'm okay.' I pull a loose thread on my trousers. The seam comes apart.

'You sound more than weird, honestly.'

'Well thanks.' I laugh a little.

'Let's hang out. Pub of your choice.'

'Probably not the right headspace for it.' I pull harder at the thread, ripping the seam further apart, my skin white through the tear.

'Yeah, I'm not asking. I got news,' Patti says. 'It's not all about you, you know.'

So I go because Patti is insisting and also now I am curious. She is already there when I arrive, two pints and two packs of crisps in front of her. Tomorrow I'll start not drinking. But no way am I eating the crisps.

'So. You and Tabatha?' I ask, flicking an eyebrow. The pub smells weird like all other pubs, spilled beer and wet wood and sweat.

She punches my arm and says, 'That obvious?'

'We had a feeling. You guys always have good chat.'

'We do.'

'So you're dating now?'

'Okay slow down. Only just hooked up last night.' She pops a crisp in her mouth and it crunches loudly, her tight curls bouncing as she chews.

'Yeah no rush,' I say. 'Not like Tabatha has other suitors.'

'Please shut up, I'm working my hardest.'

I laugh. 'I have to say you're reasonably cute together.' Patti punches my arm again, pleased I think.

Later, Henry shows up. His relaxed manners around Patti makes it apparent they've been meeting without me this summer and I get unduly jealous. We gang up on Patti, tease her some more, drink a bit but not excessively. No one mentions Sam. We high-five and I walk home and wash my face and look in the mirror and go to bed, thinking that tomorrow the wretched lump will already be smaller.

Then, despite myself, I text her.

Die Hard 2.

She doesn't reply.

77 DAYS LEFT

Sam

It is so loud no one really talks. Instead we shout four-word sentences and hope the recipient can make out the condensed information. 'I like the band!' and 'Yeah, very noughties nostalgia!' and 'Another glass of red?' and 'Look, Felicia is here!' and sometimes just 'Tequila!'

It has been forty minutes and already I want to leave. But it is Friday night and I have no better option and the last thing I want is to go home to my sublet in Solna. At least here, there is a chance of something happening. The night still vibrates with potential, hasn't yet capsized into AM desperation. And although just a faint tremor of a vibration, it is more than what's obtainable on the sofa watching *Sweden vs Norway*.

I am here with Camilla and Elin C, friends from school that I kept in touch with through my Stockholm bachelors but didn't through my London masters. Two years I had been back in town and never reached out. But after this London summer stint, I for some reason did. It was an act of last resort, let's be honest, my Stockholm contact list slim and disused. I was not good at keeping in touch.

Elin C's brother invited us to the party, a fusion of formal dance and forest rave. Very student society. The building is a warehouse cum party venue in the middle of nature. We had to share a minibus taxi to get here. The ride took fifty-five minutes which makes me feel claustrophobic because I can't leave when I want to. I would have to order a taxi and wait for the car and for someone to share it with unless I felt like wasting a thousand kronor on fare.

We are sitting at a table far back and my legs are crossed and do their restless shake. A band is playing on a low stage and behind them a large screen flashes psychedelic imagery. Although this is a ravey crowd, the band is playing real instruments. Some kind of raspy interpretation of Brit pop so foreign I can't yet tell whether I like it.

Outside there's a pavilion with another dance floor. The techno tent. Its electronic beats mingle with the band's pop drums and the effect is disillusioning, like the world is out of sync with itself.

'The bass player's hot,' I shout to Camilla across the table.

'What are you on about,' she shouts back. 'Bass players never are.'

Elin C giggles. I find the remark unnecessarily mean-spirited, but also puzzling. As if your looks determine your instrument inclination. Maybe they do, maybe there's a whole instrument-picking band hierarchy I know nothing about. Beauty before skills.

Elin C turns her head nonetheless. 'This one actually is hot,' she says.

Camilla tosses her hair behind one shoulder and looks for herself. 'Well damn.'

Elin C giggles again and the faint vibration of potential drama picks up.

The bass player has brown wavy hair tucked behind his ears. He is wearing black trousers and white socks. He is tall. And his face is faultless. So pretty he confirms Camilla's theory. You'd definitely assume him to be the singer.

'He's just your type,' I shout.

'What?'

'He's just your type,' I shout louder, my throat straining. Every so often, the bass player looks over at us.

And now I really want Camilla and Bass Player to have an intrigue of sorts. Out of my present friends Camilla would have the highest anticipated success rate. She has confidence enough to approach someone this good-looking, and a reason to allow herself the fun. Her long-time boyfriend recently left her for a much less physically attractive girl. This makes Camilla doubt the appeal of her own personality.

Since picking up our friendship again, I have been doubting it too. She just isn't very nice. I remember her as fiery, funny, up for anything. But now I find myself drained after seeing her. She tends to intentionally misunderstand and contradict you for her own amusement.

Entertaining herself with Bass Player might take the edge off, or at least give us something to dissect at coffee tomorrow. She has a talent for telling droll cringy stories from her personal life. There will be things to laugh about and I will forget how twitchy I am.

It has gotten worse, my twitchiness. Like a perpetual craving but with nothing to crave, nothing to look forward to. An impatience cul-de-sac.

Camilla disappears and comes back with brushed hair and a fresh lick of lipstick, then sits down and attempts to catch Bass Player's eye. And eye-catching she is. Although not very nice, she is impressive and I have always been proud she is my friend. Back in school, she raised our group's status quite a few notches.

But now we are adults and I don't have to care about group status anymore. It's uncertain whether adults belong to groups at all. Regardless, I am sure of one thing. This group, I don't belong to.

•

A few days after landing in Stockholm I started a new chat and invited Camilla and Elin C. Their immediate reaction to this is impossible to know but their revised reactions were positive.

We met up for coffee the next week in a grotty subterranean café on Södermalm, a place we often went to back in college. It looked the same. Same glass bar with the sandwich-cakes and pastries. The tea selection in metal containers, the Bardot-esque playlist. The same girls around the table drinking the same foamy cappuccinos. A little older, a little meaner.

First we covered a mashup of old memories and current situations. Both of them had decent office jobs. Camilla owned a small apartment. Elin C rented together with her boyfriend, and they had started discussing children, 'but seriously this time'. I was shocked. I stared at Elin C, trying to find anything remotely nurturing about her. I couldn't. None of us were, with our reckless bodies and self-absorption. Our stomachs didn't seem like safe spaces for a foetus. I knew they went hard on the weekends, I'd seen the photos. In honesty, this was my reason for getting in touch again, the certain absence of substance-use judgement. Also I was curious about them, naturally. The deadly lure of the high school reunion.

'What do you mean by seriously?' I asked.

'Well. As of two weeks back, I'm off the pill.'

'Jesus,' I said and Camilla shrieked and clapped her hands and said, 'I'm so jealous!' She leaned back in her chair and whipped her hair behind her shoulders. 'You know, if that shit Nicke hadn't dumped me we might have been off the pill together.'

Maybe I looked strange because Camilla said, 'What?'

'Nothing. I'm just surprised.' I replaced my coffee cup on its saucer. 'We're only twenty-eight.'

'Well yes. And we don't want to be old mothers do we.'

Elin C said, 'I still can't believe Nicke,' emphasis on Nicke, 'dumped you,' emphasis on you. I glanced at her stomach, picturing something already growing inside but it seemed strangely grotesque so I stopped. I thought about Luc doting on our bodies even after a normal

alcohol hangover, assuaging the guilt with ample hydra-
tion. I couldn't imagine how he'd dote on a body with
a foetus. Insufferable surely. But then I felt quite good,
because I didn't share Elin C and Camilla's situation.
They were thresholding. Acting as adults climbing the
property ladder and inventing baby names, at the same
time as holding on, with white-knuckled optimism, to
their youth. Their weekend stunts and their shot trays.
They were gunning for both, neatly dressed delinquents, a
strictly scheduled post-studentism. And rather efficiently
too, moving forward into adulthood even with the constant comedowns blunting their brains. I was just pleased
I wasn't torn. I didn't have to spin plates, their brand of
adulthood being years into my future. I did not lose sleep
over being a young mother.

Our coffee cups emptied, we left the old memories and
moved to gossip. They both apparently had horrid bosses
and horrid girlfriends and horrid siblings. I thought what a
strange hobby, talking ill about people, since it wasn't even
marginally enjoyable.

Elin C shared an unintelligent thing her boyfriend had
said, a mispronunciation of the word entrecôte, and my
hands were fiddling in my lap. I picked up a packet of stevia
and tipped it back and forth, back and forth, the granules
rasping the paper. I wanted to tell Elin C to stop, that she
was being disloyal. Then I wondered if I was guilty of any
disloyalties of my own, like when telling Tabatha and Finn
about Luc's sex proclivities. Good things, but intimate. I

didn't know if he would find that disloyal or too personal. And I wondered how many private things Henry and Patti knew about me.

Instead of giving Elin C sympathy, Camilla started contradicting her upon which Elin C became defensive. We were forty-five minutes in. I was so wired at this point I went to the toilet and flushed cold water on my wrists. When I came back Camilla targeted me.

'Now what about you, any boy gossip?'

Nothing on this earth could have made me say Luc's name in this company. 'Yeah, no, I'm not dating right now.'

'Liar. We've seen your instagram. Who's the hottie?'

'Oh no one, just a casual thing in London. We're not in touch or anything.'

'What's his name?'

'Should we get a drink? We could share a bottle of wine,' I said and waved to the energetic waitress.

'Wait, am I making you nervous?' Camilla asked, smirking.

'Yes.'

An abrupt silence. As if okay for Camilla to make me nervous but not for me to admit the fact.

The waitress came and I ordered a bottle of pinot noir. Our lips got wine stained and still the tension didn't ease. By the time we hurried to the metro station, collars up and hands in pockets, I was exhausted by Camilla's silent hostility.

We were going north. The train's overhead lights were harsh and every time the doors opened, the draught made my bones feel damp. The pinot made it look like we'd been drinking blood. Camilla's long hair was static and moved around her head like a sea anemone. A modern Medusa.

I couldn't stand the atmosphere. It felt like I was giving her a gift every second I let this continue. As if she was quietly taking notes and memorising details to relay at other coffee dates with other friends for another serving of sympathy. I recalled things I had said today and pictured her sharing this with others, then realised I didn't actually care at all.

It was a relief seeing my stop roll in and I couldn't bring myself to hug before getting off but neither of them stood up anyway. I walked home to my flat in Solna. Since seven months back, I had been subletting from an old couple taking a year-long trip around the world, meaning Europe and Marrakesh. I hadn't asked the couple before sub-subletting it over the summer and yes I did feel bad about that. The flat was fully furnished, nice but stuffy, the elderly aesthetic only furthering my sense of being displaced. The floor so well-rugged I hardly ever heard my footsteps.

My third day back, I had reinstated myself in my office cubicle. Brand strategist at the second largest PR firm in Stockholm, known for high-profile clients looking for fresh. I hadn't expected to but I committed to the job, feeling fancy now as alumnus of the London agency. During concept meetings, where unconventional and even strange ideas were welcome, I felt sharp and focused. My twitchiness eased and I could just sit.

At night I sometimes expanded the ideas, flipped them backwards, evaluated their merit. I liked the strange concepts since they were challenging and engaged me longer, because when not occupied my mind wandered without permission. Nine hundred miles it wandered, back to London. And I found myself in bed unable to breathe normally, scrolling Luc's instagram. He hadn't posted much since August so I looked at old photos. Some I had commented on when he first posted them. A few were even of me.

Looking at these photos gave me the same feeling as time-travelling movies. Disorienting, the human brain simply not sophisticated enough to understand the implications and paradoxes. As if something that seemed impossible, wasn't. One month ago I was the Sam in Luc's photos. It was hard to believe she ever existed. And if she had, where was she now?

The other night when scrolling I went to Luc's profile and tapped the icon for tagged posts. I saw the photos of Luc other people had posted of him. The latest one was a selfie. With a girl. They were smiling to the camera, their cheeks pressed together, Luc's eyes half closed. I haven't opened instagram since.

And now I am scared to. I can't unfollow him because that would make a statement, so my choice is to either risk seeing him with this other girl or sacrifice social media altogether. Even if muting him he would still be visible in our mutual friends' posts. I could start a new account. But I struggle to see the point.

We haven't talked. The day I left, Luc sent me a Bruce Willis text late at night. I didn't reply. I wanted to but somehow it felt irresponsible. A quick clean fracture seemed more compassionate than ceaselessly re-snapping the same splinter. We had always agreed to not long-distance this. I am sure he is fine.

And now he has the instagram girl. I should be happy for him. Luc has so much surplus affection he would be miserable without a recipient. I want him to find someone. Just maybe not so soon.

•

I have visited my parents three times since moving back. First dinner with Mamma and Pappa. That was the day I left London and I had been so shattered I couldn't contribute much. A week later I had Sunday lunch with Mamma and Pappa and my younger brothers, Matei and Peter. It was better. Even before my summer in London I hadn't seen them in ages, Christmas probably. We were not close, never talked about serious or painful things if we didn't absolutely have to. I think my parents were just pleased to have me back and didn't want to remind me of the life I had once again rejected for Stockholm. So no probing about Luc or leaving London.

Their flat was warm, in temperature and colour scheme both. Sofas, rugs, artwork, everything ranging from burgundy to ochre to burnt sienna. I couldn't tell the ochre from the burnt sienna but Mamma could. Pappa retired last year. Mamma still had five years to go.

At twenty-three, Matei was now a full-scale adult. Even since Christmas he had changed and it was shocking to spend time with him and his masculine voice. He was tall and had longish black hair curved behind his ears, and although I was his sister I could tell he was good-looking.

Peter was only twenty-one and still scrawny. His elbows pointed like spearheads. He had gotten a first-hand flat contract with two friends this summer, as if to prove to all of us he had grown up. He didn't fool anyone.

Mamma had baked her thick, chewy rye bread and from the smell seeping into the dining room, I could tell Pappa had cooked his special. Sarmale rolls, mushrooms, and zacusca. My saliva glands stung.

'Bon appetit,' Mamma said once the food was on the table. I attacked the sarmale.

'So,' Matei said, spreading a thick layer of zacusca on rye, 'how small does Stockholm feel after London?'

'God, tiny,' I said and then realised this was rude. 'But so clean. Like, the air doesn't hurt your lungs here.' When I cut into the tight cabbage roll steam poured out and smelled of rice.

'I think London is over,' Peter said. 'Like in terms of business and work opportunities, you're probably better off here. Stockholm has one of the largest international tech scenes now.' And then he said, 'It's true,' as if someone was objecting.

'Like you'd consider London anyway,' Matei scoffed. 'You're way too self-conscious to move anywhere you'd have to speak your imbecile English.'

'What's wrong with my English? Hey, what's wrong with my English?'

Matei smirked and rolled his eyes and I had forgotten about it, the constant taunts, the poking where it hurts. It made me realise they had been hanging out without me, which wasn't that strange, why wouldn't they. I scanned their faces and yes, it was apparent, the easiness about them. Mamma's physical fussing around Peter, Matei objecting to Pappa's opinions even before expressed, their dynamic fixed and only intermittently interrupted by my sporadic presence. They were family. I was like a distant aunt only showing up when in need of money. But they made an effort, even Peter. I had returned, again, and we were back to family of five. No one acted like this was out of order. But likely they assumed I would be leaving again.

Pappa filled my plate with more cabbage rolls without asking. Him knowing the size of my appetite caught me off guard. My throat grew tight and it became hard to swallow, the tiny rice grains catching and sticking on the way down. I wondered, if I also made an effort, how many Sunday lunches would it take to not feel like the distant aunt. Would I go to parties with my brothers and plan summer holidays to the cabin? Would I take Pappa to the cinema and shop for winter coats with Mamma? Find a boyfriend to introduce to them in some pasta restaurant on Södermalm.

Get married, create my own family sub-unit of five. It was physically possible, I knew this, yet it seemed make-believe to me, supernatural.

'Maybe we could turn this into like a bi-weekly thing,' I said. 'Sunday lunch I mean.'

'That's an idea,' Mamma said. 'Don't expect me to bake again.'

Peter stood up and suavely placed his napkin on his empty plate. 'What, you're never around and after one lunch you suddenly get feeling?'

'Alright alright, we'll see, we'll see,' Pappa said, not agreeing or disagreeing with anyone.

'I'm around,' I said.

'When are you around?' Peter was out in the kitchen now, yelling his replies through the open door. He was slamming something like he was washing up although we did have a dishwasher. 'First you study in London, and that's fine, whatever, but then you were back here for two whole years and still I never saw you. Then you leave again, and what, you're back now?'

'Well evidently,' I said and swooped a hand in front of myself to demonstrate which he couldn't see anyway. I heard I sounded mopey and it wasn't attractive.

Peter stopped slamming and after a moment he asked, 'For good?'

I couldn't answer that and I felt bad so I just let the anger flash and said, 'Peter will you stop being a dick,' and Pappa said, 'Hey now, what's up with this nonsense,' and I said sorry and we left it at that.

My brothers went home soon after and no one has suggested Sunday lunch again. But then a few days ago, I showed up at the apartment unannounced. Mamma was still at work and Pappa seemed surprised to see me. We hardly ever met just the two of us, and his hug was stiff and tentative, like he worried something was wrong or that I was leaving again. I got a sting of guilt but resented it because I hadn't even done anything wrong.

He took my jacket and showed me to the formal chairs by the window that we never used except on Christmas. I sat down and he went to the kitchen to make tea. I closed my eyes and listened to his activities. Slippered feet, opening and shutting cupboards, his movements slow. He was getting old, and I had somehow failed to notice.

I could smell the tea well before he placed the tray on the table and sat down on the other formal chair. He poured. It was spicy with pepper and cinnamon. He put a cube of sugar in each tiny glass cup. I didn't like sugar in my tea but he had always served it to me like this so I didn't say anything. We stirred with tiny silver spoons. He cleared his throat.

'So, sweet daughter, let's talk,' he said, readying himself for whatever might come. He placed his hands on his knees.

'Jesus Pappa. Listen I'm sorry if I worried you but there's not like any specific reason for my visit.'

He looked perplexed. Then lifted his cup to his lips as if to hide it.

'I was just, I don't know. I wanted to see you,' I said.

'Ah. That's nice.'

'Yeah, just see you. Talk.'

'Are you sad?' he asked slowly, weighing his words. We locked eyes.

'Yes.'

'Oh sweet thing. If you are sad, I am sad too.'

'Thank you Pappa.' I could feel hot tears in my throat so I drank spiced tea to swallow them down.

·

The band announces their last song for the night and Camilla prepares for the next phase. Then the applause starts and ends and the band packs up their instruments. Camilla walks over to the bar and leans in a way that flatters her body. She orders two drinks and offers one to the bass player. Back at the table, we intently watch this unfold. She really is rather bold. They talk for a while and he glances over at us, then he says something to his bandmates and they all come over to our table. Bass Player sits down next to me.

Camilla flirts and she is doing a good job. But soon, to both our surprise, it becomes clear that Bass Player is pursuing me. It is not procedure, guys picking me over her. I can't think of any other time this has happened. But Bass Player is so unstealthy we have to face facts.

Camilla is not pleased and quickly starts ignoring Bass and me both. My stomach draws tight as if vacuumed, and I worry there will be consequences for this, hostile coffee dates. Though even that could be considered a kind of pastime I guess, to keep my brain occupied.

I am too drunk and numb to care right now and Bass is very pretty. His hand is on my thigh and I don't remove it. He is warm. It is cold outside. My flight home had departed in summer and landed in autumn. Stockholm autumn. Bleak, windy, wet. Not romantic autumn with red leaves and coffee to go and long scarves wrapped three times. Now my hands are always cold and I had forgotten the Stockholm-specific shade of sky. Concrete grey.

Bass's hands are radiators, I want him to thaw me. I wonder what kind of duvet he has. Since leaving London I have not dated or kissed or even flirted but maybe I should. An amuse-bouche to cleanse the taste of Luc, get some selfies of my own for instagram. Reclaim the space.

We go outside, Bass and I, each clutching a beer bottle. The sky has many stars and the air is jarringly cold. I exhale white smoke. It won't snow for another few weeks but the wet path looks shiny, treacherous. I test the ground with my shoe and the grip is bad. My ears are ringing from the loud music before and my senses feel generally overburdened.

The techno tent is packed with dancing people in small clothes and exposed skin, kept warm by the cardio or the pills. We look but we don't join, being past that stage of the night. We are rounding off before the big finale.

'Are you cold?' he asks.

'Yes, very. Aren't you?'

'I don't really get cold. One of those warm-blooded peo-ple.' He wraps himself around me. I keep my arms and hands tight in front of my chest, sandwiched between our torsos. He really is warm. And I am drunk. And he smells like clean wood even though he has been sweating on stage.

'So, how come you play the bass?' I say.

'What do you mean how come?'

'This is stupid maybe but isn't the prettiest band member supposed to be the singer? Star quality, I mean, for market-ing purposes?'

He smiles, pleased. And then he kisses me. It feels pecu-liar. His lips are large and his mouth is dry, his tongue mov-ing rapidly inside my cheeks. 'If you're cold, we should get some real heat into you,' he says and pulls me back towards the main building. I wipe my lips with my hand.

We do three shots of tequila in quick succession. We kiss again. On the dance floor, in front of the now-empty stage, people dance to bubblegum hip hop.

'Let's go back to my place,' he says and I don't bother with a witty retort.

I stumble a bit walking to our table, the tequila in my legs now. Looking for my jacket, I say goodbye to the others, Camilla currently on the drummer's lap. I wonder if drum-mers are considered pretty or ugly. This particular drummer is not nearly as pretty as Bass, which makes me cheerful. Bass is by the door, apping a taxi.

'Should be here in fifteen,' he says and hands me his drink. I don't need any more but can't find a reason to stop.

He kisses me again and pushes me back against the wall. He is being intense and it is meant to be sexy I guess and I neither like it nor particularly dislike it. This evening is more about participation than evaluation. Tomorrow, at coffee, maybe I will do the evaluating. If I can make it amusing enough for Camilla not to feel bitter. I think I will prefer a humorous retelling of these events anyway.

'It's here in a few minutes, let's go,' Bass says.

To meet our taxi, we have to trek down a gravel path too small for cars. The ground is slick with ice and my soles are slipping. I am freezing and unsteady, intent on reaching the car and its heating system. Bass is rushing too, passing on my left. Slightly ahead of me he loses grip and skids on the ice and starts flailing to regain his balance. For a moment there it looks like he will make it. But then the flailing starts again and he is down on the ground with a smack.

He springs to his feet and pretends it is funny, but it has to hurt and be at least somewhat mortifying. I ask if he is okay and brush dirt off the back of his jacket with my naked hand. My bottom jaw is shivering now and my hand feels numb. Even though falling over is human and it could easily have been me skidding and flailing, I still find that I pity him. And this makes me not attracted to him anymore. Those flailing arms exposed his humanity, tragic or comic or both. He might be pretty, but he skids on ice just like the rest of us.

The taxi is warm. I hold my hands up to the vent and hot air blows sensation back into them. When my jaw stops shaking I register that for the next fifty-five minutes, I am trapped in a taxi with a bass player I am no longer attracted to. He has himself not registered this.

I look at his face to analyse what makes him pretty and conclude that it is the symmetry. But now with pity in the mix the symmetry has no real appeal. Luc's harsh cheekbones and wide lips, while somewhat weirdly proportioned, give him charisma that makes you go oh, that man, he will be fun to kiss, he will elevate the conversation. I try to remember a single thing Bass and I have discussed tonight. Something besides drink orders and taxi pickups and you look nice and yours or mine?

Even at seventeen eighteen, that first night we met, sitting next to Luc at the messy dining table, our conversation had flowed quite decently despite my stumbling English. About the hybrid in the driveway and Scandinavian clothing brands and whether politeness or political integrity was the worthier pursuit at a dinner party. It had felt like an intimately private conversation. This summer too, I could say anything I wanted and he would agree or at least not be horrified. I liked it best when we did not agree. Those talks could be dropped and picked up over days, sometimes turning existential. Like whether hetero relationships could ever be gender free, or if authenticity was of any relevance when buying bubble tea from a German named Rex.

Bass moves closer. He has mucus in his eye corner. I lean back and look away, wishing to sleep and wake up in my own bed. His lips are on my neck, my cheek, my earlobe, making childish kissing sounds. I hope that he will stop if I don't move. He doesn't. His lips tickle and I feel nauseous and I am very drunk and I don't want his mouth on me.

I sit up straight and turn to face him. 'Listen. I'm sad to say I'm not really feeling this.'

'Oh. Really?' He backs away.

'You're lovely and everything, I'm just not into this right now.'

'What, and you couldn't have told me that before we left the party?' He looks sullen. I have seen this look on guys before and now I am even less attracted.

We figure out which metro station is between our flats and tell the taxi to drop us there. The rest of the ride, I pretend to sleep. The heating is on but I can't get rid of the cold completely. I pick on a broken nail, shocked by the pain when I tear too far.

At the station I pay the taxi with my card. Nine hundred something kronor. Bass says he will transfer me half through his phone and we go inside the station to keep warm. He swipes at his screen.

'No battery. Shit, sorry it's dead.'

I just stare at him, no energy to comment.

'No worries,' he says. 'I'll go to the cash machine. There's one outside, be back in like two minutes. Wait here and stay warm, okay?'

I wait twenty minutes, too listless to simply leave. Bass doesn't come back.

•

Between my station and apartment building there is a grove. A paved path runs through it and although lamplit by night, I find it scary. But walking home in the cold, deserted by a stingy bass player, I don't care enough to look over my shoulder. An hour in a warm taxi has turned my tequila intoxication into a premature hangover. I am ugly drunk, cannot walk straight and pretty sure I would slur if forced to speak. I had thought leaving London would mean drinking less, but not so. To be honest I can't find sufficient reason not to.

Halfway home, I stop. The tequila is not sitting right. I turn left up a slope, soon crawling more than walking, my fingers digging into cold moist dirt. I pause, stay on hands and knees, and vomit. Holding my hair back with one hand, I lose balance, and drop the hair in the sick. And I can't think of a single person in this whole country I want here, getting me home.

Walking to my building is slow progress. Back in the flat I take a hot shower, shuddering at the lumps in my hair, shampooing two and three times. Then I put on a dressing gown and warm socks, and go to the kitchen. I heat soy milk in a pot. Pour it into a mug. Find cocoa powder in the pantry, a leftover from my retired landlords.

At the kitchen table I stir three heaped spoons of cocoa into the hot milk and then I call Diwa. It is four in the morning in Stockholm, 3am in London. This seems irrelevant, all things considered.

'I saw Pappa the other day,' I say when she picks up. 'He said call Diwa, so here we are.'

'Why did he say that? You okay Sami?' Her voice is gluey but alert.

'No. I don't think so,' I say and sort of hiccup. I try the cocoa. Way too hot still.

She asks me many questions and I can tell I am too drunk to make a lot of sense but this I can't do anything about. I scoop a spoonful of cocoa from the packet and strew it on the table. I form a heap shaped like a pyramid with my fingers.

'You're breaking my heart here Sam, because I can hear you are hurting but I don't know how to fix it.'

'I don't think this is a fixable thing. I mean, fixing doesn't seem like a possible outcome at this stage.'

'You're always like this in Stockholm, we know that already. You should get out.'

'Yes, that would be nice.' I demolish the cocoa pyramid and spread it out evenly on the table and doodle things in the powder with my fingertip.

'Here's a thought. How does Greece sound to you?'

'It sounds nice to me,' I say and hearing the slur in my voice does not mean I can intercept it. I lick my chocolate finger.

'Next-next Thursday, Milly and I are going to the villa for like a long weekend. Why don't you come?'

'I have work that day,' I say, stupid.

'Yeah, obviously you do. But really though, do you care?'

76 DAYS LEFT

Lucas

I start my shift at Darling by cutting an energy bar into eight pieces and placing them in a row behind the till. Every hour on the dot I eat a piece, as a way to mark time. Now there is one piece left before I will close up. Today it's an apple cinnamon bar, my first-choice flavour. Still I have managed to stick to the schedule.

So far getting my life together has been semi-successful. Healthwise, I'm there. I go to the gym four mornings every week, I don't drink much and no smoking at all. Henry and Hitesh and I have playstation nights and I cook dinner. They are grateful for the most part but sometimes they order pizza and I put their uneaten portions in boxes in the fridge.

My stomach is flat again which is how I prefer it but I wouldn't openly admit this. I pretend my usual good shape is by accident, not the result of gym sessions and macronutrient calculations. It's like men aren't supposed to care too much about anything. When seeing my old friends from school, they take the piss out of my clothes and my staying in shape but they never say a word in summer when we go to the beach.

The first time I really noticed my body was because I was embarrassed by it. This was back when Dad and I had eaten bad food for a year and swelled up like marshmallows. I guess it was a sign we were moving forward from Mum's death, the fact that we could even get embarrassed again. I saw him hunch as if trying to shrink and although I would never confess this to anyone I had not only been ashamed of myself but of him too. It was unbearable seeing other people eye him derisively whenever he put fat food in our supermarket trolley. Still I get anxiety sweat worrying he had noticed me noticing them. That he knew I was ashamed, but even more so that I had registered his own shame, that I had to see my dad degraded.

Mum had always been the anchor so without her we drifted. We needed an agreed-upon stability to stick to because Dad and I, if not careful, we slippery-sloped. When we started losing control we rapidly lost all of it. So I reinstated weeknight dinners and Dad bought bathroom scales and it was nice seeing his pride return as his weight came down. I sometimes think this is how we finally got over Mum. It is strange though, Dad always having been such a painfully self-aware person, to see him lose it that quickly had been dramatic.

But now I am far from that slippery slope. And physically I feel great.

Though I wonder how Sam is doing. I hope she is also partying less, waking up without puffy eyes and day-after anxiety. I try not to worry about this but although the gym is a useful distraction, it has turned out to be impossible not to worry about Sam.

I hear the shop's heating system whirr through the music. However loud I play a song the whirring is always there, a locale-specific tinnitus. And it brings me back to the reality that I still spend my days tending racks with thirty-two pieces of clothing. I ignore the whirr and stare at the screen by the till, willing time to move quicker but it doesn't oblige. It is almost time to close and there have been nine customers in today. No one bought anything.

I finally close up and put the last slice of energy bar in my mouth and ban the thought of doing it all over tomorrow. The cinnamon stings my gum.

Mid-October and at 7pm it is dark outside on the street. I walk towards Dalston Kingsland station without any plan. It's Saturday night and neither Henry nor Hitesh is at home so the flat will be dark when I turn the key. I take the overground and get off at Shoreditch.

The streets are filled with people in different states of disorder. I want to be swallowed by the crowd but the heat and noise just make me feel remote. As if wearing a VR headset convincing me this is real but if reaching out I'd only touch air. Paradoxical, not believing a virtual world to be real but the real world to be virtual. Digital age delusions.

On my phone, I am still logged in to Sam's spotify. I can access her playlists, see which new songs she adds and old songs she revisits. Like a musical diary, a track of her mood.

She has mostly added sad songs in minor and I am conflicted. I want her happy of course, but don't know how I would react if she added nothing but upbeat blippy music. I do know that I feel guilty about my own covert activity, skulking her playlists. It is invasive, I get that. I still don't want her to log me out, so I make sure not to do anything to annoy her. I put my earbuds in and listen to her list of Lou Reed songs in order of preference. When I reach 'Perfect Day', I turn it off.

The wretched lump in my ribs has not perceptibly shrunk in the weeks since Sam left. I am almost always able to stand it and trust it will go away but in this moment I have doubts. Maybe it will not go away, what then. I am sad, of course I am. But I got over Mum dying and that was much much sadder.

There is a new sneaker shop on the street corner in front of me. I go inside, pick up a high-top sneaker that I can't afford, put it back. And then there's a tap on my shoulder. I turn around. Evelynn.

To my surprise, I am thrilled to see her. She looks the same, same blonde fringe, same sleepy eyes. I reach out to hug her and she's not made of air, she is organic and she hugs me back.

We talk over each other, stumbling, and it is awkward at first as inevitable with exes. I ask, 'Are you busy right now? Should we get coffee?'

We go down a side street and into a standard café with big velvet armchairs and an abundance of cacti. She talks to the staff as if she comes here often and she asks if I wouldn't prefer a negroni to coffee. 'Yes, sure,' I say, suddenly in a great mood for alcohol.

We sit at a secluded table in the back. It is dark in here but not so dark I can't see her intentionally tanned skin through the intentional knee rip of her light-wash jeans. While she texts her friends she'll be late, I conclude that although I am happy to see her, I am also happy just for a reason to form words with my mouth after a grim day of solitude in the shop.

Evelynn is giving me the brief on her family. We had been nineteen, dating for a year and a bit. I don't remember what initially attracted me to her but I vaguely recall our first kiss, cider-coated tongues behind her friend's garden shed. I don't know how the kiss started or ended or what had provoked it. Even our breakup was unmemorable. She was always kind and all. We just didn't fit.

The dinner party where I first met Sam was still graphically detailed in my mind. Her accent, her long johns and the creepy feel of stubbled legs, how her tongue seemed to investigate my mouth. I remember adding my number in her phone, spelling my name Luc like an idiot because I hoped it would induce character. As far as I know she is the only one thinking of me as Luc.

Evelynn and I are both energetic and laugh at things that aren't very funny. The conversation halts and stops often and this makes us scatty so we order more drinks and finish them quickly. After an hour we have already had three cocktails each. I should eat something. But this feels good, the first time in weeks I'm not constricted as if my skin's too tight. The lump is there but it is benign, doused in vermouth.

By now Evelynn and I both know we have nothing much to say to each other and we both know that we both know. Yet for some reason we are adamant to go on, enjoy each other's company. Maybe it's a sort of loyalty, not ruining the fond memory by admitting the obvious lacklustre chemistry.

'I should get going I guess,' she says and checks her wrist as if wearing a watch, which she isn't. 'I'm late meeting up with the girls.'

We split the bill and head outside. The warm light from the coffee shop spills through the window onto her stubby nose and now I remember this being what initially attracted me, I had found her nose cute. It still is. And I am grateful to have run into someone who genuinely cares about me. We hug goodbye and I hold on for too long. My throat is tight and my tear ducts sting so I stay in the hug to catch my breath. She pulls back a little and then my lips are on hers. It is a forceful kiss, more eating each other than anything. Our teeth clack together, our tongues tangle. And I am thinking, is this really happening.

'I'll get us a car,' she says and waves to a black cab. And although I already question this decision, I give the driver my address.

•

I had set out to quit Darling before October twelfth. Now it is the seventeenth, and I have missed my deadline by five days.

I studied mechanical engineering because of a documentary I saw when I was fifteen, about an innovation making electric cars thirty percent more energy efficient. Since then I have seen all the documentaries and read many books. When applying to universities engineering seemed the natural choice, combining my fascination for mechanics with my fear of climate change.

But green jobs are even scarcer than anticipated and the positions I have applied for have come back as rejections, even after my latest environmental engineering course and the painstakingly readjusted cover letters. Every position takes an age to apply to, researching the company, rewriting my sample letter to be personally addressed to the person in question, coming across as skilled in exactly their respective fields. At first I was optimistic every time I clicked send, feeling I was so obviously the perfect candidate for the job. But by now I have started to feel the hours spent on each application to be a waste. People have got jobs before, I tell myself. How hard can it be. Still, for every automated rejection in my inbox, my agitation grows and I become harsher on myself.

I know that many companies, even eco-unfriendly ones, are employing engineers as sustainability consultants. I have two former classmates with jobs like this and from the looks of it, the whole thing is a sham. They put you in some cellar office and invite you to meetings and listen to your objections and pretend to take them into consideration. Just to have on paper that they are sustainability consulted. Taking a job like that would be the antithesis of my intention with the degree.

I have emailed my old professor, Jonas. I hate self-promotion and being a nuisance, but I know he likes me and I'm hoping he has an industry contact he could pull or at least agree to be my CV reference. Yesterday he replied to my email. Very happy to hear from me and would love to discuss my future over a quick campus coffee. I am grateful for the reply and don't mind coffee and small talk if it means getting his advice. Actually I am looking forward to it.

.

I open the door for Evelynn. The hallway is dark but I turn on the lights and the flat isn't quiet because Evelynn is chatting about nothing really. I hang her jacket on the coat rack and show her to the kitchen.

I pour us each a glass of Hitesh's red wine but before we have tasted it, she kisses me again. I am thinking maybe this is good, I should get it over with. Sleep with someone else. Clear my cache. Evelynn is cute and a kind person, better this than the apps.

We are on my bed and she takes off her top and bra. I don't ask myself if I want this because I don't want to ruin it with an honest answer. Instead I rush off my t-shirt and trousers and we kiss frantically and I put on a condom.

I wish we had some music on. The sounds we are making are too loud, wet, I can't concentrate. She is moaning and wriggling under me and I start to worry I might not come and this horrifies me, because the most important thing when having sex with a girl, is to come. If not, you indicate something's wrong with her because guys are supposed to always finish. And I always do. I've never not. So this is new to me and I don't have any tricks. I decide that whatever it takes I will come and not make this weird.

My phone is on the nightstand and I open Sam's spotify. I choose a playlist with good sex music. Then I close my eyes and focus and move at a fast even pace and I zone out and think of another time with another girl and then finally, blessedly, I come. It is such an impressive accomplishment that I actually laugh and Evelynn grins back. It can't have been enjoyable for her either but at least it's over and although somewhat weird, it's not extremely weird.

I pull out and lie down and take her hand, panting, and she is just about to say something when my phone rings.

I look at the screen. Sam.

It has not been ten seconds since I pulled out of another girl, the condom still on, and she calls.

I feel physically overpowered, like there are too many things for my hands to deal with. I let go of Evelynn and stand up and put my phone down, scared I might accidentally pick up. It shakes and skids across the nightstand from the vibrations and I don't know how to explain the severity of the situation to Evelynn. I pull the condom off but don't have anywhere to put it. I can't go naked to the bathroom and throw it in the bin and come back to the bedroom naked because I can't be naked in front of Evelynn any longer. I drop the condom on the floor, wince at the wet smack, and put on trousers, not bothering with underwear.

'Who was it? Something wrong?' Evelynn asks.

'Yes, sorry,' is all I think of saying.

'Do you want me to go?'

'Sorry for being rude, but yeah, I kind of need to deal with this. It's important. Sorry, I know I'm being a dick.'

She chuckles and starts dressing. 'Lucas, you have never been a dick in your life. Don't worry, I'll let myself out.' She kisses me on the cheek. 'Hope it works out, whatever it is.'

I follow her to the hallway and stand there while she puts on shoes and jacket. I look down and see my heartbeat through the skin.

She leaves. I exhale and make sure the door is locked for some reason before going to the bathroom. I wash my face and hands and try to calm down. Back in the bedroom I throw the duvet over my bed to cover the sheets Evelynn has been naked on. I take our wine glasses to the kitchen to rinse and put upside down on a towel. I sit down on the edge of my bed and stare at my phone. Maybe just wait and call back after a shower and a glass of water and some food. After changing the sheets. I can still taste Evelynn. I am sticky from the condom. At least I hope it is only from the condom.

And then my phone rings again. I stand up. For a second I deliberate.

I pick up. 'Hello? Sam?'

The voice on the other end says, 'Okay so how does Greece sound to you?'

I am so disoriented I just stare at the wall, mouth open.

'Luc, are you there?' she says.

'Hello? Yeah. What the hell?'

She laughs. 'Sorry about the surprise call.'

My breathing is off, short and panty. 'Can you make sense please.'

'So I talked to Diwa last night,' she says, then tells me she has been miserable in Stockholm and in fact ever since those last two miserable days in London together and now she is going to Greece and needs me to come spend some good or at least okay days with her to alleviate her agony. She speaks so rapidly I am having difficulties following.

'So, you're going to Greece,' I say, the only thing I understand for certain.

'Yes. Ten days. And I am wondering if maybe you want to come.'

I let this sink in. I drop my head and look at the floor and there is the used condom. Limp and pale, containing the by-product of awful sex. Of me trying to get over her.

Sam says nothing, waiting for me to talk. But I hear her breathing.

'I thought you wanted a clean break,' I say finally. 'Isn't this a breach of our no-contact agreement?'

'That particular agreement isn't imposed on Greek soil.'

I pick up the condom and carry it to the bathroom, throw it in the bin and close the lid firmly, wedge the phone between my ear and shoulder and count the days of my annual leave while I wash my hands. And with that, I am lump free. As I dry my hands I say, 'You're so fucking weird.'

She laughs and I go to the kitchen and put the kettle on and for this call to end, she will have to hang up because I never will.

70 DAYS LEFT

Sam

The sun does not wake me. The birds do not either. I wake up because my body is sleep satiated.

Outside the window I hear the neighbours having breakfast in their garden. It is a safe sound, like listening to your parents talk over the TV after you have gone to bed.

I arrived at the house yesterday. My flight to Athens landed early in the morning so I took a bus to the ferry and the ferry to the island. I dragged my luggage through the village and up a slope, and a short walk later I got the key from the folded old woman next door.

The white stone house seemed small from the outside. Two floors, windows shuttered, at the end of a street lined with heat-resistant trees. The front looked out over the street, the back onto a garden and the ocean below.

Milly had said to choose whichever of the three bedrooms upstairs so I put my bags in the room with the best view of the ocean and the garden, walled and secluded, except from the birds. In the tiny blue-tiled ensuite, I took a shower and shaved my legs and sprayed my perfume once. I dressed in a beige strappy sundress and white cotton underwear.

Luc was supposed to arrive in Athens early afternoon and take the ferry across at five. It was hot for late October and felt like being teleported back to summer. And I wondered if all this was such a good idea, too many variables to predict a likely outcome.

I made our bed with clean linen and bought dinner things and retsina and bread for breakfast at the village market down the slope. Today was Friday and Milly and Diwa wouldn't join until Thursday, leaving us a week in the house by ourselves.

There was still time before Luc's ferry, so I investigated. The house wasn't big but open-plan and sparse, prototypical Greek with white crumbly walls and floor tiles cool under my feet. The furniture was low to the floor and completely flat, no bulky sofas or puffed cushions. Milly's parents had bought the house in the nineties and it looked like a yuppie's take on a traditional Greek villa, which I guess was mostly accurate. I loved it.

Not sure what to do next, I went out to the garden and took some arty photos of the ocean with my phone and posted one on instagram, humorously hashtagged bliss. Then I edited my caption and removed the hashtag because it really was blissful here and I didn't want to sound ungrateful. I kept scrolling my feed, not really looking at the photos.

To get time off work, I had lied. Which is against my nature so I played it safe by inventing a reason my manager couldn't dispute. I told her my uncle had died and I was needed in London for the funeral and to help my aunt with the aftermath. My manager was very understanding and that made the lie worse. Whenever Uncle Abdel did happen to die, no matter the cause, I would in part put it down to this piece of bad karma. The moment I landed on Greek soil, I changed my instagram settings to private so my manager wouldn't stumble upon un-funerally pictures of turquoise seas and sunscreen.

Walking up and down along the garden wall, I refreshed my twitter feed over and over, occupying my hands from picking at my fingernails and my mind from deliberating how to greet Luc. Hey, hello you. Moronic. Without reaching a conclusion, I put on sandals and skidded down the slope to meet Luc by the ferry.

It was just a tiny dot on the ocean, growing slowly larger. I shaded my eyes with my hand and pictured Luc contained within this dot, that something so small and solitary could safely deliver him to me. As it came closer I searched the deck for his silhouette, convincing myself I could make him out although it was impossible at this distance. I waved nonetheless.

Noises and smells seemed unusually strong to me, vanilla and diesel and men screaming orders, but I forced myself not to get nervous. My legs were shaved, I smelled nice, and there was ouzo in the fridge. I hoped he wouldn't be awkward because if he was, I would be too, by cringe contagion.

The ferry signalled its horn and I flinched, while people both on board and on land got busy securing it to the concrete pier. From the stern, Luc appeared with a nylon sports bag and a carry-on. He was wearing sunglasses. I waved. He couldn't see me because he was looking in the wrong direction but I kept waving since I wanted to be already waving once he noticed me. He did finally. And he smiled. I stopped waving and grabbed my shoulder for balance.

He walked quickly through the crowd and dropped his bags by my feet and hugged me tight with his lips on my neck. I tangled my fingers in his hair and inhaled through my nose and if he had let go right then I would have collapsed to the ground. It felt like I had tricked the universe by coming to Greece, stealing a pocket of time that would stay unrecorded, unlogged.

We went back up the slope. I rolled his carry-on and the wheels sputtered happily on the gravel. We sputtered too, excited small talk about his journey and the house and the village below. I touched him a lot, casually stroking his hair, squeezing his arm for emphasis, because I couldn't quite believe he was here. I had been holding my breath in the harbour, knowing he was on that ferry but still not completely trusting it.

When we arrived at the house, I closed the door behind us and this was a mistake. The air sucked as if vacuum-packed and complete silence fell on us. No more birds and wind and Luc's sputtering carry-on, the simple ease between us gone. I could tell he realised it too, his back too straight, arms stiff at his sides. I cleared my throat and the sound was roaring.

'Do you want something to drink?' I asked.

'Yeah, water would be nice.'

I poured him a glass from the filter jug and when I handed it to him, we both kept our distance. He turned and walked into the lounge and I followed. He stopped by the window, I was metres away.

'How was your trip, flight okay?' he asked.

'Yes, it was fine.' Then after a moment I said, 'So. What's the plan, are we back to normal? Having sex I mean.'

'Jesus Sam.' He laughed a single hah and touched his forehead. 'Not much for formalities are you.'

'What, you want me to finesse it?' It felt like I had bubbles in my throat.

'Surprised you know the word to be honest.'

'We only have ten days. I don't want to waste time finessing around each other like we're shy.'

'Fair enough.' He licked his lips. 'But maybe at least work up to it?'

I paused. Then I said, 'Go on then.'

He tilted his head and we locked eyes. 'Come here,' he said, a shock to my body. I came close enough to touch and he took one of my hands. My arm went tingly. He ran a thumb over my knuckles. 'Usually I would come even closer,' he said, 'before kissing.'

In the silence I could hear my ears pulse. He moved in until our bodies barely just touched. My hair went static and it was almost too much.

So I kissed him. And it was Luc. The specifics of his mouth, his tongue, the rhythm was so familiar it startled me. He tasted faintly of peppermint like he had recently chewed gum. I wished I had too. He placed a hand on the back of my head and I bit his lip and he pulled me closer until our bodies touched everywhere. I moved back and slid the straps off my shoulders and the dress fell to the floor.

He looked at me, quiet for a second. Then he said, 'I've fucking missed you.' And those warm confident hands were on my skin, my ribs, my breasts, low down my back.

I opened the doors to the garden. He leaned back on a sunchair and I got on top of him and pulled the t-shirt over his head, the low-hanging sun leaving long shadows on his chest. He took his phone and wallet out of his pockets and found a condom. Being on top is not my favourite but maybe this is because I have never been on top on a sunchair in Greece. He gripped my hips and I put my hands on his chest for leverage and tried to go slow. The salty wind was in my hair and tickled my skin. I wanted to be loud but thought of the neighbours.

That first night, we didn't mention the past or the future and just got used to being in the same place. With the sun halfway slit by the horizon, we went for a swim which was cold and thrilling, then ate dinner in the dark garden.

Later in bed I showed Luc some Swedish TV, the humour of which he didn't seem to appreciate even though there were subtitles. We lay on top of the covers in our under-wear, drinking ice-cold retsina, the windows opened fully. Loud insects and lapping water and Swedish dialogue our soundscape. We ate popcorn too salty for Luc and not salty enough for me, the tiny white grains spilling onto the covers, making us itch when we moved.

The retsina finished, Luc asked if I wanted another drink. I shrugged a sure and he went downstairs to the kitchen. I scrolled my phone until he reappeared with two tumblers filled with pale yellow liquid, lemon slice on the rim.

'My own invention, sweeter this time,' he said and I laughed.

I took the glass. 'Here's to okay days,' he said. 'To okay days,' I echoed. We raised our glasses and sipped. It was sweet. Too sweet for me. But I drank the whole thing just the same.

∙

Luc sneaks in, opens the windows, and hands me a cup of strong black coffee. The smell is intoxicating. It is our first morning in the villa, and I am already awake listening to the neighbours' breakfast noises and archaic-sounding language outside. I stretch my arms and roll my ankles and moan. Luc pulls a chair up and blows on his coffee, then puts his feet on the bed and rocks his chair on the back two legs.

'Wish I woke up every morning with you bringing me coffee,' I say.

Luc looks away and says yeah.

I think I've just misstepped, bringing up the future like this. The futility of it, spending ten days only to eventually again break a half-healed bone. I flip the duvet off my body, the sun already relentless through the open windows.

He picks up his phone. 'Should we see what twitter has been up to?'

'Why not,' I say and I hope this will become our holiday thing, him reading me headlines and twitter witticisms in the morning.

I truly enjoy holidays, relish them as if a taste to attentively savour. The way Luc and I already seem installed, finding our closest little shop on our way home from our swim last night, to buy orange juice and olives and toilet paper in. The way we're developing vacation-specific habits, like coffee and twitter news in bed.

This is why I love temporary locations. On holidays, I am relaxed. I sleep well, read whole book pages. My fingernails unmutilated, long enough for varnish. I am not on my way anywhere else because I already am elsewhere.

It is the place, but it's also Luc. There is a togetherness about it, factoring someone else into my day. A procedure I am not exactly practised in.

I sip coffee and make dry remarks on Luc's tweet-read to entertain him, reacting to most headlines with 'this would never happen in Sweden.' He reads a headline, 'Sad dog gets a sister and it changes his life forever,' upon which I conclude, 'This would never happen in Sweden,' and finish the last of my coffee.

We shower and dress in swimwear under our clothes. We skid down to the village and walk past the market along the harbour. Then we start climbing street after street leading up the small mountain on the other side of the island. Over the ridge is supposedly an unspoiled pebble beach where not many people come due to the trek. The streets are endlessly zigzagging upwards, lined in white houses with blue shutters. I stop by an off-licence to buy water and ice lollies. The heat today is dry and aggressive and melts the ice quicker than we can lick it, sloppy drips of mango marking our progression like a breadcrumb trail.

Luc asks for a photo of us together so I flip the camera and we smile in front of another white house with blue shutters. This reminds me of the photo on his instagram, the selfie with the girl.

'Have you slept with anyone else?' I ask.

He actually jumps, a physical jolt.

'Don't,' he says.

'No it's okay, I won't mind. I mean, we weren't together.'

'Why, have you?' His lips look sticky with sugar, the ice lolly in his hand out of place in this conversation.

'I haven't, no,' I say. 'One close call but I didn't want to. We kissed but that was it.'

'Oh.'

'Yeah. So have you?'

He looks panicked. I can tell he has and is now deliberating whether to tell me or refuse the conversation. I know he won't lie.

Finally he says, 'I have. Once.'

The heat is ruthless, constricting. The sun so bright it illuminates everything glaringly, our shadows black by contrast. There is no softness anywhere today, no shade on the street to hide in. A mango lump drops on my hand and makes its way down my wrist. I don't have a tissue so I rub it on my shorts.

'Who with?' I ask.

'My ex.' His forehead glitters with sweat. 'Evelynn.' And then the story bursts out as if festering inside him, swelling, just waiting for the moment to pop. I am shocked. Though not as shocked as Luc himself telling me that when I called to invite him here, she was in his bed. That when I called again, the filled condom still lay on the floor. It's a lot. He apologises and says it was bad timing and the sex was awful and the day had been grim but that my phonecall had counterbalanced the bad and it had ended up being an overall decent day. Starting bad, ending brilliant.

I blink.

He slows down but I want to hurry up the sloping streets and out of the sun. I am physically uncomfortable and wonder if I should be angry, like he has betrayed me somehow. I am vaguely sickened. But mostly I feel an unbearable regret that this happened to him.

It's a lot.

'And, will you see her again?' I ask.

'God no. No it was awful. I'm sure she felt the same way. I had to think of you to be able to come.'

'Stop. Jesus. Just stop, okay. No more details.'

'Sorry.' He rubs his face. 'I've just felt so wrong not telling you, I mean, I know we're not together and we can sleep with other people, but it was literally impossible not to tell you.' We go around a zigzag bend and still there is only street. Nowhere to hide from the sun, no shady hillside in sight. I am panting now and it is hard to talk and climb at the same time. My insides are cooking and I think that this can't be healthy.

I slow down and sigh and turn to him. 'It's fine. Let's just stop talking and get to this beach, okay.' I take his hand to show him we're good. But walking up that sun-scorched street I can't stop thinking about sending him back to London. Alone. With his nylon bag and his sun-bleached hair.

I stop at the end of the street, to my right is the leafy hill-side finally.

'If you came back to London though,' he says, 'there'd be no need for me to sleep with other people.'

'Sure.' I swing his arm back and forth. 'But I can't switch countries every time I fall for a boy.'

He stops and exhales as if bracing himself. 'Right. But if you're set on Stockholm, you could at least let me visit. I might like it even though you don't.'

I bite my lip till it hurts. Then I say, 'Luc, I sort of hate the person I am in Stockholm. You would too, trust me. She's cynical.' And although it's shocking thinking this I fear I might not like a Stockholm version of Luc either.

He pulls me in tight and exhales with his sugar-sticky mouth in my hair. 'Pretty sure I'd like you in any city to be honest.' I pull back and he looks sort of agitated. 'Seriously though, if you hate it so much, why would you stay there?'

I shrug. 'I probably won't.'

'So this isn't about staying in Stockholm, it's about not staying with me?'

'Indeed.' I sound hard, the conversation irritating me now. 'Honestly Luc, do you really want me back in London, like full-time.'

'Yes.'

'I don't believe you.'

He walks up to a house door and sits on the front step. I join him, the stone hard on my bones, the sun burning my thighs.

'Why?' he asks.

'We're so different it's absurd. And getting older we'll only grow further apart.'

'Or we could grow closer.'

'After ten weeks this summer you found me exasperating. Imagine ten months or even years.'

'I annoyed you as well.'

'You did yeah.' I feel tears stinging which is irritating so I give my head a few sharp shakes. He squeezes my knee but doesn't say anything. 'I loved this summer,' I say finally. 'Like I think of us and it makes me nostalgic. I don't want to force a relationship and grate each other until we kill it or until we can't look at us nostalgically anymore and start hating each other.'

'No I get that.' He sighs. 'Speaking for myself here, last month has been grim. I won't bore you with it. But it's such an insane contrast to how I'm feeling now.'

'No, I agree. But we'll get over it.' I tap his leg with my fingertips. 'I would only hold you back. And you would me.'

He gnaws his lip and then he says, 'That's the thing, I'm not sure we would.' He clears his throat. 'Yeah we disagree on that.'

This is curious so I nod at him to go on.

'People who are close, they don't just keep grating each other. They can change, over time. Like mellow each other out.'

'As in you calming me down, me loosening you up?'

'Maybe.'

'But, is that even desirable? To mellow out. Like, your structure and routine and fixations, would you want to mellow them?' I search his face for his reaction. 'Because honestly, I don't think I want to slow down, I don't want to be like you.'

'Wow Sam.'

'No seriously now, do you want to become like me? You don't.'

'I don't. But I don't know why, because loosening up, it sounds nice. It sounds like something I should want for myself.'

I lean my head back against the door and close my eyes. 'Yeah. I mean, I want that for you.'

'And I definitely want you calmed down,' he says.

I scoff. And I feel it then, that familiar tingle, the urge to throw myself headless. It is mad to me, that in this conversation, I am somehow the cautious one. I turn to face him. 'So, our working theory is that our differences would either hold us both back from the lives we want, or evolve us into calmer looser future selves? So either catastrophe or quite sublime.'

'Or both.'

I fully fill my lungs.

'I mean, it's a risk,' he says. 'But consider the alternative.'

'Which is?'

'Bland. Tolerable.'

'Maybe for you but my life wouldn't be.'

'What then?'

'I don't know, rootless?' I say, but what I'm thinking is manic.

'I'm not trying to be cute here but I have been looking at the job situation in Stockholm.'

'Why, what's in Stockholm?'

'I mean, you are.'

Without blinking I say, 'Allegedly.'

He stares at me for a moment then lifts his shoulders in a who-knows and smiles with half his mouth.

Our time on the stone step has only lasted a few minutes. Disoriented, I notice the ice lolly still in my hand, slowly dripping sugar like no time has passed at all. We stand up and face the leafy hillside. I throw the remains of my melted lolly in a bin, then wipe my sticky hand on my shorts again. He laughs and calls me a mess and finds a bottle in my rucksack and pours lukewarm water on my sticky hand. I take the bottle and wash the sweet taste out of my mouth. And when we finally make it across the ridge, the ocean on the other side is obscenely blue and looks cold and salty.

47 DAYS LEFT

Lucas

She is on the floor with her limbs out like a starfish. I lie down next to her, my head on her arm. 'It's not much but it's ours,' she says. Empty except for a few bags and boxes, one small bedroom, a galley kitchen next to a living room, a peach tiled bathroom with shower. It is not how I pictured my first flat. Still, it's sort of great.

'Till you get a new job anyway,' Sam says, full of optimism.

Last week, we viewed three other places before this, all in East London, each worse than the previous. One had a combined bedroom-kitchen and not much else. One with bathroom mould so widespread I first thought the ceiling was painted a mottled grey. The third flat we viewed, the final one before finding this place, was a souterrain with dark red walls that made walking down the stairs feel like entering someone's stomach. The place was fuggy with garlic and cigarettes and stale wine, and when the estate agent showed us the bedroom a man flew up from a tangle of sheets like a jack-in-the-box. Just standing there

143

naked-chested with nostrils flaring to everyone's surprise. I looked at Sam although I knew I shouldn't and our laughter erupted with those snorting sounds you make when you try hard not to laugh and the whole thing was very inappropriate so we left quickly and went to a café in Stoke Newington to cool off. I ordered for us both while she planted herself by the window.

When the coffees arrived, Sam was complaining about my reluctance to let her pay a bigger portion of the rent to increase our overall budget.

'I know it's just a temp position,' she said, 'but still, I make more money than you so I should pay more. Let's look at percentage instead of total.'

'Yeah, I'm not comfortable with that.' I tasted my black Americano. Sam was having a foamy soy latte.

'Why?' she asked. 'It's only fair. And if you earn more later on, you'll pay more.'

'I hear you. It makes sense and all, and fine if we'd been in this situation further down the line. I just can't start out unequal like that.' I blew on my coffee which was hot. 'Besides, we've only viewed three places.'

'If this is some masculinity thing, I'll be so annoyed.'

'Obviously it's not. Hell, I'm not that insecure.'

'Okay then.' She huffed. 'But send out those CVs soon please because I'm not living in a souterrain stomach flat forever.'

'Sam, don't worry, we'll find a place.' I wanted to envelop her, like physically give her reassurance. Her hand fiddled with a napkin, tearing the paper into shapes. The place was quiet except for the milk foamer once in a while hissing air. 'Hey, who do you think was more freaked out, us or the sleeping man?'

She snickered. 'Us for sure.'

'You reckon he comes with the tenancy?'

'I should hope so for that price.'

When Sam was in Stockholm I had worked on my CV, meticulously drafting and redrafting. 'Can I see it?' she asked now and ordered another soy latte plus an oat cookie. Four hundred calories at least.

I had looked forward to showing it to her. Her marketing expertise was hugely helpful of course, but also her confidence in me made me keen not to disappoint. I had met Professor Jonas for a quick campus coffee just before Greece and he said he'd keep an eye out for any opportunities. But that was the extent of my contact list, a very limited black book. One name. Lately in the far back of my brain, I had been entertaining applying for jobs in less ethical companies as a starting point. To get out of Darling before my mind was lost interminably. I was adamant to find something well before this level of desperation.

Tabatha had told Sam about a maternity-leave temp position opening at the agency Sam had worked at over the summer. She was offered the job before the position was even advertised because the team leader remembered Sam, plus Tabatha's mum was a golden ticket type of reference. I could tell how anxious she was to start next week. I was pleased for her, and also I envied her a lot.

I took a deep breath and got my laptop from my bag and slid it across the café table. I opened the CV document and flipped the screen up so we both could see. Sam took a bite of the cookie and held it up to me. 'Want some?'

I wondered if it was expected of me, to prove I was relaxing my fixations. I broke off a piece and put it in my mouth and the chew was alarmingly loud in my ears. I couldn't say whether I liked the taste, to me mostly sugared butter, but in this instance taste seemed inconsequential. I swallowed and tried not to think about it.

'So okay, I love it already,' she said, scrolling up and down the two CV pages. 'It looks impressive. Very modern. Very designed.'

'Too designed?'

'Maybe a tad,' she said and scrunched up her eyebrows, scanning my face to see I wasn't hurt. I wasn't. 'Maybe skip those lines there,' she said.

'Got it.'

Then she read through the whole thing carefully. Humming. Sometimes uhuh-ing. She marked a couple of things in red.

'Well, I'd hire you,' she concluded and smirked and broke off a piece of cookie and put it in her mouth. Crunching noises filled the space between us.

'Too bad you're not hiring.'

'One thing. I think you can add something charming about why you studied engineering in the first place, that documentary with the battery guy? Would make you come across as a real person instead of just one of a hundred applicants.'

'And that wouldn't be, you know, obnoxious?'

'No definitely not. Since you have such limited experience, what else do you have to offer than your winning charisma?' She looked at me expectantly. 'You're not begging for a job. You're informing them they'd be lucky to have you, that's what a cover letter is for.'

'Yeah, no, I'm no good at that stuff.' I rubbed my eyes till I saw white orbs moving under my lids.

'I know you aren't,' she said and chewed and the cookie crunched. 'Don't worry, I'll help you. Let's make a list of people you should try to get in touch with.'

I squinted at her, not sure what she meant.

'You know, networking. Are you even on linkedin?'

'Oh, well no. I wouldn't bother someone unsolicited like that.' I felt warm, my armpits moist.

'One million engineers want the same job as you. How will you get the position if you're not willing to nag a little? I don't see you have a choice.'

And I thought okay, getting a linkedin account wasn't so bad, just to silently skulk, learn the important industry names. 'You got a point,' I said and she looked pleased and again I was grateful for her simply being in the country.

•

The next day we saw Milly and Diwa for lunch in Angel. We met early because Sam and I had another flat viewing that afternoon. The restaurant was much larger on the inside than it looked from the street and Diwa and Milly were already seated when Sam and I arrived, even though we weren't late. We hadn't seen them since they joined our final weekend in Greece and although I didn't know them extremely well I thought asking us out for lunch seemed kind of formal. So yeah, I was curious.

Diwa had moved in with Milly earlier this autumn and Sam had been staying in the near-empty Kentish Town flat since Greece, getting out of the way whenever it was shown to potential buyers. It was weird seeing the place now, in gloomy autumn, next to no furniture, as if the summer we spent there was years ago, not months.

We hugged and talked over each other and both Milly and especially Diwa seemed frenetic, almost a bit high. The chairs screeched when we sat down and Milly poured us all sparkling water from a large bottle before raking a hand through her hair.

'I'm having the pesto sandwich,' Diwa said without looking at a menu.

'Oh me too,' Sam said.

I ordered a rice bowl and Milly a burger with sweet potato fries. Although the energy was festive Sam didn't suggest wine. It all felt very adult. And also I thought, sort of like a family gathering. I drank some water and looked at Sam.

Even before the food arrived Diwa said they had news. 'Not exactly news yet really, more of a concept at this stage.' And Milly said, 'An idea really.'

'Spit it out,' Sam said and laughed.

'Don't lose it now,' Diwa said, 'but we're trying to start a family.' She held on to the table and looked at Sam for a reaction. 'Diwa, jesus!' Sam said and I said, 'Oh wow,' and I was very happy and wanted to find good words for what I was feeling. We didn't stand up but kind of half hugged over the table and said congratulations and more of the one-syllable exclamations. I think they understood how we felt without any particularly good words. Then the food arrived and we all leaned back and simmered down.

'So how does it work exactly?' Sam asked.

'Anonymous donation,' Milly said and dipped a sweet potato fry in ketchup.

'No I mean as in, who will be the mother?'

'Obviously, we'll both be,' Diwa said slowly, with an edge.

Sam waved a hand, unfazed. 'You know what I mean.'

'We haven't decided yet,' Milly said. 'If we have two we might do one each.'

I chewed rice and swallowed too quickly and said, 'I think it's great. That you can like, choose who does it.'

Milly smiled at me and Diwa said, 'But seriously so difficult. It's such a huge decision.'

'You mean practically? Like whose career to pause?' Sam asked. 'Or do you mean like healthwise.'

Diwa let out a single laugh. 'Yeah I mean sure Sami, but I was more thinking in terms of who's going to miss out. On being pregnant. From what I hear it's quite the experience.'

I found myself wishing Milly would be the one missing out, that Diwa would be the pregnant one. Because what I wanted was to meet a kid with her genetic makeup, which was also Sam's genetic makeup. I looked at them now, chatting, taking too large bites of their sandwiches, chewing too few times before swallowing and interrupting each other without a trace of politeness. Sam would love that kid and if she ever had a daughter of her own they would be cousins and best friends just like Diwa and Sam. I wasn't sure how it worked with donors, if they would choose hair colour and skin tone or leave it to chance. But if Sam and I became parents, my guess was her genes would be dominant and our daughter would look just like Sam, only with hair a few shades lighter. Maybe if you checked close you would see some of me, in the mouth or the slant of the eyes. It was a staggering train of thought, all of it. And still totally reasonable. It was a physical possibility is what I mean.

Milly was telling us about her parents' comical reaction to the news and how they had repeatedly failed to grasp the idea of the baby not sharing both Milly's and Diwa's DNA, that it wouldn't be a genetic combination. There were a bunch of jokes to be had on this subject and Milly and Diwa were fairly outrageous but also their jokes showed, by sheer number, that they had been talking about this for some time. I wanted to tell them to hurry up getting the donation.

'So does that mean you're not a family now?' Sam asked suddenly. 'I mean, since you said you're starting a family by getting pregnant?'

Diwa sighed. 'It's an expression. Don't be literal.'

'No I wasn't, I was genuinely curious if that's how you feel.'

Diwa grinned wide then. 'Oh I see,' she said. 'For the record Sam, yes I do consider you family, don't worry. Although I have to say it doesn't exactly flatter you to get jealous of a conceptual foetus.'

Sam rolled her eyes and mumbled something like, god so stupid, and Milly said, here we go. It was a great scene really, I enjoyed it.

Diwa paid for lunch and when we objected she said to pay her back with dinner in our new flat once we got one. We left them in the restaurant with their coffees because we were in a hurry to get to our viewing in Leytonstone.

Walking to the station the air was cold and sunny and we had to squint our eyes. I was light both in my legs and in my head. The cold felt good when I breathed.

I found Sam's hand and brought it to my lips. She said, 'I feel a bit bad.'

This seemed strange so I said, 'Bad how?'

'Don't you think Diwa was a bit disappointed? By my reaction?' Sam didn't slow down so I couldn't see her face. 'Like, maybe I was being weird.'

'No. No you were fine, just a bit shocked. Diwa would understand that.'

'Still though, I want a do-over.'

I could see the tube entrance ahead, we would make the viewing on time. 'Just call her later. Tell her all the irresponsible auntie things you will do, she'll like that.'

'She will,' Sam said, sounding lighter. 'Oh I would make such a great aunt wouldn't I.'

'You would yeah.' And as we jogged down the steps to the station I said, 'Hey whatever this flat is like, let's just take it okay?'

•

Our new place is the one-bed we viewed that afternoon, an unfurnished flat in Leytonstone. It is clean with white walls and budget wood floors. It smells of paint and rubber, brand new. Nothing about it is unique. Pragmatic mediocrity.

We don't have much to unpack. The sofa will be delivered in a few weeks, and we are picking up some of Diwa's rejects tomorrow. Kitchen table, chairs, a bookcase. The rest we will thrift. On the floor is a box with *books* in red marker. I drag it towards me and make colour-coordinated book piles that I stack in different windows. I step back and evaluate the room and our few possessions look nice together, as if meant to be mixed.

Sam unzips my suitcase and hangs jackets on the hooks in the hallway. One night in Greece when setting the table for dinner she had looked up at me and plainly asked if I still thought it a good idea for her to come back to London and I said, 'Yes, yes of course I do, are you joking.'

Now Sam sits down next to me on the living room floor. I ask her how she's feeling. She says, 'Great,' and picks up her phone. 'Let's start a shopping list, emergency items.' She thumbs words on the screen.

'I can't believe you are here. I mean in this flat, with me.'

'It is rather wild, isn't it. Last month I was doing tequila shots in the woods with a bass player and just look at me now.'

'Hey now, none of that.' I go over to the suitcase and pick up bathroom things and pile them on the floor. 'I don't want to picture him in here.'

'No? Prefer to invite your ex instead?'

'Ah, see, I might prefer your bass player actually.'

Forty minutes ago the estate agent handed us the key, took a victory lap around the living room, and left us to our destiny. We had already signed a contract thick as a Stephen King novel and it made me nervous since there was no way to read all of it before signing. But also proud because it was one of those adult moments. No more flat-mates. And I was only twenty-seven. By London standards that's fairly advanced.

Sam puts on my black sweatshirt as a dress over an oxford shirt and sheer black tights. I lock the door to our flat and we take the train to central and press into the crowds of John Lewis. On the higher floors, the crowds disperse. We stroll the aisles, carefully considering our options. Sam picks up a noodle bowl and holds it up to me with a face that says 'look, cute'. I budge.

She finds a set of six Iittala wine glasses that are simple and elegant and glint when she rotates them. They are expensive. She says she is not leaving without them. The disparity of our bank accounts will become an issue, I realise this. But today I don't care and I am dying to give her these wine glasses but I can't afford them. I shift my weight from side to side.

'My housewarming gift to you,' she says, and so solves my dilemma.

'I haven't got you anything,' I say.

'The noodle bowls, stupid.' She nudges my shoulder.

The pillowcase aisle is empty and she is giddy and so sexy in my sweatshirt and we kiss pressed against the shelves. It doesn't matter that the flat is small, I don't want space between us anyway.

Picking out two of everything like a Noah's Ark of tableware to eat breakfast and dinner and drink wine and wash up and sleep together gives me a pleasant shiver right there in aisle four. Like playing house, but without playing.

The queue is long and I entertain Sam by telling her lame things. I say be prepared, I will serve her food in these bowls for an undetermined number of dinners. And I think, later when our circumstances have changed, when we've bought a two-bedroom on a street with trees, we will romanticise this specific day, our current lack of finances by then only nostalgia inducing. How soft-hearted and condescending of this version of us we will be. Likely we will still have some of these items in our remodelled kitchen. The three surviving wine glasses. The one bowl I didn't break washing up. I try to express these thoughts but I'm not sure I'm making much sense. She says that at this price, more than three wine glasses better have survived. Maybe some of the people in the queue hear us going on like this, I don't know.

We take the train back home which is a nice thought. When we exit the station with our large plastic bags the sun is out and our new street looks warm, neighbourly.

'We should invite Dad over,' I say.

'Oh yes, let's.'

'Will be good for him to meet you finally, see the flat.'

'Too bad your mum can't see it,' she says. 'I will never meet her you know, it's weird to think about.'

'I've thought that too.' This is a sad conversation but I am happy Sam brings it up like this, impromptu and not so serious.

'Do you think she'd like me?'

Although it's bleak, I say, 'Honestly, I don't know. I mean you're a ridiculously likeable person so I'm sure she would.' I scan Sam's face and she just nods upwards, go on. 'But I don't know what her exact opinion would be, like what specifically about you she'd single out.'

'You don't remember her enough?' Her voice is completely normal, as if discussing which takeaway.

Although far from as comfortable, I say, 'You know how grieving people say they can't remember someone's face and how it kills them? Like, I remember her face fine, it's her personality I struggle with. She was just there. Very present and kind. But her idiosyncrasies? I don't know.'

'Yeah that's a hard one.' She puts down her bags and squeezes my upper arm. 'Although to be fair, my mum has plenty of idiosyncrasies and I still don't understand her half the time.'

'But Sam,' I say and put my palms around her face. 'My dad, he will love you.'

She looks up at me. 'He will?'

'Oh yes. I mean eventually. First he'll be extremely awkward around your, you know, more abrupt sides.'

'That's terrible Luc.' She looks at me with childlike sincerity. 'I'll tone it down.'

'No god, don't. We'll laugh about it afterwards and then he will call me the next day saying something like how interesting you are. No no, refreshing.'

She shoves my chest and starts walking again. 'Actually, I think I might like that.'

Later I join her in the shower but I hurry. Then I place an order on my phone and I put on a clean shirt and a pair of trousers not too suitcase creased.

When Sam turns off the shower and goes to the bedroom to dress, I have already laid things out on the living room floor as a solution to the lack of tables. Our new plates and glasses, a condensating bottle of Cava. My phone plays a blippy French pop playlist she likes.

She walks out the bedroom wearing a vest and a pair of black trousers. Hands in her pockets, hair wet, barefoot. She makes an excited noise when she sees the picnic scene. Then she sits opposite me in lotus position, her knees bobbing up and down.

I open the Cava with a pop and fill our new wine glasses. 'No Champagne glasses,' I say. 'Let's add that to the shopping list.'

'No this is perfect Luc.'

It is dark outside and we have no lamps so her face is only illuminated by the kitchen fan and the streetlights. Passing cars send flares across the room making her eyes flash now and then. I am determined to make her feel at home in this space.

There is a sharp ringing sound.

'Is that?'

'Our buzzer?' Both of us grinning now. We have a joint buzzer and this is the sound it makes.

19 DAYS LEFT

Sam

He is in the bathroom with a basket of wet laundry on the toilet lid, the drying rack half filled with white t-shirts and socks and underwear. His earbuds are pushed in and the overhead light is harsh on his skin. He sticks his tongue out and moves it around because he is concentrating. It is Saturday morning and this scene looks so mundane I can't tell if it is heartwarming or depressing. A bit of both probably.

'I'm bored,' I say and lean against the doorframe with my arms folded. I regret saying it when hurt raps across his face. My blurts seem to hurt him quite often. As if my personality somehow is his failure, and by living together I should have by now developed a slower, more considerate disposition. 'Let's do something,' I try again, softer. 'We never see your friends.'

'We see Henry and Patti and Tabatha like all the time,' he says, methodically hanging my damp bras, untangling the straps, each one amply spaced on the rack. Items so familiar to him they have lost their seductive power. Breast support, not sex accessories. Again, both heartwarming and a little sad.

'What about your old friends, I still haven't met Robert,' I say and nudge him on the shoulder. 'Are you ashamed of me? Not as cute as your exes?'

An hour and four texts later, we are invited to cocktails at Robert's that same evening.

The last few weeks with Luc have been beautiful. And though they've not been smooth, we have both adjusted, mellowed out. I sometimes get fidgety staying in at night, but often I find it restful too. I wake up with amplified energy, which can be a good thing depending on which direction I release it. Luc seems mostly pleased too, moulding his routine to fit around me. We give and we take and yes so far we seem better for it. But we still aren't smooth. He doesn't handle emotional outbursts very well and sometimes I aggravate him on purpose to get a reaction, release tension, move on to good makeup sex. He hardly ever shows anger and when I do I feel vicious by contrast.

It is early December and we have yet to buy Christmas decorations. I think maybe it's best to get them myself because Luc has hardly any money and I don't want to do the budget version with sad plasticky baubles and fairy lights that explode the third time you plug them in. I will be in Stockholm on the actual day so we'll have our own mini Christmas the week before.

I take a shower, and once done with the laundry, Luc slides open the curtain with the phone in his hand.

'Okay, so I just heard back about the agriculture consultancy job. They're going for someone else.'

My stomach drops. 'Oh mate, I'm sorry Luc.'

He places the phone on the basin and undresses and joins me in the shower. 'It's like, I'm twenty-seven, shouldn't I be done with this.' His voice sounds raw. 'Months are just going by and I'm standing completely still here.'

We have worked on Luc's CV together and its current status is as good as it's going to get. But jobs are scarce and he lacks experience so the few replies have so far been rejections.

I pull him close and place my chin on his shoulder. We're right under the showerhead and the water splashes into my eyes and ears and mouth.

'What if I'll be folding clothes in the shop forever,' Luc says in a rare show of pessimism, his voice echoing through the falling water. I kiss his neck, gently. Thinking of him alone in that clothes shop eight hours per day makes my heart ache. He is so clever and charming and talented, but talent with no contacts is like a wheel without a car in this city. I am only happily employed because of Tabatha's mum after all.

He pumps soap into his hand, two clear blobs.

'Sooner or later you will get the job, I know you will.' The water is too hot so I turn the knob.

Luc's stress about our wage discrepancy is obvious and although I first suspected it a masculinity thing, I now don't. I think it's about the things money enables. Luc doesn't attempt grand romantic gestures. There is no running at airports or shouting from rooftops or passionate fighting and making up. Luc's specific brand of romance consists of small but perpetual acts of care. Going to the Conran Shop and letting me handpick Christmas baubles, mixing and matching as I wish, this would be Luc's idea of a gesture. And we could still do that, if not for his misconception that it matters which credit card makes the payment. It doesn't.

•

My mouth gets burned by mulled wine.

'God that's hot,' Finn says. 'My tongue lost like three layers.'

I laugh and blow my styro cup and try another careful sip.

'Also hot?'

'Also hot.'

We are at Mare Street Market and it is festive with blinking lights and stalls wrapped in pine and holly. I link my arm through Finn's. We are wearing many layers of clothes and it is nice huddling together blowing our hot drinks in the crisp afternoon. We've had lunch, just the two of us. Luc didn't join because he went to the gym after the job debacle this morning and he wanted to eat something efficient afterwards, meaning food you have to peel, measure, and cook yourself. Finn and I had mushroom risotto which I figure wasn't even that unhealthy. But Luc will often want to peel and measure when he's anxious and the rejection email had been sufficiently anxiety-inducing so I left him to it.

It is fine because it's lovely to be alone with Finn and he is the best partner for my current type of wild mood, as he has almost no self-assigned rules. Although today will not turn into one of those wild days since Luc and I have cocktail plans with his childhood friends. We have borrowed Milly's car and will buy a Christmas tree before driving to Robert's flat.

Finn asks if Luc and I are getting used to sharing one living space. I tell him it's great. Really great. He stops and stares at me until I expand.

'It's December. It's not like you know, summer,' I say carefully. Although immigrants both of us, I figure we should adopt the Brits' love for a good weather euphemism.

'But is it cold dark midwinter or is it cosy hot-chocolate winter?' Finn asks. 'Oh fuck, it's not panto is it?'

'Jesus, it's not panto relax,' I say and laugh. 'It's the cosy one. Hot chocolate.'

'But winter still can't beat summer?'

'That's it.' We walk towards Broadway market, locals in jackets too thin, tourists in jackets too thick. It smells of cinnamon and nasty cheese. Once swallowed by the market crowd it gets noticeably warmer. Finn and I, arm in arm, moving through other people's exhaled air. Marketplace miasma.

'I'm not complaining or anything. Luc is gorgeous, like extremely affectionate. It's just, we are still finding our rhythm I think.'

'Sure,' says Finn and the conversation ends there. Finn wants you in a good mood and when you aren't he usually ignores this or distracts you until you're happy again. Not that I'm not happy. Things are just different from last summer when we had a time limit, a ten-week holiday. Luc had been carefree, trusting in autumn to bring back normalcy.

And I see now how much he loves the routine everydayness. While I still miss summer.

That miserable month in Stockholm I'd longed to be back in London, back with Luc. I got precisely what I wanted. City, boyfriend, job, flat. So the flat is not great but it is a start. When we improve the living situation I will be content, and soon it will be spring and then summer again. Another summer in another flat with the same Luc.

But first Christmas in Stockholm. I don't like leaving Luc. I still haven't met his dad but from what Luc has told me they seem a bleak pair. Luc wouldn't want his dad alone for the holidays so I haven't asked him to come with me.

Finn and I walk through the market to the southern end where Luc picks me up in Milly's car. I hug Finn goodbye and get in the passenger seat and Luc drives to a garden centre where we spend an awful long time choosing our Christmas tree. We put it in the car boot and it is dense and slightly bent and kind of great. It is a real tree and it fills the car with the scent of resin and wet needles, putting artificial pine car fragrances to shame.

Robert is Luc's friend from school. This is the first time I will meet him and I am excited. Luc has mentioned him when telling childhood memories and they share a lot of history so I figure he'll be another number in the Luc equation.

'A small warning,' Luc says, driving, looking at me instead of the road.

'What's that?' I say and grab his shaved chin, turning him back forward.

'Robert is not exactly, well, he, we are like,' he clears his throat, 'we don't have a lot in common really. He is into football and that, bets on games a lot. He's more of an anecdote type of person.'

'Bets on games. Anecdotes. Got it.' I sound flippant but Luc feeling the need to warn me is slightly unsettling.

We park the car outside a square apartment building in a residential south-east London neighbourhood. I clutch the neck of the wine bottle I've brought as we take the stairs to the second floor. Now red wine seems like the altogether wrong thing to bring to this place, I will come off as a douche. Should have gotten a couple of good beers, in bottles.

Luc rings the doorbell. There are voices in there, low music. Someone shouts something and then the door swings open and crashes into the wall with a bang before swinging back. I catch it so it won't slam shut again, almost dropping the wine.

'Lucky,' the person yells and collects Luc into an embrace of sorts, banging Luc's back so hard I hear the hollow of his lungs.

'Hey Robbie,' Luc says in between bangs. 'This is Sam.'

'Hi,' I say, taking a half-step back to dissuade any further embraces. 'Nice to meet you finally.' I hold out the wine bottle like a peace offering. 'This is for you,' I say. He doesn't accept it. I have been in the company of Robert for all of ten seconds and I am already sweating. His aggression is sheer. Sharp. Badly hidden under a toothy grin. I

165

wonder why we are here. Then I remember I was the one suggesting it.

'Red wine, fancy,' he says and takes the bottle. He gives me a quick up and down assessment, the smile fades and he turns around. I am searching for Luc's eyes as if islands in a storm. He takes my hand. 'You okay?'

I nod.

'Linda and Gael are here too,' he whispers. 'We don't have to stay long.'

He leads me to the living room. A thread of fairy lights flashing red then blue then red again are taped to the wall, both colours alarming in their alternating heat and cold. There is a miniature Christmas tree in the window, sprayed with synthetic snow.

In a large leather corner sofa, Gael and Linda are sitting, each with a beer bottle in hand. I have met them once before, they seem nice. Standing up, we all kiss each other's cheeks. I appreciate that Gael and Luc are cheek kissing when they meet. I think it's the done thing in Spain where Gael is from, but Luc also looks natural and kind of aesthetic doing it. And in this room, it staves off some of the surplus testosterone. Robert is body-slamming the kitchen by the sounds of it. Out he walks with a shiny black tray, five whiskey glasses filled with urine-coloured liquid.

'Scotch and soda,' he says, proud as if his invention. Whiskey makes me ill but Robert is not a person you easily say no to, so I reach for a heavy ornamented glass when he holds the tray in front of me. The bottle of wine is alone on the table, ignored. I want to hide it.

'My two best friends, both all coupled up,' he toasts, glass raised. 'Now we just need to find me a girl and we'll all go on holiday together. Cheers.' He drinks. I taste a small mouthful. The whiskey stings my upper lip. I hate the flavour.

We sit down, Robert dragging a chair to the opposite side of the large glass table, then turning the music volume up. Post Malone. Linda and Gael both look small on the sofa, as if shrinking, eaten by leather. Robert is too large for his chair, though not actually a big man he looks sort of swollen. Everyone is drinking quickly, glasses clinking on the table. I don't dare ask for a beer so I sip my whiskey, ignoring the nausea. Better drunk and sick than sober stiff in this company.

The setup somewhat resembles a piece of experimental performance art. Robert more or less monologuing, the rest of us subdued, like we're dodging his attention. I am surprised by my own reluctance to speak. We are five adults, yet I don't remember feeling this intimidated since like eighth grade.

Robert is refilling our glasses in the kitchen. I summon up courage to ask for a beer, imagining the cold bitter taste washing away the whiskey. But I deflate, look to Luc for help.

'Oh,' he says. And then louder, 'Robbie, you mind grabbing a beer from the fridge?'

Robert stops his pouring, goes to the fridge, grabs a bottle, slams the fridge door shut. Soon he is back with his shiny tray again.

'The beer's for Sam.' Luc nods towards me.

'Of course,' Robert says.

'Cheers,' I say, reaching for the bottle.

'You know, next time just ask me yourself. I don't bite unless asked.' He smiles and all I see is teeth and I picture myself actually getting bitten, his teeth sinking into my arm, the feeling of skin popping open.

I don't say anything. Luc doesn't either. He is chewing his lip as if considering his options.

'Or maybe you'd rather have a glass of wine?' Robert waves at the rejected merlot on the glass table and scoffs as if I've brought a bottle of Krug and caviar blinis to Glastonbury. And unreasonably I get an anger flash towards Luc. He could have told me not to bring the wine. Now he looks damp, like he's regretting the wine himself. And I don't envy him, having to stay sober because of the car.

'What about you, Lucky? Glass of wine?' says Robert.

Luc shrugs. Linda and Gael are both still as mannequins. I wonder if cocktail night at Robert's is always like this. Maybe I did something to provoke it. Wearing too much black. Worse, matching with Luc, also in black. Maybe bringing merlot to this flat is a declaration of war in itself.

Then I wonder if maybe it is Luc. My Luc is not their Luke and the two don't seem to synthesise. His reluctance to introduce me makes sense now. It has only been half an hour, and I don't see how we can last at least another two.

Robert's poor hosting skills aside, he is generous with his alcohol. As soon as a glass is near emptied he fills it again. We get drunk, it's a blessing. Robert grows worse, still the alcohol makes his presence less menacing. Gael and Linda actually dare making a few jokes at his expense, half of them well received.

It even seems Luc starts to relax. Then later, things go bad.

·

Coming back to London from Greece, I had brought my suitcase to Diwa's and put my thin summer clothes in the washing machine. I would stay in her flat until Luc and I found a place. It was strange being back at Diwa's almost empty flat, most of her things already at Milly's, only deserted pieces of furniture left. It didn't have an echo but looked like it should. I had so many memories from these rooms. My first night with Luc, reading the personals over iced coffee, Bruce Willis game in the bathtub.

I lay on the memory foam mattress and scrolled my phone for flats to rent. Pappa called.

'Hey, everything okay?' I sat up and his face filled the screen and I could see the laughter lines around his eyes and worry lines on his forehead.

'Yes sweetie, I'm fine. Just wanted to talk again.'

I had called him and Mamma from the airport in Athens the day before to let them know I wasn't coming back to Stockholm. The terminal was noisy and my parents quiet and it hadn't been a long call.

'Oh. Sure. What's up?' I said.

'Well yesterday maybe I didn't sound as happy as Mamma. About you moving to London again?'

Neither of them had sounded happy exactly. Neither of them had sounded much more than perfunctory curious.

'That's okay, it was a bit of a shock maybe,' I said.

'Yes, it was. So that's why I am calling now, when the shock has gone.' His jaws clenched and unclenched like he was chewing phantom food. 'If I can be frank, it made me sad to hear you won't be here. You were back so short a time and I know you weren't happy, but I had hoped that maybe some time would pass and you would get over London and that boy.'

'Luc,' I said automatically.

'Luc, yes.' He looked away. 'But you know I thought for a long time last night and I talked to Mamma too, and I feel a little bit ashamed.' He rubbed his stubble, his hand covering his mouth. I didn't know what to say, surprised by this turn of events.

'I was about your age when I left Bucharest,' he said finally. 'And although we have family there I don't go back often and how many times have you visited? Three?'

'Three.'

'What I wanted to tell you is that, actually, I'm happy in Stockholm. I have adopted the city as my own. And I will always be Romanian, of course, but I am also a Stockholmare. It is possible to be both. And I think that, more than a Stockholmare, you are a Londonare.' He nodded and I chuckled at the sound of the word Londonare.

'Wow, okay. Thank you Pappa, for saying that.'

'I'm happy you're not disappointed with me about yesterday.'

'No of course not. And you're sure you and Mamma won't feel like, lonely?'

'Lonely, why would we? You know you have two very sweet brothers right here in Stockholm?' He pointed a finger at me, enlarged by being so close to the camera. 'Even without you, we are a family of four. That's more than many people have. And also you're coming home for Christmas?'

'Yes, will definitely see you for Christmas.'

'Good good, that's important to Mamma.'

'And to you.'

'And to me.'

•

I come back inside from Robert's balcony after smoking. Since returning to London I have stopped smoking completely almost, but Gael had been fiddling with a pack so I asked him for one to get a break from the room. Now I close the balcony door behind me and sneak back to the sofa. Robert is monologuing again. Gael and Linda are holding hands. They look like schoolchildren, him in a shirt and cable knit, her in a peplum-collar blouse. Luc is staring at his phone. I sit down, kiss him on the cheek, and he smiles the confused smile of a feverish person.

'No I swear, it's been a goddamn while since I met a woman even remotely attractive,' Robert says. 'Back in school, girls used to know how to look good, like how to dress and that. Now they all dress like angsty little boys.' He turns to Linda. 'I don't mean you obviously Lin, you're gorgeous, like always. But I swear, you're the only decent woman I've seen in weeks.'

Although he is talking to Linda, this is blatantly directed at me. At Luc. I don't move a muscle of my angsty boyish being because I don't want Robert's attention. My mouth fills with water.

'To be fair it's not just the women.' Robert grins good-humouredly. 'I mean look at you Luke, you're dressing weirder every time I see you.'

'Fuck's sake, I've always dressed like this,' Luc scoffs.

'I don't know you could be right, maybe it's just the effect of the pair of you together.' He waves a hand over us, then he laughs abruptly. 'I mean your poor dad Luke. I'm sure this is what he had in mind when picturing you as an adult. Pillar of the community, family man, beautiful wife. Skinny vegan working in a clothes shop.' He laughs again to label the comment as humour.

Luc says, 'You're on form tonight Robbie, making a good first impression.'

Robert turns to me. 'Has he met you yet, love? Luke's dad?'

'Not yet,' I say.

'Isn't that curious. Nah I'm just messing, don't worry I'm sure he'll adore you.'

I pull my lips to a facsimile of a smile and I squint my eyes and say, well thank you. Then I excuse myself to the toilet.

I close the lid and sit down and touch my forehead which feels hot. My ears burn and I'm sure they are red and I need them to cool to not be physical signposts of Robert having an effect on me.

Luc had told me his dad would love me. Exact words, love me. Now it seems obvious that was optimistic. And why would he want me for his son, what do I offer? I fill with self-loathing for believing it. I thought we were doing well, that I was pulling Luc in a wholesome direction. But my direction now seems maybe wrong, away from a life that suits him. I feel intensely confused. Like spun around too quick. The room gets heavy and my lungs press inwards, reluctant to take air. And it all feels useless suddenly. Like wishful thinking.

I dab my ears with cold water and smooth my shirt and go to sit next to Luc on the sofa. Hey, I say quietly and touch his arm. He lifts his eyebrows, and then nods towards his wristwatch and then the door. I give a slight nod to concur.

'And that time you tried to push Helen off on me, remember that?' Robert asks Linda. Gael snickers.

'I mean Helen? The ugliest thing in North London?'

Everything goes still. No one speaks, as if the room is in shock. I can't process that Luc doesn't speak.

They all know Helen. She is Linda's friend. She is Gael's friend. A shy, short, sliver of a person. We ran into her in a pub once, she seems kind. Her eyes are wide apart and her teeth are too small. She is not beautiful. Also, she is Luc's friend.

For Luc's sake, I say nothing. For Helen's sake, for my own, I am dying to. I want to cause a scene. But I will not make things difficult for Luc by standing up to Robert, not knowing the subtleties of their relationship. I can't tell if I should feel proud for holding my tongue, or ashamed.

Luc is staring at his phone screen, jaws working. There is a void in the room where his words should be.

Finally, Linda speaks. 'Know what, Helen is the best person you'll ever meet. You don't even deserve her going on like that.'

'I don't deserve her?' Robert says. 'Like I would ever go for that. Is that how you see me, desperate enough to stick it in just anyone? I mean, Helen?'

I grip Luc's arm.

He puts his phone down, swallows, stands up. 'Hey, listen Robbie,' he says. 'We're heading off. That's enough of your incel rants for one sitting, you need to check yourself mate.' He sounds completely calm but I know on the inside he is not.

Robert stands up too and they go into the kitchen, talking so low the individual words lose contrast and reach me like a rumble. Robert stares at me through the open door. I can't sit still. I get up, kiss Gael goodbye, then Linda. 'Okay, thanks for tonight,' I say. 'This was weird.'

They both laugh nervously, as if me addressing the elephant is more disagreeable than the elephant itself.

'Bye guys, see you soon yeah,' Luc says, not worrying about hugs or kisses or handshakes. Robert is still in the kitchen. The wine bottle is left on the table like a graffiti tag. I don't say goodbye.

We leave, and by god do we leave. We skip down the stairs, two three steps at a time. We fly out the apartment building, across the parking lot, into Milly's car. He starts the ignition and we drive. Five minutes later we stop at a minigolf car park. It's only just after ten. I am proud of Luc but also worry he's drawn a line he can't undraw. I am shocked by it all, this evening something we will need to unpack. But after this morning's job rejection, I can't put him through another dramatic conversation.

The car park is sparingly lit, Luc's profile only a silhouette against the car's window.

'I mean,' he starts.

'That was,' I say.

'Yeah, that was Robert.'

'He's not coming to the wedding.'

We lose control then. I laugh so hard my stomach cramps and I am in actual pain. Luc's lips are fixated in a horrible grimace, the only thing moving is his twitching nostrils and his bobbing shoulders. It is not remotely attractive yet a joy to witness. His face blurs as my eyes fill up.

'For clarification,' he says, 'I love girls that dress like angsty boys.'

We have constricted, giggly sex in Milly's car, the Christmas tree rustling in the boot. It is physically not good for either of us, more frustrating than anything. But we need the camaraderie. To prove Robert hasn't plugged a thorn between us. But of course, in some sense, he has.

0 DAYS LEFT

Lucas

I am on my way to the airport and this time it's to pick up my Sam. Not that she really is mine, but more so than anyone else's on this motorway. There are not many of us on the bus, listening to the driver playing Eros Ramazzotti on repeat. It is New Year's Eve and I have not seen Sam for twelve days and now I think I should have got her something, flowers. My antiquated iPad is in my tote bag, brought for entertainment on the bus, although I have not used it. I pick it up and open the notes app and type a name in bold letters.

I get off at terminal two and navigate the crowd up to the rail separating arriving passengers from loved ones and chauffeurs holding small whiteboards with names. Some, like me, instead hold up tablets with names. It is crowded and warm in the terminal and although the space is vast, the acoustics are surprisingly muffled, as if people are speaking into individual tin cans.

The wait is so long I start to wonder if she will show up at all. If I'm at the wrong terminal or her flight got cancelled.

I check the information board for the sixth time and then a seventh time and then she appears, like magic. Though of course she does because why wouldn't she. I wave but she doesn't see me, and there's like a stitch in my chest because she looks small and vulnerable. I don't know where her usual poise has gone.

She turns and sees me. I can't move forward because of the railing, so Sam has to make her way with bags that look heavy and I can't give her a hand. Finally she reaches the partition and stops just behind it. There is rail between us. She looks at the name on my iPad.

'Bruce Willis?' I ask.

'I wish.' She kisses me, her lips landing just at the corner of my mouth making it hard to tell if she was aiming for my lips or my cheek. I hug her tight over the rail and then lift her bags, which really are heavy, over the steel. She crouches and slips underneath it.

She looks pale and uncomfortable.

'Are you alright?' I ask. 'You look, sort of, clammy.'

'I'm okay. Well not really,' she says. 'Think I got food poisoning maybe.'

And for some reason this news puts me at ease, my shoulders sink and I exhale fully. Food poisoning I can handle.

'Probably the Christmas leftovers should have been thrown out earlier.' She swallows. 'Yeah, actually, let's not talk about food.'

'Ah mate. And you were flying like this? Let's get you some water.' I put her rucksack on top of the wheeled luggage and with my other hand around her waist as support, we walk slowly towards WHSmith.

'Hope it's one of those twenty-four-hour things,' she says. 'Maybe feel better if I get some sleep. I really want to go to Tabatha's tonight.'

'Yeah, let's get you home and rest first.'

She falls asleep on my shoulder on the bus. And then she falls asleep in our bed. I close the curtains and put a rubbish bin lined with a plastic bag by her side on the floor. I prepare lunch but she wants nothing but ice water and cucumber. Then she is sleeping again, in foetus position on her side, knees drawn tight to her stomach. Lying on the covers next to her, I am bored on my phone, trying not to wake her by moving. Still it's great to have her home.

I text Patti to warn her we might not come to her and Tabatha's New Year's dinner tonight. Then I go to Tesco, closing the flat door quietly behind me. After many hungover days on the sofa together, I know what Sam fancies when nauseous. Basmati rice, peanut butter, pitta bread, corn kernels, cucumber. A lot of orange juice. By the tills, New Year's knickknacks are on display.

Nowadays, there are fewer nauseous days on the sofa. We still go out and get stupid drunk and sometimes Sam goes without me if I don't want to pick up another hangover, but often we stay in. Which usually means me starting dinner while Sam takes an after-work shower and then sits at the kitchen table with her knee to her chest in front of her laptop, working some more. After dinner she will do the dishes while I sit on the counter and talk and then we will some-times watch something but usually have coffee at the table in front of our laptops, me applying for jobs, her researching whatever current client, knee to her chest, foot tapping the floor. I don't think this is what I had pictured when wishing her more calm, because even when at home she is mostly intense. But now I am starting to see her intensity as multi-faceted, that there are different types of fervour. And likely this is just Sam, this is how her brain is wired.

There are some things that slow her completely. Kneading her calves up to her thighs. Unhurried, lazy sex. Japanese anime about moving out in the country.

Back home from the shop, taking my shoes off, I hear her turning in bed.

'Hey you,' she says, barely audible.

I whisper even though she is awake. 'How are you feeling? Good sleep?'

'Yeah I feel better but still crampy.'

'Let's cancel then.' I sit on the edge of the bed. Her skin looks moist and unhealthy in colour, with lips so drained they blend into her face.

'I think we need to. But in principle I'm against it.'

'I'll text Patti.'

When Sam is in the shower I heat a pot and cover the bottom with olive oil and corn kernels. Soon popping sounds evoke hundreds of other movie nights. One of the universal happy sounds, like laughter and *The Simpsons* theme song.

She comes in wearing sweats and I put a silver paper hat on her which looks ridiculous next to her pallid face. I light two sparklers and give her one. We just hold them, not sure what we are supposed to do. Still they are nice to look at in the dark room, the flares shooting off like tiny silver fireworks. I've hung a Happy New Year banner in gold paper over the TV. She is very cute on the sofa with cone hat and bare feet.

'Movie marathon?' I ask.

'As we already have the popcorn.' She nods to the table and hugs her knees. I sit down and hand her a hot-water bottle for her stomach and look at my phone. 'Okay let's see,' I say and find the list on my app.

'What you got there?'

'Just a list of films you've talked about watching, or mentioned in like conversation,' I say, a little self-conscious suddenly.

'You've made a list?'

'Well, yeah. Easier to remember.'

'Shit you're cute.' She stretches her legs and puts her feet in my lap, pinching my stomach with her toes.

'You wanted to watch The Way We Were, right?' I ask. 'And you still haven't seen Crouching Tiger, though All That Heaven Allows is Christmassy so maybe we should try that.'

'Wow, that's quite a heavy collection there. I was thinking like a Lord of the Rings triple bill or something?'

'Christ, sure. What can I get you besides popcorn?'

The toasted pitta sounds tasty when she bites into the crunchy crust, and the first movie is extremely cosy, all

Shire and hobbits and second breakfasts. Her body is warm pressed to mine and the colour is gradually returning to her face. But halfway through the film I glance over and she is holding her knees so tight her knuckles look white. And I can tell, can't I, that something is wrong.

'Sam, it isn't just food poisoning is it?'

•

I missed her intensely over Christmas. Just like every year I slept at Dad's on Christmas Eve to wake up and do breakfast and presents together. Christmas is a thing that changes when one of your parents dies. It used to be the three of us in robes and slippers all morning and then afternoon at my one remaining grandparent's. But she is in a retirement home now, not completely lucid.

After breakfast Dad and I got dressed and went to see Grandma for a little while, then back home for an early dinner. The day was a string of hours, each long enough to existentially count as a day itself. This extensive session with Dad made me question my normal everyday life to be true. Sam's whirlwind movements seemed impossible in a realm this slow.

I doubted Dad got more pleasure out of Christmas than I did, but we still went through the motions. He put on the same CD of mixed Christmas hits. He decorated with the same plastic Santas and supermarket snowflakes. He set the table with the ivy-patterned wax tablecloth and the fine china from Grandma, his style of decor so haphazard and conflicting the result almost making some kind of eclectic sense.

Dad and I remembered all our traditions, we were stubborn in this, the only family thing intact after Mum died. Every Christmas he made the effort. Hot chocolate in front of *It's a Wonderful Life*, the annual awkward phonecall to his brother in Glasgow, mince pies. Although completely lacking holiday cheer, we performed the ritual out of loyalty. Before Dad had even set the table I was itching to leave but this made me feel so bad I stayed well after dinner. He brought out the Christmas whiskey and a box of fancy pralines and clicked on the TV.

Although full of dinner, I ate many chocolates and drank a lot of whiskey, my only weapons against the hours. I overindulged. I regretted it even while doing it, getting me warm and uncomfortable, so I stood up and opened the window and swallowed cold air like water.

Sipping my whiskey, I looked at the neighbouring windows, wondering what was happening in there. Were they also bored and full of whiskey and turkey. Unused to meat, the dinner sat awkward like a lump of wet cement slowly hardening in my stomach. I tried not to think about it.

I hadn't eaten meat in six months. Over the summer I got used to cooking vegetarian with Sam but even after she went back to Stockholm, I kind of kept it up. It wasn't a statement or anything. Even so it was good to make a diet decision not based on superficiality. It made me feel like a slightly better person ethically but also it was doing something nice for Sam. I knew she was surprised and pleased by how easily I had given up meat. Like a natural-born bunny, she said. I liked it, not the bunny comparison, but the way she made me more, like, open.

We had invited Dad for dinner in our flat early in the new year. I hadn't lied when telling Sam he would like her. I knew he would, after the initial shock. I was less sure how he'd feel about me with her. Probably confused because I was not so outgoing with him, his reservation contagious. But so was Sam's bluntness. Maybe she would coax things out of him, like Mum had.

Dad placed a hand on my shoulder, a rare incident of physical contact between us. We shook hands as hello and hugged goodbye, otherwise we never touched.

I nodded to the ink-black sky and shockingly I said, 'Do you think she's up there?' immediately wishing to take it back.

'Well. No, I guess I don't,' he said.

'Me neither.'

'Nice enough thought though. Makes me a bit jealous of religious people.'

'Yeah I get that.'

'So. Where do you reckon she is?' He removed his hand, leaving a warm imprint on my shoulder, the conversation so unexpected I needed a moment to think of a reply.

'Maybe like how it is before you are born? Maybe she is there?'

'When you die you join the unborn? Like, oblivion?'

'Christ Dad, sounds a bit grim when you say it like that.'
I laughed.

'No it sounds okay to me. Not a bad place to be really.'

'Where do you think she is then?'

'Well I don't actually think she's dead at all,' he said, straight-faced. And for a moment there I feared he might be suffering some early-stage dementia or similar.

'What do you mean she's not dead?' I asked, steeling myself.

'Depends how you define dead of course.' He held his palms up as if to reassure me of his sanity. 'But me and Mum, we were together a long time and I knew her in some ways better than myself. Like even now, when I watch a film or go food shopping, I listen to her opinion more often than my own.' He refilled our glasses and we drank simultaneously. And we both stared intently at the ink sky as if looking for her even though neither of us believed she was up there but staring anyway because it gave us a reason not to look at each other.

'So I can't consider her dead really, since I still get her reactions to things, and I let her make decisions for me sometimes. I'm sorry, this makes no sense at all. But as long as someone is alive who knows her like that, I reckon she's still around.'

I said nothing for a while. He was right, it didn't make sense to me. But whatever, it did to him. The night air was cold and nice on my skin. I looked for stars but the city lights were too bright.

'So. What would she think of us right now then?' I asked finally.

'She'd think we were absolute dunces talking like this and tell us to put on the kettle, enough of the whiskey.'

We closed the window and Dad made us a cup of tea and now I was glad I hadn't left early.

•

'It's not food poisoning,' Sam says.

I stand up. She looks pleading, though for me to say something or be quiet I am not sure.

'What then?' I ask, but really I don't want to hear what she will say next. I want food poisoning and me taking care of her and tomorrow she will feel better and we will go on like normal.

'The reason I'm not feeling great,' she looks away, 'I had an abortion. In Stockholm.'

I blink. The New Year's banner glimmers. Sam starts to cry. Silent big drops roll down her cheeks. I stand perfectly still.

'I wasn't going to tell you,' she says.

'Oh.'

'But now, seeing you, I couldn't not tell you. Sorry I wish I could.'

I try to calm down but I am shocked and somewhere in my foundation there is a crack. I repeatedly hear the word no in my head. No no no no. I swallow.

'It's just, for me, this is not such a huge thing,' she says, 'but I thought it would be for you and I wanted to save you the unnecessary grief. I'm really really sorry, I should have told you earlier.' Roughly she wipes her cheeks with her palms. She looks wrecked, her face blotched in many different colours.

'But when would this even have happened?'

'I did the test just before Christmas and had the thing, the appointment, a few days later.'

My mind wants safe ground so it starts calculating. 'But we always use a condom. Like every single time.'

'Yeah I know.'

'So how could it?'

'I don't know, one must have broken?'

'Wouldn't I notice if it broke?'

She doesn't reply at once. She looks at me with dead calm, her eyes still wet. 'Is there something you want to ask me?' she says slowly.

I think about this. Do I worry she has cheated?

I don't.

'Are you okay, as in, physically?' I ask.

'Yes fine, just cramps and nausea.'

'And it can't affect you getting pregnant in the future?'

'No, nothing like that, I can get pregnant again. But Luc,' she stands up and takes a step towards me, 'the thing is, I don't think I want to. I mean ever.'

I try to understand what she is telling me but I am still processing the thing, the appointment. And that she booked it and went through with it without me knowing. This seems impossible. My thoughts are scatty and it feels like I am swaying. 'Are you saying you don't want children, like ever?'

'It's just, getting a positive on that test felt so wrong. And I can't see it ever feeling otherwise.'

'And you didn't plan to tell me.' I get tired, too tired to talk anymore. 'I want kids,' I say, but I am not sure she hears me.

I have always seen having children as an integral part of the human experience, as if not having them would mean some hole left unfilled. It is shocking to me that she doesn't.

'I didn't realise how wrong it felt before this,' she says. 'But now I know.' She is standing with her back straight, not moving closer, hands to her sides.

'But like, this is me too, you don't think I have a say?'

'Of course you don't have a say.' She turns suddenly and walks into the kitchen. 'It's still my body.' I follow her but really I wish we'd stop talking. 'Would you want me to get pregnant if it felt wrong?' she asks and turns to face me and her remorse is replaced by a hardness, the change so abrupt it's frightening. 'Like push me into becoming a mother and then resenting you for it?'

'Of course not, why would you even say that.' I bite my teeth. 'But can you not see this affects me too.'

She walks past me into the bedroom.

'Please will you stop running,' I say and grab her hand. She pulls it back. I am exasperated now and it feels like I am not awake. Like I will any moment open my eyes and she will be sleeping off food poisoning next to me in our bed. 'I don't understand you,' I say. It feels like this isn't us, the panic almost in my eyes now. Out of everything, this hurts the most, her twisting my words, making me sound like one of those men. I look into her face, try to find Sam. But I don't. 'Why would you even say that.' I sit down on the bed, spent, floaty.

She is quiet for a long while.

Then, of all things, she says, 'I love you Luc.'

And there is like a rift. She has never said it before and she chooses this moment. It is a betrayal, using those words now. Too late to stop the fracture, it's as if we have pushed until we heard a snap. I don't know how to mend it.

I go to the bathroom and I close the door and I flush cold water on my hands, wrists, arms.

·

One day in Greece I came out of the shower and found Sam sunbathing in the garden. She had pulled a sunchair to the edge of the wall, getting a view of the ocean below.

She was leaning back, one knee up, arms behind her head. On a folding table was a Dorothy Parker short story collection and a glass of iced tea with three half-melted ice cubes. She was wearing nothing but sunglasses, knickers, and a wide-brimmed straw hat. Her breasts a pale contrast to her tanned body as if wearing a white bikini top. She looked serene and languid and fucking glamorous.

This close to the ocean there was always a breeze and despite the warm sun her nipples were hard. I wanted to touch her breast, see if her skin was hot or cold. But also I wanted not to disturb her.

This very moment was the most relaxed I had seen her. She was still as a photograph. Her hands lax, no fidgeting. Her nails unharmed. The only thing moving was the brim of her hat rolling in the breeze. She might have been asleep, the sunglasses hiding her eyes. I thought, she is in her right element, this woman in front of me. Removing her from here seemed a violation.

I sat down on the ground next to her, smelled salt from the ocean. I picked up her book and leafed through it. Tasted her iced tea which was tart.

I realised then with a simple certainty, that continually seeing her like this, in her right element, would make me content in life. As if I had bigger ambitions for her wellbeing than my own. Or maybe that her wellbeing was a prerequisite for my wellbeing. And I imagined I would be good at it, facilitating this relaxed frame of mind, languid and happy. Just as she grounded me, made me heavy and solid, I would make her at ease, stop tearing her fingers.

I had been stupid. Her languor was not my doing.

It was Greece. It was summer in October.

She was relaxed, in her element, only when in a state of evasion. And our cramped flat, hanging laundry, keeping budgets, was escapism inverted. It was peak realism.

I had been halfway through a short story when she spoke, still not moving.

'You like it?' she asked, meaning the book.

'The view? I do. Especially the hat.'

'Oh? Not the tits then?'

'Them too.' I laughed and placed my hand on her left breast, moving my thumb up and down. Her skin was warm, despite the breeze.

•

I look in the mirror but that makes the dizziness worse. I get a blood pressure vision drop so I lean against the wall for stability and slide down to the floor. I place my hands over my face. And I cry.

It is physically painful, like my ducts are too tight for the tears. All my muscles tense, my stomach and face cramp. It gets worse by trying to stay absolutely silent. The tap is still running water. I keep my eyes closed.

I have lost Sam once already, to Stockholm. That month in London without her had been greyscaled. I operated like normal, I went to work and paid bills, I cut fat and built muscles, but I couldn't see a good reason for it. And then on that ferry from Athens, spotting her in the harbour waving, I was back to colour. We are not an easy fit, sometimes we hurt each other. It doesn't change anything. I still want her.

I stand up and open the door and go to her in the bedroom. There is an open bag on the bed. She is packing clean clothes. This completely throws me.

'Sam,' I say.

She doesn't look up. She says, 'I ordered a taxi,' as if this is sufficient.

'Don't. Let's talk, okay.'

'I need a moment. Like, away from here.'

'It's just, you leaving.' My voice is strained. 'I didn't think I was one of the things you'd ever run out on.'

'I am not happy here,' she says, her back to me.

'We will get another flat, soon, promise.'

'It's not about the flat. I mean of course it's not.' She shoves clothes into the bag.

'What then?' I don't dare to move.

'I just feel like I don't fit here. Like I'm damaging things.'

'What are you even talking about, of course you fit.'

She grips the bag and closes her eyes for a second. 'I think it's best if we don't say anything else right now.' She closes the zip with a jarring sound. 'I need to go.'

And she brushes past me and puts on her shoes and gets her coat and is out the door.

She is halfway down the stairs when I have my shoes on. 'Please,' I shout, 'just stop.' She doesn't.

The taxi is outside waiting and she throws her bag in the backseat before getting in herself. I grab the door just as she moves to close it.

'Please. Don't leave. Just stay here a while longer with me, please Sam.'

'I can't, I'm sorry.' She looks away and grips the door handle. 'I will talk to you later, okay.'

I let go of the door and although I shouldn't, I say, 'If you leave, I think maybe that's it,' because I am desperate for her to stay and come upstairs and talk to me.

She shakes her head many small times. Her eyes fill. Then she closes the door and the taxi drives away.

PART II

180 DAYS UNTIL

Lucas

Two months now, we have been over. And okay life isn't stellar but it is manageable. I set alarms, I go to work, and six mornings per week, I'm at the gym. I would prefer going on Sundays too but I don't since that would mean I'm one of those people, the addicts.

The view from the group session room is nice, on the fifth floor overlooking the East End industry brick. Today with the morning sun just now coming over the rooftops, the brick lights up like when you blow on embers. Brown and red and orange. I stretch my quads and today I have good energy, I can feel it in my legs. I jump on the spot two times.

There are mirrors on two walls, windows on two. Ballet barres line the room and although I have no interest in this exercise form myself, it does give the room a certain dignity, as if we all straighten our backs and mind our posture by proxy.

My usual spot is free which is a nice start to the day. Close by the mirror but far away from the instructor,

Allan. Australian and big and loud with thighs so large his shorts look panicked, like they will rip if put through one more squat.

'Hi,' someone says to the right of me. A blonde woman about my age that I haven't seen before.

'Oh. Hey,' I say.

'So is it very hard, this class? It's my first time.'

'Well yeah it is fairly tough. You couldn't like skate through it I guess, but you can modify, don't worry.'

She places her mat next to mine and stands tall, stretching both arms over her head. I see her face in the mirror. She is likely a few years older than me, blonde hair in a sleek ponytail. Shiny, neat. She is almost my height, very fit. Her shoulders are round with muscle and two abs are visible through her top. She looks strong but light on her feet, a calibrated balance of strength and cardio training. My guess, dancer or martial artist.

She is wearing a light grey top, long-sleeved and high-necked with a zipper in the back. Matching grey leggings with reflective strips. Now self-conscious, I look in the mirror. I am wearing a black t-shirt and black compression tights under bright blue shorts. Next to this polished blonde my shorts glare. They look adolescent. I smooth them with my hands as if that could wipe the colour off.

It is a calisthenics class with only body weight, always leaving me shaking and coated in sweat. We are doing burpees and the blonde next to me is sweating but explosive, like a bullet in her grey gear. She really needn't have worried about the intensity level and I hope I hadn't come across as patronising when I said she could modify. Her burpees are cleaner than mine.

Near the end of the class I am completely wrecked because I have exerted myself, glancing in the mirror often, checking my form. The final exercise is press-ups to plank, three sets. Clapping press-ups followed by a two-limb plank back to clapping press-ups.

I like the static positions best. When moving I can use momentum as a cheat but when static there is nothing between me and the lactic acid except self-control. The pain feels healthy, making me stronger and more resilient. Although what I like most is that it plants me in my body. My mind and my personality and my plans for the future matter none in this room, the only possible focus is the pain and how to cope with it. Most efficient is to blank my head and trust my body.

Mid-plank, instead of blanking out, I picture Sam on that sunchair in Greece. How lazing in the October sun had seemed her natural element. Now, here, finding quiet in my screaming muscles, I think this must be mine.

The mat turns mottled with drops of sweat. My shoulders burn, my plank is straight, the music hides my panting.

•

Two weeks I'd stayed in the flat after Sam left. It had not been a good time.

The first three days I didn't go outside and I didn't tell anyone what had happened, in a horrifying state of outright denial. Also, I wondered how it would make us look, in our friends' eyes, that we had lasted so short. If they had guessed all along, maybe even talked about it, our ill-fittedness. Sometimes I would wince thinking like this. It came in spikes, the shame. I feigned sickness to get off work. I called her phone many times. She didn't pick up.

The fifth day, I lay on the sofa watching videos of teenagers spending money on expensive cars they could then wreck in later videos. On the table next to me was one of the noodle bowls from John Lewis, coated in residue cereal and milk now yellowed and hard and crackelated. I had thought we would bring these bowls to our next flat, my image of that future so clear it seemed like a lived-through memory. But it wasn't and now it would never be and this seemed like an error. Picturing the erasure of this future distressed me so much I honestly panicked. I sat up and maybe I would vomit or break something. I suddenly couldn't be in the flat, her things still here, our books mixed together, soon to be divvied. I texted Gael. *Do you want to get high?*

It was only afternoon and Gael would be at work, but with some kind of junior management position in his father's company his attendance wasn't reinforced. Besides his availability, he was also the only person in my phone who wouldn't judge this show of self-destruction. I pictured how Henry would grimace if he saw the text, with his fresh shave and his budgeting apps. How Patti and Tabatha would talk about me pityingly, spending slow lazy nights at home together, like I had with Sam just months ago. I was offended by them, their seclusion, their intimate uninterest in others. Even though I could identify my resentment as backhanded envy it still didn't blunt my upset. I figured they would move in together soon and I didn't think I could be happy for them.

Gael and I hadn't spoken since cocktails at Robert's and he would find my text odd, also because I didn't ever do blow or any of it. I disliked how it blurred my identity and made me say and do strange things that felt tragic the next day. But now I needed to lose some identity, couldn't stand one second longer being myself, lucid and present. Gael wanted to lose himself too so we made plans to meet up. A shower would have been sensible but I had to get out of the flat.

By 8pm the world was off its incessant rotation and my lungs filled to their normal capacity. Gael was funny, I was glad to have texted. We walked to Hackney Downs and met up with three of his friends having meze around low silver tables. I wasn't hungry but ate a dolma when offered, swallowing without chewing almost. We talked a beautiful conversation and I felt close to Gael's friends even though we'd just met. I was speaking quite a lot but no matter because everything I said was intelligent.

Then I heard a laugh. Two tables away. The sound so familiar my instinct was instant. Glorious gut-wrenching joy. I stood up. The person laughing had her back to me, black messy hair, hands flying for emphasis. She was a little too loud and she turned her head and she bit her bottom lip.

Not Sam. Diwa.

Even without the coke this would have been a brain disruption, my glorious joy cut off mid play.

I walked over to the table, it seemed urgent and wise to say good things that would prove to her how well I was doing. Opposite her was a woman and a man, maybe late fifties.

I put my hand on her shoulder. 'Diwa?'

She looked up and said, 'Lucas, hi. Wow.'

'You must be Sofia and Abdel,' I said to Sam's aunt and uncle. They looked politely surprised and I shook their hands.

'Mum, Dad, this is Sam's, you know, she told you about Lucas.'

'Yes of course,' Sofia said. 'I've even seen pictures online.'

'Nice to meet you Lucas,' said Abdel.

This is going well I thought and said, 'Yes you too, I wish I'd met you earlier. I know how important you are to Sam and it would have been better to see you when, under other circumstances I mean.'

'It's okay. It's fine.' Diwa reached out and held my forearm, making me take a small step back which felt too far away so I leaned forward, hands on their table.

'Still I'm glad to get a face on you both. And I want to say that Sam, she is a very good person. You should be proud of her. But I don't have to tell you, you already know her very well.' And it was nice to talk to them, in a melancholy but significant sense, like all was as it should be.

'That's great Lucas,' Diwa said and slowly stood up.

A hard thump on my shoulder and Gael was behind me twisting me around saying, 'Alright buddy, time to go.' Their table rattled comically.

He pushed me towards the exit and when I turned my head to say goodbye, I saw Gael mouth to Diwa, 'Sorry,' and roll his eyes.

And reality altered. I viewed the interaction through Gael's eyes, then Diwa's eyes. And I realised what I had just done. We were out the door and I started jogging down a side street. 'Hang on,' Gael shouted after me. I stopped by a lamppost and held on with one hand and leaned over, my head swimming towards the ground. Gael dunked my back saying, 'Wow man, that was priceless,' and I vomited finally, the dolma coming up my stomach almost intact. Just after eight at night, all these normal people on their way home from work. And I was the disgrace being sick on the street.

I woke up on Gael's sofa and the remorse was mind-breaking. And unreasonably, I blamed Sam. She had wanted me eased up and I had tried my hardest and it had been excruciating but also a relief of sorts. I had been sloppy drunk countlessly, ugly dancing in front of her scrunched-up laughter face. I had told her stuff about Dad and cut ties with my oldest friend. I had eaten food I didn't want to, covering me in cold sweat and self-loathing. This was the hardest part. But I did it anyway because I had planned to be with her always. And still, she had left. And last night I lost it and got high and reached a new low. Because when I lose it I really do lose it.

•

After leaving Gael's sofa that day I went straight home and put the flat up for sublet, then rang Henry and Hitesh's doorbell unannounced. We sat in the living room and Hitesh got bottles of IPA from the fridge, which I declined.

'So can I move back in?' I asked.

Henry raised an eyebrow.

'Well,' Hitesh said, 'we do hate the new guy.'

Sam only returned once to the flat, to pack. I was at work and came home and her things were gone. Ten days later I was back in my old room unpacking my own things. Boxes with stuff, a suitcase of shoes and clothes. Then at the bottom of my gym bag, was Sam's stupid chocolate shirt. She had left it in the wardrobe. I tried to interpret this action but there were too many possibilities. Out of spite, to show me she didn't want the memento. Out of kindness, leaving me something to remember her by. Out of indifference, the shirt meaning no more to her than the shampoo she left in the shower. Out of hope, that they'd one day reunite.

I unfolded it and put it on a hanger. There was a lump in the breast pocket so I stuck my hand in there and fished out a stick. Her lip balm. I removed the cap and grapefruit scent instantly transported me back to the summer. To tube rides, sharing earbuds, Flora Purim. To making out in the music booth. I put the cap on and summer stopped. Like pausing a movie. I placed the lip balm in my nightstand drawer and haven't touched it since.

A couple took over what was left of Sam's and my six-month contract. I texted her saying I had found new tenants and that we were clear financially and she replied, *Okay, thank you,* and that was the last time we were in touch.

I didn't understand why she had kept the abortion secret, which was not okay and also not like her. The lie had been shocking, an unexpected pain, but I'm sure I could have forgiven her not telling me if she had only explained why. Although the immediate issue had been the abortion and the lying about the abortion, the real reason it all became so enormous was that she didn't want children, and I do. This wasn't something we could explain away or resolve with an apology, this was a difference in direction. An either-or. It didn't matter how much smoother our relationship had become, how much less we chafed. This was a clear rift, we couldn't meet halfway. And in the midst of it that night, talking about the abortion, realising something had broken, I couldn't stop myself looking at her stomach. Now empty. But a week earlier, not.

I could understand the situation getting out of hand, us panicking, saying the wrong things. But even so. I never thought she could leave like that and then not talk. Not even as friends. The day after she got in the taxi, I called her. Four times. She didn't pick up. Two days passed, three, five, and she didn't pick up. I wanted us to apologise and talk things through so that if we were over, at least we were over in a sad but beautiful way. Like sympathetic companions in our joint breakup, taking interest in each other's pain management, that sort of thing. But after my night with Gael I told myself whatever, it was for the best, no one was to blame. We were too different. And the life she wanted was not mine.

Still, I knew that all this about sympathetic companionship and wanting to talk things over calmly, it was self-deception. Because what I truly wanted wasn't to be over beautifully, it was to not be over at all. I wanted us together, beautifully or uglily. And my sad devastated state, my losing it with Gael, was the panic of knowing that my image of the future, it would never happen. And that I somehow had to get over it.

So I have been pulling myself up, trying to resume the shape of myself. Last week Professor Jonas emailed, asking to chat over coffee. We met in the same campus café as last time, back in autumn. Bright white with plywood furniture. Students making their lattes last hours, working on essays, streaming stuff on the good wifi.

Professor Jonas was five minutes late. I had already bought a black coffee and he ordered a chamomile tea before sitting down. Mid-forties, he had a young face only slightly aged by brow lines. He was one of the cool lecturers for sure, I mean he wore vintage Skechers didn't he. He asked everyone to call him Paul.

'I might have some news,' Paul said after the polite things.
'Oh. Really?'

'One of my old schoolmates runs a team at a major car company and they are looking for an engineer. I mentioned your name.' The arch of his eyebrows told me he wasn't sure how I would react when he told me some details of the employment and the employer.

I knew it, a rubbish company. Factories all over the non-western world, aggressive lobbyism working against every forward movement in international environmental agreements. This was an obvious token position, eco engineer on paper, nothing more. Knowingly greenwashing a company for a payslip.

Shockingly, my first reaction was a sharp thrill. A real job, working as an engineer, using my brain, earning money. But however desperate I was to get out of Darling purgatory, I knew I couldn't apply for this. I thanked Professor Jonas and apologised for wasting his time. He assured me he understood and I absurdly insisted on paying for his chamomile tea, leaving coins on the table he didn't want. Then I went home and watched *Who Killed the Electric Car?* again and tried to feel good about my decision.

•

I shower and wrap a towel around me and open the locker and put my gym bag on the bench. The blonde with the ponytail left when I was rolling my mat so I hadn't found out how she liked the class. I fill my bottle with water and shake it to mix the protein powder, hemp and pea and brown rice protein amplified with several micronutrients. It tastes like shit. Actual sewage. Unsuccessfully camouflaged by sweetener and vanilla.

I want to tell Sam about sticking to vegetarianism, she would be pleased. She would also roll her eyes at me turning her political statement into a fitness regime. But it is not just for health. I might not be currently helping the planet with my degree but at least I do so through diet.

My hair is still wet as I finish the bottle of sewage waiting for the lift.

'You again,' she says, the blonde with the ponytail.

'Oh, hey.' I pull my hand through my hair. 'So how did you find it?'

'It was good. I'm knackered now though.'

'Well it looked like you were doing just fine there.'

'You were watching me, were you?'

I actually blush. 'Watching is a strong word.'

She laughs.

'So, where do you usually work out?' I ask.

'A place around Old Street. It's not a gym, only classes.' The lift pings and the doors open and we get in. I lean against the wall, fold my arms, then unfold them. She stands straight, at ease. 'I normally go three times a week. Capoeira.'

So a dancer and a martial artist.

'They're remodelling so I'll probably come here in the meanwhile.'

The lift pings again and we go through the lobby and I hold the door for her. She stops on the street.

'Are you taking the same class tomorrow?' she asks.

'I'll be here yeah. See you then?'

'Gabrielle,' she says and holds her hand out. I fumble with my water bottle and take her hand. It is warm and strong. As is mine.

'Lucas,' I say.

'Lucas and Gabrielle. Kind of excellent names, haven't we?'

'We have. We're lucky that way,' I say. And my face cracks open in a cheeky grin. It has been so long I had forgotten the joy of it.

151 DAYS UNTIL

Sam

The elevator pings and the doors open and I get in. I lean against the wall but instead of pressing eleven as usual, I press eight. Today I start my new job. From placement to maternity temp to permanent employee. I swing my arms to energise because up there are my new colleagues and I want to blind them with my brilliance.

The agency's offices are located on floors seven, eight, and eleven in a large glass building on the South Bank. I like it here. The streets are walked by a clashing blend of suits and tourists. There are dark shiny restaurants run by talked-about chefs and food trucks selling tacos with fermented ingredients. The BFI is just around the corner.

You can see the cityscape from our offices. London looks blue and old and majestic from this distance. Handsome even. Seeing the city like this, it's impossible not to feel like it is the centre of the world. Sooner or later, everything and everyone comes to London. True metropolitan magnetism.

I take a fortifying breath and remind myself that I am exactly where I'm supposed to be, because I am a little nervous. I haven't worked with this team before but my new manager Preya is reputedly no-nonsense.

There is a foyer on floor eight and a caffeinated receptionist shows me to my team's hot desk office. She leaves me in the doorway to a large room with tables in rows, one desktop on each. It's extremely lit from the overheads and the air has an electric smell and texture. There are about thirty chairs, maybe ten of them currently occupied. Some heads raise, some are fixed on desktop screens, no one stands up or says hello. I have no idea what to do now. Luckily I'm not shy.

'Hey, I'm Sam? It's my first day?' I say to the closest head, which reluctantly removes its gaze from the screen.

'Vicki,' the reluctant head says and stands up and shakes my hand. She is my height, short bleached hair, dark roots, brown eyes squinting when she sizes me up.

'What should I do?' I say in a low voice.

'Yeah sorry I'm being rude.' She tells me to take any desk I want, then points out the kitchen, bathroom, Preya's office, quiet room, gym in the cellar. I wonder why a quiet room is a department necessity but decide against asking, in case the reply should be a disconcerting piece of information to be handed on the first day.

She leads the way to an empty desk and pulls the chair out and somehow manages to look offensively smart in her white button down and tweed trousers. I sit and she leaves. Clicking my desktop for a while, I try not to be too obvious in assessing my surroundings. I wonder if there is an unrealistic deadline to meet because people are saying very little and hacking very quickly on their keyboards, the clacking loud and urgent. I feel a bit useless now, ignored at my desk, my brilliance completely unflexed.

Then the man in the chair next to mine leans over and introduces himself and I forget his name instantly because I am focusing on my own words too much. When I tell him I'm not new exactly, just a transfer from floor eleven he says, 'Fancy. Who did you blow to get up there?'

'I'm sorry?' I stare at him and feel my eyebrows shoot up.

'I'm only teasing.' He waves his hand dismissively. 'We have a kind of high-ceiling convo culture here, you'll get used to it.'

'Yeah maybe stay off the sex jokes though, better safe than sorry?' I laugh but I am rattled.

'Don't. Now you sound like Vicki.' From his emphasis on the Vi in Vicki it is clear he is not an admirer.

And then, Preya walks in. From her reputation I had expected strict, close-fitting tailoring and impenetrable facial expressions, but she is the opposite. Loose-hanging shirt, hands in pockets, sloppy ponytail. She throws some wit at people while walking bad-posturedly towards her office, determined to be one of the lads, laptop case on a long strap bouncing her thigh. I think, why the reputation? She seems approachable enough. I am about to stand up to introduce myself when she stops at a desk and loses the smile. 'Is this the alleged excellence we hired you for,' she says and points at a woman's screen. The woman doesn't turn around but sort of slumps and says, 'It's not finished.' I cancel my introduction and stay in my seat.

·

In Stockholm two days before Christmas Eve I had peed on the stick and the stick said pregnant so I called Diwa. She listened as I convinced myself to get the abortion. I tried three places. Two were closed for the holidays, one had an appointment on December twenty-seventh, only five days later. Apparently not popular to end pregnancies in the days around the birth of baby Jesus. Understandable, but as I am neither religious nor sentimental, I was only relieved they had the opening.

The day before I peed on the stick, I had met up with Camilla and Elin C for drinks. Not because I wanted to see them but because I needed a pause from the solemn kindnesses of my parents' home. We had gotten drunk and then high. When the stick said positive, I thought about the foetus, how the substances affected it. About the other times I had intoxicated my system since the germ-cell division started. If I kept it, in what state would it come out?

I was sitting on a brown padded bench covered with swishing hygiene paper when the tall doctor informed me that the foetus was the size of a mung bean. I wish she hadn't told me this because somehow the likeness to a legume made the foetus more human, not less. I preferred thinking of it as nothing more than a cluster of cells. It has no brain, she assured me. It can't feel a thing, it's not a person yet. Stop talking, I thought.

I took the first pills right there and two days later I would take another set and that would be it. No surgery, no scraping, just four pills. When Luc used a condom, he prevented a baby. That time I'd taken the morning after pill, I had prevented a baby. I saw this as no different. And I was not going to overthink it.

Walking back to my parents' after the clinic, I directed my attention to my stomach. I wanted to feel something different in my uterus, some proof that the pills were working. I almost convinced myself there was a murmur but in truth I could feel nothing.

I had the overground rail on my right and a patch of grass on my left. Three speckled bunnies chewing, frenetic in classic bunny fashion. They stopped dead as I passed. Bunnies were everywhere in the area, descendants of pets people had tired of and let loose. Overpopulation seemed as good a revenge for neglect as any.

I nodded in salute. They concluded I was no threat and continued their frenetic chewing. I wondered if bunnies actively wanted offspring, or just enjoyed sex, lacking readily available contraception.

That night Matei and Peter and Matei's new girlfriend Monika came for Christmas smörgåsbord leftovers. I set the table before they arrived. By now it was mostly the healthy dishes left. Creamed kale, white bean salad, pickled things, brown cabbage. Looking at the white beans was slightly nauseating and I instinctively touched my stomach a lot. Mamma boiled dill potatoes and pan fried all the leftover meats, which gave the flat a disorienting smell of summer barbecue. On a silver tray Pappa placed tiny glasses, the smoky ones with minuscule snowflake patterns. I lit the twenty or so candles in the apartment.

The doorbell rang and I opened while Mamma and Pappa wiped their hands and removed their special red aprons. Matei introduced Monika. She was wearing a black sparkly long-sleeved dress, and what I first clocked as shyness soon seemed more like situation-specific decorum. I reckoned she would show her true self merely one schnapps in.

We congregated in the living room where a Swedish boy choir sang through the stereo speakers. Mamma sat on one of the formal chairs by the window and Pappa poured elderflower schnapps from the frosty bottle straight out of the freezer into the smoky snowflake glasses. I was glad to have taken the pills already and be able to sing the schnapps ballad and taste the aggressive taste of clear alcohol without guilt. It was over. I couldn't damage it anymore.

Matei was so sweet, doting on Monika as if a convalescent, asking if she was too cold, too warm, thirsty, okay. She seemed to vacillate between feeling proud and embarrassed by his extreme attention. I saw an amused glance stolen between Mamma and Pappa. When Monika went to the bathroom I pinched Matei's rib. 'Someone's caught the bug,' I whispered. 'Soon you'll be asking Mamma to bring out the guitar.'

'Jealous much?' he said and pulled my hair, quite hard. It brought back memories, the feeling of follicles objecting to violent treatment. I laughed and went in close, my cheek on his collarbone, arms wrapped.

'Stop it,' he said and pushed me off. 'Don't be weird.'

Everyone else had moved into the dining room but the bottle was still on the side table by the window. Matei poured three glasses to the rim as Monika came back from the bathroom, and we gingerly clinked the tiny glasses. I spilled some on my finger.

'Skål,' Monika said somewhat theatrically.

'Skål,' we mimicked and downed the icy liquid. My brain lulled.

Peter was the goody two shoes in our sibling troop so he was busy in the kitchen, red apron and all. He still had two thirds of his original schnapps left, now thawing on the dining table.

I sat down between Pappa and Matei. Even the healthy Christmas leftovers were superb and I had not yet tired of the meat-free meatballs and sweet spicy mustard. Only eating this food once yearly, its taste and texture acted like a portal to all previous years, the time in between evaporated. The mustard teleported me to childhood Julaftons, to navy velvet dresses and white stockings, Grandma's enthusiastic but ill-executed piano playing. I swallowed and my stomach cramped and I touched it. It was fine, just a small cramp, period pain sized.

Matei and Monika were teasing Peter about something he had said about the stock market at a recent party and I wished I had also been at the party. Mamma defended Peter out of habit, him being the youngest, and Peter was duly annoyed by her overprotection. This was not anything special or unusual. But it made me feel like when you are hungry and then the hunger stops and you get that nauseous hollow sensation.

Pappa raised his snowflake glass and picked up another schnapps ballad. An old Swedish folksong about a woman drowning herself in a lake, as they used to back then.

'Skål,' Pappa said after the final note and I downed my full glass. Nowadays it was just four pills, no lake needed.

Their faces still recovering from the sharp alcohol, I placed my glass on the table and said, 'I had an abortion today.'

It went quiet, only the soft sound of Christmas psalms from the neighbour's TV. I licked my lips which still stung from the alcohol.

Pappa's face was marble, only his eyes moving.

'What in hell, Sam,' Matei said.

'No, no, it's fine, it was just the pills. No scraping or whatever.'

Matei looked as if he wanted to cover Monika's ears with his hands but she seemed unflustered. 'The pills are nothing. You'll be back to normal in a few days, easy,' she said. 'Or so I've heard.'

Everyone looked at Monika, but two and a half elder-flower schnapps in, she was beyond decorum. I liked this new girlfriend, I decided. I hoped Matei wouldn't mess it up.

Mamma said, 'Alright come on Pappa, help me clear the table.'

He placed one hand on the table and one on my shoulder as if for leverage, but softly squeezed two times before letting go to join Mamma in the kitchen. Peter slow-clapped at me, shaking his head. I gave him the finger.

•

To her credit, Diwa told me insistently to talk to Luc before booking the appointment. I hadn't. 'You don't think he deserves to know?' she asked on the phone. 'It's his cell-cluster too.'

I was sitting in my parents' living room on the formal chairs by the window, a cup of tea in front of me that I hadn't touched. It was warm in the room and I pushed off my slippers. Mamma and Pappa were out Christmas shopping. I wondered how Diwa was taking this, me ending a pregnancy while she was trying to procure one herself. She must have made the connection but she didn't let on. Anyway, I wasn't feeling ungrateful.

'It's not about him deserving or not,' I said. 'I'm trying self-censorship this time, you know, sparing his feelings instead of blurting stuff without filter.'

'You sure that's it?'

'Honestly I would feel better telling him, but it would only make him sad. Besides, the other thing is more important.'

Luc had only his father. No siblings, dead mother, senile grandma. When I was with Diwa he seemed envious, like he wanted family members of his own. Peeing on the stick, seeing it turn positive, I knew I did not. I was going to end this pregnancy but also I would never have another one on purpose.

Before the stick I had not once longed for children. When asked I replied not yet. I had figured I was young and not ready but that I would be one day, like a click. A biological operating-system update, version one point three upgrades including maternal instincts and increased levels of oestrogen. But I didn't want this update. I would opt out.

Telling Luc about the abortion meant also telling him about not wanting children ever. I was dying to call him the moment the tiny display showed a plus. But he was sensitive. It was a reason to love him. And I did. In a deep, unwavering way.

'I think the news about both the abortion and not wanting kids would be too much for Luc to process at once,' I said to Diwa. It started snowing, these slow big flakes. I wanted to open the window and stick my face out.

'I agree it would be a lot but Sami one thing you're not factoring in, you're useless at lying. And I don't think it's your cleverest idea to practise that skill with something this huge. It will backfire.'

'It would equally backfire if I did tell him.' I knew it would turn into one of those occasions where I get too intense in my impatience to reach the next stage. The subsiding of guilt, the extra attentiveness. Good makeup sex. 'And telling him wouldn't change anything anyway. I'm having this abortion.'

I hated secrets but Luc was my first important relationship and I was trying to adapt, protect him from my surplus honesty.

'I don't know Sami, I think you're reaching new levels of stupidity here.'

'As soon as the holidays are over I will talk to him about not having a family, like ever. That's more crucial.'

'Your funeral,' Diwa said.

I sighed. Even though he might leave me once I told him about my permanent childlessness, he deserved the option. I opened the window and stuck my head out. Too far under the eaves, the snowflakes didn't reach my skin.

Of course, it hadn't happened that way because I had told him about the abortion anyway and he got that hurt look on his face and I was overwhelmed, panicked. Then I said the only thing I thought could mend the fracture.

'I love you Luc.'

He said nothing.

He left the room and closed the door behind him and didn't come back. And that was it. I had stayed too long in that flat, through the mundanity and the hanging of laundry and dealing with our chafing differences. I even stayed when reflexively hurting him caused such overbearing guilt I started viewing myself differently, as an actual bad person. But now I'd said I loved him, and he couldn't say it back. I took that as my cue to exit.

•

I spent a few days at Diwa and Milly's getting over an abortion and a breakup both. Diwa called it The Purge and Milly was appalled and at first I couldn't laugh at this but then I could so it was time to leave their sofa. I called Tabatha and she took me in and I was grateful to have a rich friend with a spare room.

I think Tabatha is actually pleased to have me and I do my best to go out whenever Patti comes over. Tabatha is the opposite of a loner. She rarely leaves me alone but that's a good thing since it keeps me from reading old texts and checking Luc's instagram. He hasn't posted anything yet. Our mutual friends don't mention him although I know they must see him sometimes. We are not in touch, our flat is gone, no one talks about him. It is like we never existed.

But I'm in London and I am safe and I have Tabatha. And today is the first day of my permanent position at a renowned agency. So what if the office has a high-ceilinged convo culture and I don't have my own place to live. Out the window, London is showing off. This is what I always wanted, a good job in my adopted city. I wish I could screenshot this and send to myself at sixteen.

In Greece, deciding to move back was about the city as much as the boy. Or rather, the two had become inseparable to me. Since meeting him at eighteen my London daydreams all included him. Luc was London manifest. Cool, intelligent, vast, awake. Metropolitan. Fun.

Fun to kiss.

But then living together, some things were not fun. In reality we pulled in directions much too different. We had known it was a risk going in and now it had been proven.

Catastrophe, not sublime. It was for the best surely, better find out now than later trapped in a mortgage and joint custody of dogs or furniture. This was neater, packing things in a box, subletting the flat until our contract ended. And then we would be clean cut from each other.

I turn off the desktop screen and stand up, saying goodbye to a few of my new colleagues, still in their chairs at eight thirty. I have not awed anyone with my intellect and good points but made some competent first-day conversation I think. I press zero in the elevator and lean against the wall and shake my hands. When the door pings I exit the building and in front of me is the river. End of March and I can smell spring finally. And garlic bread and hot coffee and churros with cinnamon. People are wearing new denim jackets and the river is murky brown but still I want to swim.

'Hey. New girl,' someone calls. Vicki. She is standing in an alley beside the building, smoking. 'So, how was day one?' she asks and looks like a Bikini Kill song.

'Yeah good thanks. Didn't really get to talk to Preya though.'

'Intimidating right?' Vicki says, blowing her peroxided hair out of her face. 'Sorry, shouldn't scare you on your first day.'

'I don't scare easily,' I say and resolve to prove this tomorrow.

'Fair enough.'

While we small talk, she hands me a cigarette and lights it for me. I have stopped smoking almost, this is an exception. First day, I should celebrate.

'So Sam, do you party?' She steps on her cigarette. 'I'm meeting some friends if you want to come? Team building?'

And yes I want to party with Vicki's friends and smoke out today's tension and enjoy the city I am embracing as home. 'Team building?' I say. 'We're not doing trust exercises or something are we?'

Vicki shows her teeth. 'Depends on what you mean by trust exercises,' she says and holds out a bag of pills. I take one and put it in my mouth. And then things are strange and exciting for a bit and then later we go dancing and it is fun and then skip to eating sushi without chopsticks in a good-looking place and skip to a bus seat my bag next to me and then skip and I am home alone in bed.

The opposite of sober, I lie on my back and I hold my phone up and my arms look wastefully long. Static arm hair standing right out. I can sense my nails. I am happy and dizzy and infatuated with this city and I wish I could talk to it like you would a person.

I click on my phone, send a text.

How good or miserable are you these days?

I don't know what I want him to reply. In the end, I'm just happy he does.

Mostly okay these days.

Okay. He is okay.

105 DAYS UNTIL

Lucas

And so far, tonight is going well. The waiter puts down a dish in front of me, a large white plate with a wide rim. In the middle, a beige puck. White foam around it, a purple flower on top. I could fit the whole puck in my mouth but somehow I have to make it last at least fifteen minutes.

Gabrielle looks editorial opposite me. With her blonde hair and nude dress, she matches the food. Her shoulders are bare and she wears no jewellery. This would make for a nice instagram photo. I tell her this and she is delighted.

It is May sixteenth, Gabrielle's birthday, and we are in her favourite restaurant. A serious place with black lacquered furniture. There is no cutlery, instead there are flavour-free bread squares on the table and designated personnel bringing out steaming hand towels between courses. She is having their seven-course tasting menu. Me, the vegan version. This is the first course, seven times we will go through the procedure. The waiter placing the plates in front of us, reappearing to ask if everything is satisfactory, coming back to refill our water and suggest we order another glass of wine, back again to take the plate, to finally reappear with the next course.

I am mindful of being nice to the waiter and reassuring everything is great. But I wish I could tell them to bring all seven courses at once to mix in a bowl and cover with hot sauce and eat like a normal meal, uninterrupted. I want to focus on Gabrielle and this aggressive staff attentiveness makes our conversation clipped, as if stop motion.

Gabrielle loves this place though and I am only happy to see her enjoy her day. When she is pleased she looks like she is vibrating, humming. Which is the effect I am aiming for when I place the most expensive gift I have ever bought on the table. It is small, square, and wrapped in black ribbon.

She moves her hand to her cheek and beams. 'What's this then?'

'Happy birthday. Open it.'

She does and it is a silver bracelet inside. A simple chain of heavy links.

'Oh, it's exquisite. I love it.' Which I knew she would because she pointed at it once in Dover Street Market. 'Help me put it on.'

I reach over and fiddle with the clasp and it is on her. She holds out her arm and twists it left and right to catch the glimmer from the tealight. The chunk of the chain makes her arm look graceful, smooth like new. It suits her. 'I'm never taking it off. It will be on me like a tattoo.'

The waiter appears with the second course. A white jelly sphere, stalks of chives stacked like Jenga.

Gabrielle is into food, saying we shouldn't just eat for fuel but for physical pleasure too. She likes finding new ingredients for us to try and she eats slowly, using her tongue, curious. When I cook for her she always leaves some on the plate no matter the size of the portion. I am not sure if this is a politeness thing or a tic because she doesn't do it in restaurants. I find I am frenetic cooking for her, keen to get a good reaction, the dropping of the shoulders and humming and savouring with closed eyes. I don't ever serve her food in the John Lewis noodle bowls because it somehow feels like a disloyalty but to whom I'm not sure.

Though tonight I am not doing the cooking and she is already pleased so I can just relax and enjoy seeing her indulge.

'Your hair is getting long,' she says.

I touch my neck. 'True. I have a trimmer at home if you're offering.'

'Not a chance. Go to a nice hairdresser. Treat yourself.'

And amazingly, I can now afford the treat. And this dinner. And the bracelet currently gleaming around her graceful wrist. Okay the bracelet was a stretch but it was worth it. It will be on her like a tattoo.

I got a job. And not until my first payslip did I realise just how straightjacketed by my bank account I'd been. Like when you turn off the kitchen fan and the quiet is so obvious and so nice that it's incredible you didn't notice the noise before. I had normalised my constant money worry to a screech in the back of my mind I thought was chronic.

Financial tinnitus. And now it's simply gone. To Gabrielle's credit.

It comes with a caveat. I took the dirty car job.

•

Besides capoeira, Gabrielle also runs and one day she invited me to join. Low-intensive Sunday morning jogs in the pale May sun, instantly I liked it. And now I lace up four times a week. It is different from strength training. Instead of the burn being focused in one location, the biceps or quads or shoulders, the pain is everywhere, muscles and lungs, an omnipresent discomfort.

The rounded dense muscles I got from calisthenics are stretching out, now long and lean and durable. Aesthetically I find I have no real preference, but symbolically I like it. I want to physically illustrate that the person I was has moved on. And now, slimmer, longer-looking, my clothes fit differently.

The third morning Gabrielle had joined my gym class, I inhaled and asked if she wanted to go for a walk. We bought coffee and she owned a reusable to-go cup which was a good sign and we had a lot to talk about and she was flirty and so was I. Three years older, developer for a tech-giant, clever, impressive body. I was flattered. After that, we started seeing each other two three nights a week. I realised how malnourished I was of touch, company. On our fourth date, a kitschy tiki bar in Soho with paper lanterns and Hawaii music, we talked about my hiated career.

'So you want to get a highly sought-after type of position? With everyone competing over the same few openings?' She gathered her completely straight hair over one shoulder. It shone like a liquid.

'Yeah basically. I mean no one studies environmental engineering to get a job destroying the planet is my guess.'

'And it's impossible to get this good job without decent experience.'

Her laid back but keen interest made me feel hyper. 'Not impossible maybe. But without contacts, I'd say it's improbable at least.'

'So you got yourself a catch twenty-two, sort of.' She lifted the cocktail stick to her mouth and bit down on the green olive and pulled the stick out slowly. Her face tinted red by the rice paper lamps and yet she looked cool to the touch.

'Any advice?'

'You only really have one option, right.'

'Which is?'

She leaned forward. 'Take dirty car job first. Get dream job later.' The bar went quiet as the current ukulele song ended.

I exhaled until my lungs were empty. 'You don't see any way to skip directly to dream job, without getting dirty?'

'Well, it's May now. You graduated in what, July? It's not looking good is it.' Even though she gave me no reason to be, I was embarrassed. 'And you're at that age now where it's like, if you want a career, you have to find an entry. You need a jump start.'

'Sure. But working for the industry I'm hoping to later dismantle, that's fairly poor form.'

'Those guys you told me about, the inventors or whatever.'

'What about them?' I leaned my forearms on the table.

'Where do you think they started? None of them ever work for an unethical company to learn the ropes and get industry contacts?'

She had a point. 'You have a point.'

And by then I was so exhausted by Darling and the solitude and the whirring from the heater that I think a much smaller nudge than hers would have tipped me over.

The next morning I checked online whether the car company was still accepting applications. They were. I emailed my CV and referenced Professor Jonas in my cover letter and that night I got a reply with details for an interview. It was done. And although only just a first step it was a massive one.

I told Sam about my new job in a text. It is six weeks now since she got back in touch and I was by then dating Gabrielle already. When I texted Sam about Gabrielle, she did not have much to say. *Congratulations. I'm happy for you*, was her whole reply and I was only relieved to not discuss it further. You never know with Sam. But my new job she did have opinions on. In an impish tone unsuccessfully masking her disapproval, she basically said I was better than this and they didn't deserve me.

I wasn't better than this. No one else had wanted me. She was being overly optimistic.

She did not agree. *It's a trap. Get out while you can. Take the red pill.*

The blue has fewer side effects.

Maybe true but it's the drowsy kind. Take the red. All the cool kids are doing it.

Said the woman in marketing.

Well I'm not one of the cool kids am I.

Goodnight Sam.

Talk tomorrow.

We stick to texting. No phonecalls, no emails, absolutely no video. Texting feels neat. And you can really only type short things, so there is low risk of saying too much. I make good use of the redrafting possibility, often leaving a text for a few hours before sending.

We have not discussed my cocainey run-in with her aunt and uncle but doubtless Diwa has told her. Neither have we mentioned the breakup or the abortion even once. I think about it though, that she doesn't want children while I do.

And I would be good at it. I look at me and Dad, at how Mum had been the warm and present parent. I could offer that to someone, presence and affection and stability. A home to grow up in with inhabitants who talk about things, about their lives and their views on their lives, interrupting each other at the table. There would be two or maybe three because I'd want them to experience having siblings, that unique connection you can only really get by growing up with the same parents, the annoyances family-specific. Somewhere there had been a mistake, me growing up first with a great mum and then with only a dad. He was a kind person but he wasn't skilled at active parenting. And even though I am stunned by the darkness human thoughts can reach, I sometimes do think, it should have been the other way around. She should have been the one taking care of a twelve-year-old in grief.

This wish of mine, creating a family sturdy and numerous enough to deal with things, with death even, I sometimes wonder if it's really mine at all, or just a default. If I want a family because I truly do, or because I'd been told I should. It could well be one of those existential certainties. Like going to school. Or retirement schemes. Buying a car. Or dying. One day, having kids would just be the next step on the staircase. But then I think, authentic internal want or outside expectation, does it matter? Because here I am, still wanting.

I want Sam's opinion on this because it is easy to work things out with Sam. After the breakup it was terrifyingly quiet for a while, and now, strictly texting, there is no discussing important life decisions or emotional ambiguities. We talk about her colleagues and me picking up running. Our thoughts on that MP's recent transphobe tweets.

Sam seems okay. She's got this new fancy job and I am proud of her. It is easy to be unambivalently happy for her since I've got my own decent job. We are these days financial equals, and although I reject the thought, there is a hum in the back of my head. Now, we could have afforded a nicer flat.

•

Gabrielle licks her lips and puts down her dessert fork and folds a stray hair back into position.

'This was absolute decadence,' she says. 'I feel so spoiled. Thank you Lucas, really.' She squeezes my hand with her hand and I lift it to my lips and I'm happy.

She goes to the bathroom. I still have half my coffee left. It is strong, the first thing I am served tonight without a refined understated flavour you need a sophisticated palate to appreciate.

Gabrielle comes back with fresh lipstick. She sits and tends to her remaining dessert wine. In a way, dating Gabrielle is like slipping into comfortable clothes tailored to your exact measurements. She is quintessentially British. We have the same frame of reference, she thinks before she speaks and rations her emotional output. She is very London. Chilled, dry, elegant. Gabrielle likes staying in watching films and cooking great food just as much as I do. I don't ever feel awkward about wanting brown rice or turning down a pub night. We are resistance free.

Even though it is a windy night, her hair is smooth. I look outside. The breeze blows a plastic bag across the pavement, a group of pigeons doing pigeon things. One male dancing and spinning and puffing up for a female. She seems unenthusiastic. Pigeons are not much more than city decor, backdrop, I never take note of them really. Had it been me and Gabrielle that day in the Soho alleyway, I wonder if either of us would have noticed the pigeon with the hole in its neck.

'There's a new bar close by that's supposed to be nice if you want to get another drink?' I say.

'No let's go back to my place.' She bites her lip. I get a thrill.

'Let me pay and we can get out of here.'

I ask our attentive waiter for the bill and fuck does it feel good to slide my card into the machine and fuck does it feel great to see that satisfied look on Gabrielle's face. Our first birthday celebration together. I think I did well.

I help her on with her coat and get us a taxi and we go to bed and have sex which is nice and afterwards she falls asleep and I go to the kitchen and eat cold leftovers in the light of the fridge because I am still hungry.

79 DAYS UNTIL

Sam

Six minutes from now, I am meeting Luc's girlfriend. I am sitting outside a bar in King's Cross, it is June eleventh, it is Friday, and it's six minutes to seven in the evening. Besides his girlfriend, I am also seeing Luc. For the first time in five months.

The evening sun skids off the rooftop across the square and hits my face. There are numerous bars and restaurants and cafés around here and like every Friday in every June there is a buzz. Young parents, men in suits, owners of pugs. Avant-garde fashion students from Central Saint Martins. It feels like today, summer really started. I should be off mischieving with Finn, not having civilised sauvignon with Gabrielle.

I text Finn to meet up later. To bring Tabatha. And weed.

When I dressed this morning, I packed extra makeup and a top to change into after work. I couldn't decide what to wear and regretted having left Luc the chocolate shirt. It would have been just the thing, both slippery sexy and evocative of our time together. I want him to feel a pang of remorse, not self-congratulatory with his current choice of

233

girlfriend. It is selfish and petty and not fair on Luc but I don't care because I figure it's only natural to have this attitude towards your ex's new partner.

I ended up choosing a thin black camisole without a bra. I have seen a photo of Gabrielle. I did not enjoy that.

I would much rather have met Luc without the girlfriend. Last time I saw him had been through the rear window of a taxi, his silhouette slowly shrinking as the car drove off. He had stood with his hands at his sides, watching the taxi leaving him behind, and he had looked so lost, so unmoored, my only thought was to never do this to him again.

But now we are texting and it has been safe and we have gotten back into rhythm, as friends. I am dying to talk to him because textual communication is not the same. And despite it all, despite us being laughable as a couple, I still need him around. He has somehow become integral, replying to my thoughts like no one else. His reaction to me is unique and therefore he has inconveniently proven to be irreplaceable.

Luc has of course told Gabrielle about us being in touch and hence we're now meeting for drinks, her idea. It feels like I am being vetted. That if Luc and I want to keep contact, sauvignon with Gabrielle is the price to pay.

The sun is in my eyes so I don't see them until they are right by the table. Luc is slimmer. My chest cramps for a second. Then I smile. He smiles back. He is physically close, just inches away, and through his white t-shirt I can see the shape of his protruding belly button.

I stand up and give Luc a quick hug and he introduces me to Gabrielle and she is tall and we cheek kiss. Two kisses, civilised as expected. We sit down and Luc is awkward and this makes me awkward. I pour them water and spill a little on the metal table. Luc draws his chair closer and bumps the table resulting in even more water spillage. Gabrielle seems unfazed by the dramatic scene.

She is tastefully blonde, discreet makeup, extremely relaxed. Blue jeans and Breton shirt that I bet smell like soap flakes. She would fit on a boat. Not a luxury yacht or anything gaudy but a real sailboat, a small one you have to operate yourself. I can see her pulling ropes and spinning one of those wheel things.

She signals to the waiter. 'Should we share a bottle of white?' she asks. Luc and I agree and she orders a riesling which is my least favourite grape. I make a note of our taste disparity.

They talk about a charity run they did one Sunday where people throw different coloured powder at the runners. I can't imagine anyone throwing colour at Gabrielle but they have photographic proof on Luc's phone. Then Luc asks me about work and I tell them an anecdote about my manager not eating salad.

'And then she says, "I swear to god Amelia, if you order me something detoxy we will have a problem. I have a brain, I don't need to watch my weight, I can eat real food," as if a missed opportunity to fill up on steak and chips automatically would like, lower her career drive. Like scurvy is a sign of you know, great management skills.'

Luc laughs a little and Gabrielle smiles and I am surprised because I think the story deserves a bigger reaction. I put on my sunglasses.

'What about you Gabrielle, what's your office like?' I ask.

'It's not that special really, I'll not bore you with work talk.'

The waiter brings three glasses and a bottle in a cooler. Gabrielle tastes and approves the wine.

'Well Luc wins employment from hell anyway, doesn't he. Like The Stepford Wives, office edition,' I say.

'Oh, you know about that?' Gabrielle asks and I wonder if I should pretend Patti told me. But I don't know why, as Gabrielle is already aware of Luc and me being in touch.

'Yeah I mentioned to Sam that I find it a bit unsettling how nice everyone is,' Luc says.

'Oh, of course. Well I'm glad you two can be friends, I find it so impressive when exes manage that transition.'

Luc shifts his weight.

I wonder what he has told her about us, and the image of them talking about me in bed after sex disapproving my immaturity makes me flush. I don't think Luc would do that. He is very loyal. I tell myself she doesn't know more about me than I about her.

While she is talking about a film they saw the other night, I study Luc's face. He is markedly slimmer, and it makes him look spent. Or maybe gaunt is the word. He has a couple of early summer freckles on his temples and I know what he would smell like if I leaned across the table.

The ninety minutes I spend with Gabrielle feels like twice that. I try finding common ground to lubricate the stilted conversation but really we have nothing to talk about and all my questions seem vulgar or probing although they are not. I have never experienced this in Luc's presence before. I understand it is down to nerves navigating a tricky social situation, still it's gruesome that our first meeting after the abortion fiasco is just this perpetual miscommunication. He seems hesitant. Borderline suffering actually. As if he doesn't know which foot to stand on. It makes me think of Scotch and soda night at Robert's. I drink more wine.

He is telling Gabrielle about Tabatha and Patti first getting together at my goodbye party and the irony of that and how cute and obvious they had been and I am laughing at the memory thinking it is so like him to ponder this when she puts a hand on his wrist.

'Lucas, I'm sorry to interrupt but I have to go.' And then she turns to me. 'I have dinner plans, apologies for just rushing off.'

'Oh don't worry. It was lovely to meet you finally,' I say and I'm grateful it is over.

'I'll walk you to the station,' Luc says, 'and maybe I'll head back to yours if you don't mind?'

'Sure. Let's get the bill,' she says and hands him a keychain with a large silver name tag. Gabrielle in corkscrew italics.

'Oh I got this one,' I say. 'Will stay for a bit anyway so I'll sort it when I leave.'

'Nonsense,' she says.

'Yeah no, this one's mine Sam,' Luc says. 'I owe you for so many bubble teas anyway.' He smiles and I chuckle and say, 'Alright, fine. But really you don't owe me at all.'

Gabrielle stands up. 'I think it's quicker if we just pay inside.'

They do, she kisses my cheek twice, Luc gives me a hug, and they leave.

Walking off hand in hand, she says what sounds like, 'Why does she call you Luc anyway?'

And I watch his back and that head with the tiny soft neck-hairs disappear around the corner. The thought of sending him off on slimming runs with this clean girlfriend is devastating.

It takes six minutes to walk to the station from here. I place my phone on the table, put a timer on six minutes, order another drink, and watch the seconds tick down.

With twelve seconds left on the timer, I text him.

Come back a sec, will you.

●

The other day marked a month in my new job and I still wasn't used to the climate. I missed floor eleven. I missed Tabatha, my old team.

Preya had heard I was Tabatha's mum's protégé and that did not go over well. She never spoke directly to me and if I said something in a meeting she started ruffling papers or clearing her throat. My colleagues soon picked up on the atmosphere and as easy as a few rustling papers I was made pariah.

Preya was like that friend from school who used to pick a new target every break between classes. And us other kids so relieved to not be target of the day we gratefully participated in the torment. I had been both tormentor and tormentee. But now I was an adult and shouldn't have to engage in toxic group activities.

Only Vicki was nice to me, office omega herself, too political to fit in. She seemed unconcerned by this, her face a constant mask of slight disdain and filled-in eyebrows. I took my cue from her and feigned ignorance of the weird mood by keeping a stoic expression. It was a new tactic for me, this non-confrontational head-in-sand pose. Old me would have left circa day four but the client list was unreal and jobs like this don't just come by and I wanted to prove I could hack it. Besides, it was a bad mood for everyone, not just me. I could get used to it surely.

At least Vicki was fun and her friends were welcoming and they partied so hard I felt like a lightweight. An unfamiliar feeling for me and I quite enjoyed being the innocent for once.

They had tried everything and generously offered to organise the best possible first-time experiences for me. I sampled new substances and mixes they claimed to have carefully calibrated for the perfect evening of this mood or that mood. My favourite was the dance mood. I did not like the sit still and monologue mood.

I had many thrilling nights. It was fun in a wild way and nothing too heavy and I was impressed with myself for going so hard and still managing work just fine. There were also many strange moments, when reality slipped or I lost time and I wondered if this was what it felt like to slide down insanity avenue. Even when sober, memories flickered that I didn't know just what they were. I spent all my money on rent, food, and drugs. There was nothing left to save, but I only saw this as evidence of me having a good time. Every saved pound a sign of lost opportunity, of the everyday making ground.

Finn and I had a bad moment one night when he joined me and Vicki and them. I was quite drunk by the time he showed up but only on alcohol. He wanted to talk so we went outside to the street and he was anxious because his visa was expiring and his current workplace had finally come to the decision not to sponsor him. He might have to move back to Hong Kong. I concentrated on furling my brow and sounding concerned but I was already slurring my words.

'You know, I'm not that keen on meeting up just to watch you pretend to be sober,' he said. 'Like, I enjoy actually talking to you, not just doing shots together.'

'You're right, my bad.' I was hot and wiped my face with the back of my hand.

'But seriously now, why are you?'

'What?'

'Going on like this.'

I grew incredibly tired. It seemed unfair to me, as if only allowed a taste for intoxication in case of early trauma or clinical diagnosis. I had neither, there was no psychological wound to blame, no acronym or abusive adult. I was just wired with high voltage, it had its pros, it had its cons.

'God Finn, I'm twenty-eight. It's not so unusual to have a good time.'

'Are you though?'

I rubbed my eyes and wanted him to not be mad at me anymore because now there was a threat of self-pity. 'Let's hang out just the two of us,' I said. 'Just talk, go for a walk. Tomorrow.' And all I wanted was to go on a walk through Victoria Park with Finn, laughing at ducks while not feeling a pulse in my neck.

The next day, I slept in and texted him in the afternoon but he was busy by then.

Diwa nagged me but she was older and settled. Tabatha and Patti sometimes asked me to stay home with them instead of going out but also they needed their space and I didn't want to be a nuisance. In all our texts, I never mentioned any of this to Luc. He would not like it.

There was a freedom here, from judgement. I was my own person, no one relied on me, my wildness could harm no one but myself at this point, Finn or anyone else couldn't get much more than annoyed. I had no obligation to talk to Luc about it either, owing him no details of my private life. And although comedowns were rough, sacrificing my Sundays seemed a small price to pay.

•

Luc has not replied to my text but still I wait in my chair outside the bar. I wonder what I had looked like to him, if he could tell I am a little bristled. I pick up my pocket mirror and check my complexion. I think I look fine. Not tired, or jaded, or dull.

He had looked different though and I wonder how much weight he has lost. I know he is running with Gabrielle but she only looks fresh. She is slim sure, but strong not frail. So I worry Luc is being excessive. I don't like it.

Then from across the plaza I see his silhouette.

I lean back and enjoy the view of him walking closer. He is wearing sunglasses and his hands are in his pockets and I wave. He smiles. I stop waving and sit on my hands to stabilise. 'There you are. I almost gave up hope.'

'Yeah, I'm glad you asked actually. Just had to call Gabrielle to let her know I was heading back.'

'Ah, I thought we were being illicit.'

'None of that,' he says but still smiling.

He orders a gin on ice, lime on the side.

'So, how do you think that went?' he asks.

'Is she French?' I twirl my wine glass. He seems taken aback. 'I mean she looks French and her name is Gabrielle.'

'She doesn't look French,' he says as if French is an insult.

'Yeah it went okay I think. A little awkward maybe but that's sort of inherent to the format I would say.'

'You didn't like her.'

I put my glass down. 'I hated her.'

He flinches and then he laughs a single hah almost violently. It is shocking, all of it.

'Jesus Sam. That's brutal.' He rubs his eyes. 'Glad to see your frank streak hasn't abandoned you.'

'Look I tried that whole dishonesty thing and it didn't work out so hot, remember. I am better at frank.'

'Okay fine but if you say anything like that again I can't hang out with you anymore.'

'Fair enough.' And although I loathe him saying this I also find his protectiveness sexy.

'You know, I'm ashamed to admit this really, but I am kind of pleased,' he says.

'That I hate her?'

'No, obviously. That you're jealous.'

I wave my hand dismissively.

'No, you are. And I'm sorry, it's shit of me to say but it's sort of nice.' He takes off his sunglasses and puts them on the table. Five months since I saw these slanted eyes.

'Wow Luc, look at you admitting such vulgarities,' I say and think about last time, when he couldn't say he loved me back. I wonder what he says to Gabrielle. And this specific thought makes it clear that yes, I do hate her. Which in actuality means I am jealous, a fact Luc has not only noticed but also taken pleasure from. Despicable really.

'Besides, you can't hate her, you don't know her,' he says.

'She is so, like, clean.'

'She is that.'

I remove my hair tie and shake my head. 'You do realise you have found the polar opposite of me, do you?'

'What, you would have preferred me showing up with your carbon copy?'

'I would have preferred you showing up solo.'

'Yeah, not jealous at all.' He laughs.

'Fine, I apologise for being possessive,' I say, a bit startled by my own sudden seriousness.

He hesitates. Then says, 'Well in my defence I tried you and it didn't work out, so thought I'd go for a different brand this time. Learn from my mistakes and that.'

'Charming.' I wave to the waiter. 'But yes, always the methodical one weren't you, with your lists and your measuring spoons.'

His grin is still there and I order another white wine and he lifts his glass to his mouth. My ears are hot. I feel the alcohol.

'Being serious now, you should give her a chance. She's nice.'

'You're very slim.'

'That tends to happen when you take up running,' he says.

'Is that really the best idea.'

'Stop. I am very healthy, I feel great, promise.'

'I don't like it.'

'Well I don't like your nightly routines.'

'Oh really. And who's being jealous, exactly?'

He holds up his hand like a stop sign. 'I don't mean because of that. You sleep with who you want. I mean getting smashed.'

'Stop. I am very healthy, I feel great, promise,' I say in a Popeye voice.

'Is that meant to be an impression of me? You were never any good at that you know, the voices, reading the personals.'

'You used to love it.'

'I was being polite.'

I tell him to take it back, that he can't retrospectively rewrite our communal memories. He laughs and takes it back. Although the metal chair is hard I feel intensely comfortable.

'But really, you don't want to take it a bit easier?' he says.

'How would you know anyway?'

'Patti.' He puts his hands on the table and folds them. His nails are short and clean. Hands made for kindnesses. Petting cats and peeling carrots, feeling your forehead for fever. I realise I still picture those hands feeling my forehead, should it ever need checking for fever.

'You don't look it though,' he says. 'Haggard or whatever.'

'What do I look?'

'Like yourself. Vintage Sam.' He plays with the lime wedge that came with his drink.

'Well it's only been five months, hasn't it.'

'But miserable ones.'

'Hey,' I say and search his face. 'I thought you were okay.'

'Yeah I'm okay now but it didn't start out completely great obviously.' He puts the lime back on its saucer.

I think of the night Diwa told me about, Luc high and dreadful and sad in front of her parents. So out of character for him, and me the sole reason for it. But I don't bring it up, not wanting to ruin the easy moment. I light a cigarette and the smoke burns my lungs deliciously. 'Want one?' I ask.

'No better not.'

I lean back and my legs are still, firmly planted. I roll my neck till it crunches, the sound mesmerising. The sun is almost behind the rooftops now but even shaded the air is pacific.

'Maybe just a taste of yours then,' he says finally.

I hand him my cigarette and he inhales.

'I have something to tell you,' he says.

I sit up straight and I am no longer relaxed at all. He gives me the cigarette back. I take it. I want to tell him to please shut up, please don't ruin it.

'All this time, ever since you left for Sweden back in September,' he says and it's like his speech is slow-motioned, 'I've kind of been logged into your spotify.'

I exhale sharply and box his arm. 'God Luc.'

'Oh sorry, I scared you did I?' He lets slip a small laugh.

I wave him off and tell him that of course I have known, this whole time. Like I wouldn't notice my 'recently played' songs suddenly being all Lou Reed and Thom Yorke and Nina Simone. That I'd remember listening to four Lou Reed albums in one sitting.

'And you didn't mind?'

'Those playlists are just as much yours as mine.'

'So I can stay? Logged in I mean.'

'Sure. Like, we don't have a child and we don't have a dog, why not crown spotify our item of shared custody.' I keep my eye on his face at the word 'child' to make sure this is a word we now can use when interacting. It seems it is.

This conversation has taken an unexpected but extremely pleasurable new route, and we spend ten minutes making up rules of conduct. No deleting songs from old playlists. No adding songs either. Absolutely no adding songs he associates with Gabrielle. No playing songs from our spotify for Gabrielle at all. And no having sex to our spotify, either of us.

I light another cigarette. 'I can't believe it's summer again.'

'Yeah it's gone so quickly this year,' he says.

'Half of it with you, half of it without you.'

'Which did you prefer?'

'You're joking right.' I tap my cigarette over the ashtray and I think it looks sensual, holding my cigarette like this, tapping with a skilled motion of the index finger. A speck of ash escapes and flutters high and lands on my leg. I wipe it with my palm. It smudges. A long grey line on my shin.

'You're a mess,' he says and picks up a napkin and dips it in his water glass and reaches for my leg. My shin on his knee, he cleans the ash off my skin.

His hand is warm and it lingers. Slight movements. And I want to ask him, please don't stop.

49 DAYS UNTIL

Lucas

'It's not a dungeon.' Sam laughs through the phone.

'Metaphorically it is. But okay in actuality it's very shiny.'

'Take a photo tomorrow, of your desk and your colleagues and everything. I want to picture where you spend your days.'

'Alright fine. Maybe not the colleagues.' I cough and squint up at the sun. My throat hurts.

Sam is on Tabatha's balcony, the wind making crackling noises as it hits her phone. It is Sunday night and I'm on my way to meet Gabrielle for a run. I am in the park across the street from my building and I smell new-cut grass and baked asphalt and a puff of someone's spliff drifting over. I stretch my quads, re-lace my left shoe. To not be late I need to hang up and get the tube in a few minutes.

'That's what I get for selling out though,' I say. 'I feel like a doctor.'

'In what way?'

It is early July but the grass in the park is already splotched brown from the sun and the rubbing of shoe soles and picnic blankets. Cigarette butts are liberally strewn across the lawn like confetti. The disrepair of the park, its lack of lush plants, makes it feel young and anti-social. It's a good spot really.

'Do you know anyone studying medicine?' I ask.

'Only an old school friend. She wanted to join Doctors Without Borders I think.'

'Bingo.'

'You've lost me,' she says and I hear the clink of ice on glass and sometimes she pauses as if sucking a straw. I picture her there, on Tabatha's tiny balcony in that orange bikini, the strapless one. Her legs drawn to her chest, picking on a chipped nail, trying not to smoke.

'It seems like every medical student wants to work for some NGO,' I say, 'only to end up with a big salary in a private practice somewhere in an affluent part of the city.'

'Well it's easy to be idealistic when you're still safely planted in the school bench,' she says. 'But you know, there are worse things than well-off doctors.'

'I do know, don't I. At least they are still helping people with their health and that. Look at me, studying to save the planet and then taking a job actively destroying it. It's like a doctor working for big tobacco.'

'Shit. Yeah it's not great is it.' She is chuckling now, agreeing with my self-criticism in a way that makes it tolerable. It feels safe communicating with Sam like this, sticking to phones only. In analogue, she is a hazard. In digital, she is my best friend. Neither of us have suggested meeting up in person again.

I hadn't meant it to, but cleaning the ash off her shin like that the other week had turned from routine physical contact into something not a hundred percent innocent. Once I noticed it had been too late, and I removed my hand but reluctantly and this reluctance is what makes me feel shoddy. It's like I can't touch her without it becoming sexual. Maybe not even look at her too long without my neurons sending signals to the sex part of the brain. Just out of habit. Nerve cell nostalgia.

I sit down on a bench because my legs are shaking a bit. I really should get going, late now. I send a rushed text to Gabrielle.

Running ten late. Start without me I'll catch up.

'Yes, your employer is evil and all,' Sam says, 'but like, is there such a thing as a clean payslip anyway? Either your company is bad or your clients are or the investors, you know? It's like every pound sterling passing hands is in some way the product of exploited workers in Cambodia.'

She is intense now, speaking fast. When she gets like this I don't interrupt because she is making sense of things by talking, as if her thoughts are jumbled and only by letting them out audibly do they piece together. I get to see her polish her worldview in real time which is nice.

I feel a cough that I try to hold in but comes out in painful cramps that leave me no choice. I cover the phone with my hand. Then I clear my throat.

'Are you ill? You were coughing before too.'

'Just a sore throat.'

'It sounds quite bad. Like, deep and phlegmy. Have you called your GP? You should get some slippery elm tea for it.'

'What the hell.'

'It's good, I'll send you a link.'

It doesn't sound good, it sounds vile. But I will likely try it anyway because I need these symptoms to go away. I have been coughing for a couple of weeks and sometimes my lungs feel hot and sometimes they feel cold, but I don't want to go to the doctor since they'll only tell me to stop working out.

I stand up and lean against a tree to catch the last sun on my face. I need to cough again but hold it in. When I breathe it feels like something is rolling in my chest.

'You know what I've been thinking lately?' Sam says.

'What.'

'That I would likely be a better person if I just moved to Flen.'

'Flen?'

'My go-to Swedish small town to illustrate non-urban existence.'

I chuckle. The sun disappears behind the rooftop and there's a breeze so nice on my face I wish I could drink it. My legs are heavy and I don't know how I'll get them to run today. 'Go on,' I say and I am at least ten minutes late but I can't seem to hang up so she will have to.

•

Gabrielle and I were on her sofa one night the other week. The heat pressed in through the open window although it had been dark outside for an hour. Her legs slung across my thighs, our skin stuck together whenever she moved, both of us in only underwear. We were googling.

'This one's in Surrey, early September. That's like eight nine weeks away,' she said, excited. It was infectious. 'If we just mind our recovery we should be fine.'

'We should yeah,' I said. 'So what, you're telling me I'm running a marathon?'

She gave a little shriek then and we chattered over each other planning our training for the upcoming weeks. I enjoyed seeing her this thrilled, her usual poise melted. We kissed for a bit and then went back to planning.

Running had turned into a hobby at this point and it was liberating to fully lean into it without worrying about outside judgement. I'd heard runners talk about the endorphins and the zen-like state, and I had believed it exaggerated. But it wasn't. I had to go a little faster or a little longer each time to feel it, much like any addiction I guess.

I coughed.

'Here, have some water,' Gabrielle said. I drank and cleared my throat, which was sore now.

'I'm proud of you, you know,' she said.

'You are?'

'I mean, in a few months you've turned into this dedicated runner and gone from shop assistant to proper engineer. It's like, you're quite proactive.' She closed the laptop and put it on the floor.

'Well. To be honest it's down to you really. You're a fairly motivating person.'

'I don't know, most guys I've dated have been so used to getting things handed to them in life they don't want to like actively pursue anything. A bit whiny you men are.'

'Hey now.' I chuckled and drank some more water, small sips, gingerly.

She removed her thighs from mine with a sticky skin sound and sat up and twisted her hair on her back. 'It's so unattractive, lazy inactive men who complain about being nagged whenever asked to just like, independently manage being alive.' She bit her fingertip. 'So I find it sexy that we sort of challenge each other.'

This puzzled me because if anything, I thought the self-improvement routine lessened our attraction. As if our similarity made us somewhat sterile, and combining our molecules in a tube would not create a big chemical reaction.

But there was very little to annoy me with Gabrielle. All the things that frustrated me with Sam, all the personality traits I wished she had, I'd gotten in Gabrielle. We were so well fitted and since meeting her, I had found a decent job, money, stability. Not once had our arguments caused me to get high and disgrace myself in front of Diwa's parents. So sometimes I wasn't overly excited to have sex, sometimes it took concentration to finish. I figured this was completely normal probably, the infatuation phase being over.

But comparing Gabrielle and Sam wasn't fair on either of them so I really shouldn't be doing it.

We started training for the marathon the next morning. I told myself I had the energy for it, that the stints of fatigue lately were nothing serious, that my body could handle a lot. I even revelled in forcing my muscles to submit, seeing how much they could take. It was like a punishment, but for what? I could see no reason my body deserved it. Nonetheless, afterwards I felt calm and absolved. I bought cough medicine and throat pastilles and didn't call my GP and didn't take the week off training because that would mess up our schedule before it even started.

•

The sun has set by the time I climb the stairs out of the tube station. It is only a couple of streets away, the starting point of our usual run. When I reach the canal I am fifteen minutes late. I had told her ten. She probably waited the ten minutes and then set off at a slow pace for me to catch up.

I rub my thighs and they feel fine if a bit numb. Still heavy, still reluctant to start up, but Gabrielle will be expecting me and also I need to hit my miles.

I swallow reluctantly and it is painful but I ignore this and start at a slow jog that I speed up after a minute until I'm at maximum for a run this distance, twelve kilometres. I wish I had brought water but Gabrielle will have her arm flask. My lungs feel dry like I have inhaled too much pollution, so I cough once but stop before it turns into a fit.

Fifteen minutes in and there is no sight of her. I am surprised because I had expected her to take it easy for my sake. My pulse is very high but I am not running fast enough to warrant this, so maybe I am stressed to catch up. But I know it's not stress. It's my lacking lungs.

The sky is dark on my right and mint blue on my left, trees making black fluttering silhouettes against the mint. There is no one on the path and my footsteps sound abnormally loud to me, like the exaggerated sound effects of a seventies horror movie. Tap tap tap.

Five more minutes and I still haven't caught up although I am running very fast now, borderline sprinting. I wonder if maybe she cancelled the run when I didn't show up but I check my phone and there are no missed calls or texts. I fumble with the phone and call her without slowing. She doesn't pick up. So definitely running then.

My throat is so dry and so constricted it is getting hard to breathe. The insides of my lungs burn and sort of shiver and I have never felt my lungs do this before.

I have to stop.

I slow my steps. Then I see her ahead so I pick up speed but although I am sprinting the gap doesn't close very quickly. And I realise she is actually not going slow, she is going at her normal speed.

My footsteps are so loud, she must hear them. She doesn't turn around. I want to shout her name to get her attention but my lungs will not let in enough air to make vocal sounds.

I should stop but my legs move automatically now. I cease breathing so they will have to stop eventually. It's a relief holding my breath because inhaling hurts too much anyway.

And then my legs stop.

The momentum makes me airborne for a second before I crash on the ground and now finally she does turn around and then the smell is noxious and I hear beeping machines and rubbery floors and I don't remember falling asleep but then I wake up and I'm in a

47 DAYS UNTIL

Sam

Hotel bed. It's a hotel bed. I get that feeling of waking up and it taking a second to realise where you are and then the relief of recognising the room. Except I don't recognise the room and there is no relief.

I panic and fumble with the sheets. I seem to be alone, my phone is on the nightstand. It's an expensive room.

The blackout curtains are drawn so I can't tell what time it is. I check my phone, 10:13am. There are missed calls, I should be at work. I am sweating. And also, I am naked.

Then the sounds of a toilet flushing, a tap running water, and a door unlocking. From the bathroom a person walks out, naked except for a towel wrapped around his waist. Black hair, young, smiling.

'Good morning miss,' he says and throws himself on the bed by my feet. I spring up to standing. My head takes a twirl and I hold on to the wall.

'Wow,' I say. I know his face faintly, like someone you have seen on TV. 2D, pixelated.

I am still naked and he doesn't seem to find this strange but I do, so I grab a white hotel robe off the floor and put it on. I do not sense any predatory vibrations and I feel more horrified by the situation than afraid for my safety. Like being dropped into a scripted scene but without either reading the script or being told the premise. Ad-libbing real life.

'Don't take this the wrong way,' I say, 'but where are we?'

He looks confused and is quiet for a second. 'The hotel?' he says finally. 'It's The Royal Crescent.'

'No I mean like, which area.'

'Which area?'

'Which area of London.'

'Of London?' He sounds like a puppet. No a parrot. A parrot is the one that mimics. 'You mean you don't remember?'

'No. Obviously not.' My fingers feel cold and tingly. Whatever I took yesterday, I am still under the influence. I should hydrate, eat some salt.

'Babe, we're not in London. We're in Bath.'

Everything stops. Then it speeds up again and five frantic minutes of me asking questions go by. To his credit he is very obliging. It is Tuesday morning. We met in Dalston on Sunday evening or rather Monday morning. I remember the club and I remember talking to some cute guy and I remember being in the cute guy's flat which apparently is this cute guy on the bed in front of me now. His name, he tells me, is Quentin. It comes back to me, in separated chunks. Memory tetris.

Yesterday in his flat, I had said I wanted to go to Bath because I wanted to test out living in a Jane Austen novel. I don't remember saying this and I do not feel a particular inclination to live in a Jane Austen novel, but Quentin had offered to drive me in his Porsche, again very obliging. A normal person would have said car, but he says Porsche as if the distinction is important. I do recall being in the car singing together.

We had gone to two different clubs in Bath and that's a blur, which is probably a good thing. And then we spent the night in this hotel.

'We had sex right.'

'Yes, a few times.' His eyes go big. 'Oh god you don't remember? I thought you were like, I had no idea you were that out of it. Are you sure you don't remember?' He is panicking now and I don't know how to react. My throat stings with acid.

'Please calm down. I am not saying that you whatever. I remember one time, in your flat? We used a condom?'

'Yes, condom. And my flat, that was the first time.' He holds on to this memory of mine like a life jacket.

'And then we went on for a bit in your car?'

He nods encouragingly.

'And then here in the hotel, right.'

'That's correct, well done,' he says, extremely relieved he hasn't played in the grey area.

'Do you remember everything? Since Dalston?' I ask.

'I think so but there are some confused moments. But like, no real blackouts or anything.'

I sit down on the fluffy carpet and I rub my eyes and wish he would tell me the appropriate reaction because I don't know what to do with all this.

'How old are you?' I ask.

'Just turned twenty.'

And self-loathing comes up my throat and I run to the bathroom and vomit something yellow, the taste so vile I vomit again. He stumbles in and tries to hold my hair and fill a glass of water at once. In between retches I say, 'Please, get out will you. Give me a minute.'

He leaves and closes the door softly. I should be at work.

I wait for the convulsions to stop and flush the toilet and sit down to wee. My urine comes out stinging and smells sharp of ammonia or vinegar. I might be sick again. It feels like the white hotel robe is dirtied by being in contact with my skin, like no amount of bleach could clean the depravity out. I strip it off and drop it on the floor.

Thankfully it only takes one step to be in the shower. I sit on the floor tiles and let the water fall heavy on me, fill my every cavity. I probe everywhere carefully with my fingers. Because of dizziness, a mental image of my head hitting the stone tiles makes me scared to stand up. My stomach looks hollow, hurting from the vomit convulsions. And it is like it's separate from me, another creature completely, one that I am responsible for and have abused in a number of ways. I place my hand on it, gently, just holding it there.

Quentin, or Q as he prefers being called, knocks on the door with soft knuckles.

'You can come in,' I shout. 'Close your eyes.'

'I'm going downstairs to get us some food, okay. To give you a minute to dress and that. What are you in the mood for? Whatever you fancy.'

'Oh okay, thanks. Just anything really,' I say and look at him standing there, eyes closed. 'Make sure it's plant-based, will you?'

'What?'

'Vegan.'

'What?'

'Or whatever just get me beans on toast okay. A lot of it.'

'Oh vegan yeah, sounds lush,' he says and we must still be high because none of this makes sense.

•

Before the club on Sunday, I'd been on the balcony with an iced coffee, talking to Luc on the phone about his workplace.

'It's just a temporary Trojan Horse situation,' I said. 'Learn what you can and use it against them later.'

'Yeah well. At least my colleagues are friendly and the money is good,' he said and I pictured him there in the park in his jogging gear, the occasional freckle on his forearms.

'We're like inverted,' I said. 'I love the clients and the offices and just the work really, but my colleagues are so high-strung in these complicated clothes and I spend all my energy not drawing attention to myself.' I clicked my tongue. 'Last week Preya said in front of everyone that I shouldn't be allowed to talk in client meetings because my accent makes me sound unintelligent. And no one objected or said a thing.'

'Seriously?' His voice changed. Monotone, tense, like that time in the park we saw a man being mean to his dog. 'That's not right.'

'It's the Swedish part of me she goes after, never the Romanian, so she gets away with it.'

'Sam, maybe it's time you ask for a transfer.'

I slurped through my straw and told him I wouldn't go running to Tabatha's mum, because of the nepotism thing. It was a nice by-product of the bad work atmosphere, that I could tell Luc I was sticking it out and enduring, earning me personal growth points but also steady servings of warm sympathy. 'Other than that, work is great,' I said perkily to defuse the seriousness but he didn't laugh, he coughed. I asked if it really was a good idea to go running when ill and all I could think was how much I wanted him and Gabrielle to break up. I didn't like them together. But then again, Luc and I had not worked either so what did I know.

That night having drinks with Luc and Gabrielle, I had been transparently flirtatious after she left and it was exhilarating albeit involuntary, sexy just sitting opposite him. But Luc had gone home to Gabrielle and they were still together and a few risky insinuations on my part would not change that. Which was rather humiliating really.

Still, talking to him on the phone over iced coffee was the ideal way to start my evening. Afterwards I would shower, shave my legs, do my makeup while having a glass of wine. Then meet up with Vicki and that crowd. My nonsense discussions with Luc aligned my mood perfectly for going out, setting me in an intense state of anticipation. Like a thirst I knew I would later quench.

When we hung up, the last rays of sun had disappeared and it was nighttime. I stayed on the balcony for a while, a slight breeze goosebumping my arms. I put on a soft cotton shirt over my bikini and closed my eyes and listened to the streets around me. Traffic, sirens, screaming kids, the neighbour's opera kitchen playlist. This would be the perfect sound backdrop to an urban stage play. And somehow, blessedly, London again felt like a holiday city. Like none of this mattered, no one was taking note.

Tabatha slid the door open and sat down on the other sunchair. She was having a beer and offered me the bottle. I declined, not wanting any new stimuli to upset my perfect mood alignment.

'Was that Luc?' she asked. 'How is he?'

I closed my eyes again. 'Fine I think. Quite settled isn't he.'

'And Gabrielle?'

'Yeah let's not go there.'

'Still jealous?'

'Furiously.'

'So,' she said and reclined her chair fully, 'maybe time you get over it, go on a date already.'

'I don't want to.'

'Why? Doesn't seem like Luc is coming back anytime soon.'

I made a half-hearted attempt to slap her arm. 'Wow,' I said, 'and it's like at least a week until you PMS, isn't it.'

'We've been living together too long.'

'Yeah.' I reclined my chair too. Our heads close together, both of us stared at where the stars would be if London had stars. 'I'll start looking for a flat of my own,' I said. 'It's time I left you girls alone.' I loved living with Tabatha, but it had been six months now. And sometimes when I came home late and she and Patti were asleep and I tried not to wake them going past their bedroom door, I could hear one of them turning in bed and it was such an intimate sound I felt like an intruder.

'You sure? No rush okay.' She took my hand and interlaced her fingers with mine and I wondered if she could tell by touch that my nails were torn down to the flesh, my cuticles bright pink strips of skin. I tried not to think of it since that would only make me start picking.

It was a joy seeing her and Patti together but I wasn't envious. The reason I hadn't been on dates or downloaded apps wasn't because of Luc, I was savouring being single. The irresponsible, devil-may-care freedom of it. If no one depended on me, I could disappoint no one. I could misbehave and pee in public and get a fine and pay the fine. I was the sole judge of my character, no person next to me giving side glances or ahems. And whatever this was, this rampage of mine, I wanted to just once explore it to its final stop.

'Should we watch a movie?' Tabatha asked.

'Actually, I'm going out.'

'It's Sunday. You've got work tomorrow.'

I turned my head and raised my eyebrows at her, then said, 'Don't worry, I'm taking it easy. It won't be late.' I had a rule to only go out with Vicki on Fridays or Saturdays to get a full day's recovery before work. It was something I took pride in, not ever letting my weekends spill onto my workdays.

'Have you spoken to Finn by the way?' Tabatha asked.

'The other day, why?'

'He's so stressed isn't he.'

I got a pang of bad conscience for my lack of involvement in the visa situation but I really didn't want to feel guilty now because I was in the perfect mood.

'I hate borders,' I said. 'How do I deserve to stay here more than Finn does? Just lucky I'm a Swedish pre-Brexit immigrant, that's it.'

'Yeah.' She smacked her lips. 'Anyway I'm going to the food shop if you want anything.'

'Popcorn?'

'Sure. And Sam?' She squeezed my hand which was a loving thing to do but the pressure was painful on my mutilated fingertips. 'Take it easy tonight okay.'

'Yes, got it,' I said and for some reason I teared up when she let go and left the balcony and turned on the light in the hallway and clicked the door shut on her way out.

I sat up and slurped the last of my coffee which was now mostly thawed ice. I showered and shaved my legs and poured a glass of wine and did my makeup while listening to Pharcyde and I just knew it would be a good night and my legs started their restless shake.

I had decided to stick to alcohol but once I arrived at the bar I felt so alive and Vicki's friends were so fun although also a little mean in their sense of humour. I was talking to a cute boy and was flattered he went up to me because he really was cute. And when Sandra said come on just half of a bump I asked cute boy if he wanted my other half and he said sure yeah sounds good and then we talked and danced extravagantly for a while. Then there were some new pills and I thought this is it, this is my rampage and thank god I am single and can do whatever the hell I want. And what I wanted was to follow it to the final stop.

•

Which ends up being a hotel shower in Bath. Hearing Q close the door on his way out I turn off the water and dry myself, wishing the towel wasn't so hotel soft. I don't want to inspect my clothes too intimately so I just find my underwear and put them on inside out. I shudder. Then consider taking them off and throwing them in the bathroom bin but the thought of wearing my miniskirt and nothing else on the Porsche seat dissuades me.

Qute has made the bed and pulled back the curtains and opened a window, letting clean air inside. I sit on the bed and I am covered by a feeling, close to anxiety but it's not it. I don't think this has a name. It's like tar.

I check my phone. Many missed calls from Tabatha. Two from Finn. One from an unknown number. Messages, mostly from Taba, which I skim because I am not strong enough to face her anger. Also I see my own moronic replies flash by in the thread and I actually whimper. At least it means she knows I'm alive. And she knows I'm in Bath.

In a message from yesterday morning, she says she's called in sick for me, blaming food poisoning. I am relieved because I missed a whole day of work yesterday, though it's not lost on me that this is the second time I have used fake food poisoning to cover up the effect of a pill.

I scroll down to the end of her messages and she says she is serious, I need to call her, she has bad news. That was yesterday evening. Since then, only missed calls.

I text her.

I fucked up. Call you in a minute, need to get out of here first.

And then Qute arrives with a room service man and a trolley filled with food. It's all very fancy. The room, the food, the man with the trolley. A weird mise en scène for my chemical imbalance and philosophical corruption. We eat on the bed. I try to go slow but I'm so famished my hands put food in my mouth quicker than I can chew. He looks so young. There is a bruise the size of a thumbprint on his arm and I wonder if it is me who left it on him.

'How are you feeling?' I ask, sucking my finger clean of baked bean sauce. 'Did I scare you with the initial memory loss?'

'I feel kind of bad,' he says and I worry he might cry.

'Yeah. I don't even know what stuff we took. Do you?'

He shakes his head.

'And then driving to Bath on that. We could have died. Or killed someone.'

'This is so messed up,' he says. 'But still, at moments I had such a good time. Like big parts of it actually.'

'You did?' I say and now I am the one close to tears or perhaps we both are. 'Let's just not do it again, okay.'

'Yeah I think once was enough.' And he actually chuckles. I nod.

We finish all the food. I don't feel better but at least closer to sober. When Qute is in the shower, I call Tabatha. She doesn't pick up. I call again. Still nothing. I put the phone in front of me on the duvet and will it to ring and then it does.

'Tabatha?'

'I hate you,' she says. 'Don't ever do that to me again.' And her voice is like porridge, so filled with suppressed tears it is hard to make out her words. By the echo I gather she's in a toilet stall at work. And we talk and she is worried and I apologise and I have been delusional. I can still hurt people, single or not. I get hot from shame and I tell her many times I am sorry.

Though underneath the tar and the hot shame, there is something else. An offbeat sort of elation. I'm grateful, that's what it is, because it is over. My rampage. This is the final stop. This bed, that anxious twenty-year-old in the shower, these inside-out underwear. I am done.

'What's the bad news?' I ask. 'Is everything okay?'

'Sam I'm sorry to tell you this now.'

'What?'

'It's Lucas. He's in the hospital.'

Two hours and fifty-five minutes it takes Quentin's Porsche to reach Homerton Hospital. We get out of the car and he asks if he should come inside. I tell him nah that's okay thanks and we hug in the car park and I hope I will never see him again.

39 DAYS UNTIL

Lucas

A week ago, I woke up in a hospital. Opening my eyes I saw a ceiling and then a white curtain. The hum of traffic intermingled with machine pings and PA announcements and rubber clogs shuffling through corridors. I turned my head and there was Gabrielle. I felt feverish and disoriented and she was wearing jeans and a jumper instead of her running gear which meant some time must have passed. Her eyes looked swollen, maybe from tears or lack of sleep.

My brain alerted me to severe but unspecified pain I couldn't pinpoint to a location. I grimaced. Gabrielle took my hand, saying I was going to be alright, and I thought about how she hadn't slowed her pace for me to catch up. My lips were adhered together and my tongue felt dry like bark in my mouth. Parting my lips would likely make them crack. Gabrielle must have seen my discomfort because she scrunched up some tissue, dipped it in water, and smeared it across my lips. I opened my mouth. 'The nurse said you're not allowed to drink yet,' she said and wiped the hair from my forehead, her hand cool and soothing.

A doctor came in with a clipboard and glasses on a chain around her neck. She told me I had slept, dipping in and out of feverish consciousness, for eighteen hours. I had bacterial pneumonia that had got out of hand. They had drained my lungs, my fever still high but slowly coming down. I was scolded for ignoring my symptoms, which I felt was warranted. And, at this exact point, I could no longer pretend my workouts were a health thing. My drained lungs and confused body were the proof. Not self-care, self-sabotage. I wondered if Gabrielle saw it too, that there would be no marathons.

I slept almost all the time and Gabrielle was there, reading magazines and talking amicably with the nurses. She was tireless, bringing me sushi lunches, streaming good TV, preventing me feeling lonely or bored or anxious. When a nurse or doctor took tests or informed me of results, she was my spokesperson, asking many questions, writing things down. It was an incredible relief to have her there, thorough and calm. And when I closed my eyes and drifted off, I trusted she would be there once I opened them.

Dad came when I was still unconscious and they had to introduce themselves without my presence. It felt strange when Gabrielle told me about their first meeting, the medical updates instead of small talk, the bad coffee from the vending machine. I wanted to know what else they had talked about, see Dad's facial reactions to things she said. I had never really introduced a girlfriend before. Gabrielle was now my next of kin because I had entered her as an emergency contact on my phone. Her and Dad, my next of kin.

The day after, Sam came. She rushed in as if I had moments left to live, in clothes more suitable for a club than a hospital. Ignoring Gabrielle she went straight to the side of my bed and took my hand. Gabrielle approached and explained and took command of the situation. Sam calmed down. And then it was like she became aware of her appearance. She pulled her skirt and fussed with her hair. I felt bad for her.

I must have fallen asleep as they talked because later I woke up and Gabrielle was reading in the armchair and Sam was standing by the window, looking out, hands gripping the windowsill. I didn't say anything because I didn't want anyone to talk. The room was dusky.

Sam looked a miserable mess, worried and embarrassed. Gabrielle seemed comfortable in her role as primary care-giver. I wanted to ask Sam things but she wouldn't speak openly unless we were alone and there was no chance of Gabrielle willingly leaving the room with Sam in it. So I asked Gabrielle if she could give us a minute. She said of course and smiled thin-lipped and left the room. I would explain to her later.

'Are you okay?' I asked Sam.

'Hey. You're the one in the hospital bed.'

'And what type of bed did you just crawl out of?' I teased although I was worried.

'None of that,' she said, staying by the window but facing me now. She looked defeated and small. My stomach twisted.

'Don't want to talk about it?' I asked.

'Really don't.'

'But you are okay.'

'Yeah.' Her voice wobbled. She came up to the bed and sat on the edge, careful not to touch me as if I would break.

'What happened Luc?'

'I was running. My lungs felt weird but I kept running anyway which was stupid and then I woke up here.'

'Huh. And you say I should stop running from things. Throwing stones in glass houses are we.'

My lungs asked me to cough but I declined. 'Yeah I think my running days might be over.'

'Good.' She sat perfectly still with her hands in her lap, yet she seemed twitchy, as if thoughts were vibrating on the inside that she refused to let loose.

'I really hope she takes care of you,' she said then, squeezing one hand with the other.

'And what, you would do a better job of it.' I laughed horribly, like a coughy croak. 'I mean look at the state of you Sam.' I had meant this as a tender sort of joke but it landed wrong and she recoiled further and I said sorry and she said no no it's okay you're probably right.

The door opened and Gabrielle came in with vending machine coffee. One for her and one for Sam. 'It's awful stuff, but seemed like you could do with the caffeine,' she said.

Sam looked at me, arms held as if cold, and said, 'That's alright thanks, I'm just leaving.'

Gabrielle nodded and Sam turned towards the door and I wanted to say I'm sorry, come on, please stay a while, but I didn't. The door closed with an airtight woosh and Gabrielle blew on her coffee.

Sam only visited that one time but we would talk on the phone whenever I was alone in the room. We both seemed weak, shattered. Not having it in us to voice anything serious, we talked about trivial things. Movies we'd seen. A new deli she'd tried. Comparing taste in childhood cartoons. I liked Digimon. She was more a Johnny Bravo type of girl.

'They're changing tactics,' she told me one phonecall when talking about Diwa and her attempts at getting pregnant and about 'nothing sticking' as Sam called it. 'They've decided to try with Milly instead.'

I didn't know what exactly was happening in terms of medical procedures and I figured it rude to ask. 'How are you feeling?' I asked instead. 'About Diwa.'

'I don't care, it will be Diwa's baby just as much even so.'

'I meant more in terms of, you know, your abortion. If it like, makes it weird.' I had never brought it up before and immediately it seemed like cowardice to air it in relation to Diwa, instead of our breakup.

'Are you asking if I feel guilty for ending one pregnancy while she is having problems starting another?'

'I didn't mean that exactly.'

She was angry, I could tell.

'Seriously now, I've never once felt ungrateful for ending a pregnancy I didn't want. You know, it was a mung bean, it was four goddamn pills, can everyone get over it?'

I laughed involuntarily, from shock or maybe shame, even though it would only make her more pissed off. 'You're right, you're right.'

She told me then that when the mung bean was in her stomach, knowing it was growing in there, what she felt was horror. And disgust. In fact, she couldn't remember ever picturing herself a mother or pregnant, or what a child of hers would be like. 'I don't know why that is, I'm sure it makes me very unnatural. But there we are.'

I said, hey sorry okay, and she said it wasn't just me, it had been steeping, other people had many opinions that made her tired. It felt like she lived in another environment, one with different air pressure, and I could observe it pushing down on her but not myself experience it. It scared me, us living under such different conditions, unable to ever fully understand each other. So we swam back to safety, talking about TV and movies and food she'd tried.

•

Seven days I have stayed in the hospital, and today I am getting discharged. Gabrielle had to be at work but Dad has taken the day off to drive me home. There's still some coughing and shortness of breath but I am mainly back to normal, although my doctor says it could take six months until fully recovered, which is a terrifying thought.

The sun is beating down on the car park, only sporadically interrupted by big clouds like whipped cream hurrying across the blue as if they have somewhere to be. Walking to the car I can tell Dad doesn't know what to do, whether to help me somehow, hold my elbow for balance.

'I can walk just fine Dad.'

'Give me your bag at least,' he says so I do, mostly to make him feel useful. It is crucial for Dad to be useful because this is the way he demonstrates care. If I start a sentence with Dad would you do me a favour, I can tell his immediate thought is yes, please just ask. It is a terrible power to hold because whatever I ask he will do, I know this. Like, Dad could you drive me to Spain. He would probably do it.

'Seatbelt fastened?' Dad asks before turning the ignition. I stop my tongue before it clicks. His more than usual tiptoe-ing irritates me and then immediately I feel bad for having got irritated. I draw a hand from my forehead to my chin, determined to be nice. The morning rush hour is still heavy and we will be in the car for a long time. I turn on the radio and lean back and look out the window.

In the hospital my routine had changed overnight, empty hours every day that used to be spent at the gym. The constant counting and measuring and streamlin-ing had been exhausting, leaving little room for other thoughts, which now seemed to me might be the addictive part. But a week out of this fixation my brain is too avail-able, all over the place. I wonder how my evenings will look now, my weekends.

Dad turns the volume down. 'So. Are you excited to go back to work?'

As far as Dad knows I am happily employed, because I want him to believe this. I learned a long time ago that Dad's sadness over my various sadnesses only makes my own sadness that much sadder.

'Will be good to get back to normal,' I say. 'What about you, they okay with you taking the day off?'

'Oh yes. One of the perks of being in the same office for twenty-eight years.' Dad has worked in the shipping company my whole life, one employee among thousands. He's been promoted a few times, though nothing you could call a career. But he seems content to me, somehow completely unbored.

'Did you ever think about finding something else?' I ask.

'Why would I?'

I chuckle. 'I don't know, jesus, to change things up a bit.'

He pauses, then says, 'Well, becoming a single parent was more than enough change for me. After that I only really wanted to give us a stable life.'

I make a sound in between a huh and a hm. And I think, that's what hard grief does, it turns change into a bad word. To be avoided at any cost. Normality and predictability and safety become ambitions no matter what your pre-death ones were. But honestly there's only so much stability a home can use, before turning rigid. Also, it has been eight years since I moved out.

I glance over at him and his reclined posture makes his chin disappear into his neck leaving a fold of loose skin. Whenever I see his age on display like this my heart aches. I turn the radio back up and look out the window at the other crawling vehicles.

•

There is a carton of Henry's orange juice in the fridge. I steal a glass and drink the whole thing standing up. By the end of the month, Henry is moving out. He has bought a flat so Hitesh and I will have to find a new flatmate to supply us with juice. I make a vow to leave before Hitesh does.

I feel agitated but for no clear reason and my limbs move here and there unasked, as if ready to pounce. No one is home which is good. I fill one more glass that I sip by the kitchen window staring at the whipped cream clouds hurrying to nowhere. Dad's car is no longer on the street outside. Soon he will be back in the office, saying amiable empty phrases to his colleagues, remembering their children's names and asking how they are doing up in Manchester, down in Barcelona. He will drive home, then walk to the shop to buy this and that, a newspaper. He will boil potatoes and when almost done, he will add cauliflower florets to the pot, and eat this with chicken or fish or baked beans. He will wash up, make a cup of coffee to drink in front of the TV and stay there, absentmindedly reading newspaper pages, until bed at ten thirty. I have witnessed this routine countless times and though he seems perfectly content, I have no idea what is going on in his head.

Before the hospital, my own routine with Gabrielle had been so extreme I never saw it as comfort-based, as the easy way. But working in the car industry, avoiding the humiliation of job rejections, seeing work as only a means to money, I know for certain this is the easy way. Sam had been so optimistic I'd eventually get my dream job and I had wanted to believe her so I did. But she is prone to wishful thinking and every rejection had told me her opinions of me were too high. Now I am not sure. Seriously it might just be me getting comfortable, too scared of what the rejections and my desperation would do to my self-image. My shirt itches and I smell like hospital. I need a shower.

The cold water is nice on my skin and I feel clean putting on a fresh t-shirt. I wish I could call Dad, ask him blatantly if he is happy. But he'd only get too awkward for a straightforward answer, losing himself in his empty phrases. I picture myself in his life, office, food shop, potatoes. By the cauliflower florets I sort of shudder. Stability, sure. Rigidity though. His days seem so small, shrunken.

Rating Dad's life like this gives me massive, overbearing guilt so I text him asking if I can come to lunch on Sunday, I'll cook. He says yes after a perfunctory complaint about plant foods. This makes me feel good, asking to see him.

I lace my fingers and stretch my arms forward. Then I click my neck. With black coffee and my laptop on the kitchen table, I open my CV. I have worked on this document so many times but not since starting at the car company, so I add this experience and it looks shiny and impressive. I remember Sam's advice to turn my cover letter more personal so I rewrite parts, honestly and somewhat humorously stating that I want to leave my current employment for ethical reasons. I close the document and leave it to revise tomorrow. The armpits of my fresh t-shirt are soaked. There is a buzz on the side of my neck, not a pulse, a buzz.

Though I don't need it, I finish my coffee and pour a refill from the French press. Still over-energised and in need of occupation, I research things for a bit. Humorous cover letter yes or no. Best way to network engineers. Networking faux pas. Pneumonia signs fully recovered. Working out normal amount. Non-addictive exercise forms. Sudden increase sex drive. Is meditation really necessary. Best meditation apps.

Then, alarmingly, I log into linkedin. I don't use it and only have six contacts, four people I know personally and two randoms finding me on the platform. I have never myself sent a contact request. Okay if it is someone you know, but if you do why would you need to connect on linkedin? And sending requests to strangers, people in your field, people you look up to even, seems incredibly presumptuous. Like why would they want to connect with you, what do you have to offer. The thought of that, their reaction to my request, declining it. Even without the soaked t-shirt and buzzing neck vein it is obvious, I have too much shame. It keeps me from things. But none of this matters considering my options. Either getting rejected on linkedin or working for a company killing the planet. They don't compare really so I get over myself.

I take off my shirt and fold it on the chair next to me and open the window, a slight breeze gorgeous on my arms and back. I stretch my neck again and look up my manager, twelve of my colleagues, Professor Jonas and two other faculty members. I go through my whole class at uni, then add everyone I know in person outside my industry to get my contact numbers up. The strategising necessary for digital social-climbing makes me uncomfortable but also it is thrilling. Like a game. In fifteen minutes I have twenty-one new contacts.

14 DAYS UNTIL

Sam

This is the third time I meet Cameron and it is going well. First time was at Finn's party, who is dating Giulia now and they are sweet together. Cameron is Giulia's mate. He is friendly, not flirty, with wide shoulders and large hands always pulling his collar as if too warm. Some things he says sound like they're ironic but looking at his expression you realise they aren't. He is unpretentiously into beer and eighties movies. It is refreshing.

The second time we met was a double date set up by Finn and Giulia. We went to a tiny Ethiopian place and we shared many types of food and ate with our hands and it was all very agreeable.

Neither of those times did we kiss or have sex. Today is our first one on one date, my first since Luc.

I meet Cameron in the afternoon and that alone is atypical. Instead of drinks or dinner, he suggested Tate Modern. I am not into art even slightly so I spent last night researching the current exhibitions, finding out curiosa on the artists and themes. I wouldn't say it was a fun two hours, but it means I can today make a good impression.

'Oh. I feel bad now asking you here and not knowing any-thing about the artists myself,' Cameron says after my third casual curiosa drip. And it sinks in. With him I don't have to make an impression. I roll my shoulders and decide not to try so hard.

'Actually I didn't either. I just googled a bit last night,' I say.

'Really?'

'Yeah sort of.' I fold my hair behind my ears.

'That's nice of you to make the effort. Wish I had as well.'

'So you're not really into art?'

'Not really no. But you can still come here just to appreci-ate the space.' He sweeps his arm over the hall. It is a beau-tiful and imposing building, brutalist but light and echoey. You get that same sombre mood as in a church. A place not meant for giggles or phones. I have zero inclination to tweet.

He takes my hand and it feels warm and a little rough, like oven-fresh bread. We walk down a corridor into a big room, and I am glad because this is the one exhibition I am keen to see after last night's research. Probably because it is the most accessible for philistines like me.

The artist, a photographer, spent months scouring google street view for interesting spontaneous shots. There is a refer-ence image of the white van driving up and down the world's streets, capturing snapshots indiscriminately. Therefore the photos are all unplanned. Accidental moments of art. The camera catching them impersonal, the curation made much later, by the photographer guy.

A feral horse running next to the van. A forest wildfire put out by soot-covered locals. Someone falling off a bike, captured mid-air in almost graceful bodily anarchy. A cat and a fox sleeping entangled underneath a plastic table in pouring rain. A street in Mumbai with small haphazard sheds, a girl of maybe seven playing with a doll, her shed covered in purple fabrics and pink lampshades, inviting in the midst of poverty.

I am strangely moved by the photos, by the series of them next to each other. I think their randomness, the undiscerning eye of the google van, makes them more powerful. These are moments captured but not witnessed. Until now, by us. There is something beautifully innocent about it, almost too candid to bear, and as we walk around the room I take Cameron's arm. We don't talk nearly at all. There are maybe thirty images and when we leave the room I look up at his face to see if he is also emotional.

'Wow huh?' he says. His eyes are bright and he blinks. 'If all museums were like this.'

'I know,' I say. 'That girl in Mumbai.' I stop there because my voice sounds messy.

'Yeah that was beautiful.'

'Thanks for bringing me,' I say. We smile.

He rubs his short scruffy stubble, the sound raspy but pleasant. 'Maybe consider our cultural outing done for today? Thought we could go for a pint if you fancy it?'

'I do, yes.'

It is cloudy and a little drizzly outside, but warm. We walk fast towards Borough Market, chattering about the google photos and about who the real artist is, the photographer guy or the van. Cameron tells me about the time he was himself in Mumbai, that he ate great food but didn't see the sheds. He regularly travels for work and I enjoy asking him about it. Not just the places, but the way of life, being on the move many months per year. It suits him, he says. It calms him down. I picture myself in this scenario and yes I can see how it could be calming. A swaying rootlessness. Fragmented relationships. Nothing too heavy.

I am in such a good mood now and we talk more about food and the cute Ethiopian restaurant and me being vegan. 'What about you,' I ask, 'any unusual habits I should know of?'

'Not really. I'm very normal. Like boringly so.'

'Prove it,' I say as he holds the door open to a craft beer brewery.

'I prefer lager to IPA, for one thing. Shawshank Redemption is my favourite movie. And I listen to granddad music.' He waves to the bartender and leads me to a booth by the window.

I slide onto the bench and lean forward on my elbows and say, 'Quick, your three favourite bands.'

'Creedence, Zeppelin. Radiohead.'

'Christ man, what are you, a Rolling Stone journalist?' I grin. When our pints arrive we toast and drink and it's delicious. We bicker over music for a solid twenty minutes and my taste is so much better than his but he is a passionate talker and I realise that I really do like this man.

And I think there will probably be a fourth date. Possibly even become a storyline of its own, instead of just a footnote. Sam and Cam. Music aficionados, beer appreciators, not big fans of art.

'So how's the unpacking going? You moved in yesterday?' he asks.

'This morning.'

•

The flat is a matchbox in Archway. I have room for my bed, a two-seat sofa, and nothing else. But the tiny kitchen is lovely in that rustic continental sort of style and there are two tall windows with sills deep enough to sit on. It is the first time I have lived alone and it amuses me to think I will later reference this flat when sentimentally looking back at my romantic London youth.

Diwa went with me on viewings, and she and Milly drove my suitcases and a few boxes of things over this morning. I don't own much, which is lucky considering the square metres. After a spaghetti lunch I had to shoo them out to get ready for Tate with Cameron.

Living on my own was a good step. After Bath I needed a physical change to signify some emotional growth. I had apologised again to Tabatha for making her worry but she just tutted and we were good. Finn still had visa issues, and although not explicitly apologising for being recently distant, I helped with his CV and put out feelers to my contacts at work for potential job openings. It seemed he had accepted my indirect apology.

The next time Vicki invited me on a night out I told her I was having an alcohol-only moment. And alcohol was fun enough, I tried to convince myself and my poor fingernails. On alcohol you didn't end up in a hotel bed in Bath with a boy named Q. Inside-out underwear. Vicki lost interest in me then which was a shame considering hers was the only friendly face in the office.

I kept wondering if this was normal for people staying in the same job year after year. If it always wore you down with its intricate colleague hierarchies and unchanging scenery. I had resolved to stick it out for once, so even though my instincts screamed for flight, I stayed put at my desk. For the past few weeks I had exerted myself to earn a promotion, to impress a manager from another department. Preferably on floor eleven. Preferably Tabatha's team. I wouldn't even mind her being my senior if that meant I could see her daily because the worst thing about moving out was ending our tribal kind of intimacy. I knew so much about her now. Her sleeping pattern, her preferred make-out music, her smells, cycle, signs of annoyance.

One night last week I sat on my bed with a full pot of Assam, researching the clients and their every competitor to prepare myself for tomorrow's meeting. I wanted the promotion sure, but also the research itself was oddly enjoyable.

I had just showered, my wet hair a loose twirl on my back, slowly soaking the fabric of my waffle robe. It was after eight and I had worked all day but I wasn't tired. When not chemically doused, my brain was an athlete. Recently I had been fascinated by products transcending their brand name to become a product name. Aspirin, Tic Tac, Super Glue, Plan B, Ziploc. I deconstructed these brands' early marketing strategies to redesign for digital.

I poured some tea which smelled earthy and nice but was too hot to drink so I placed it on its saucer to cool. These last weeks, I had realised that the tension release I would get from a night out was possible to emulate with intense research. The thrill of building new neural pathways was addictive, and I would come to hours later, my legs still and my fingernails untouched. I couldn't tell if these obsessive sessions were healthy or not but it was this or Vicki's bag of pills. This kept me out of Bath at least.

Though my nights of voluntary rabbit-holing didn't keep me from checking socials. Midway through an article my phone demanded attention next to me on the bed. I picked it up and opened instagram and clicked one of Luc's photo tags through to Gabrielle's account. We didn't follow each other but her account wasn't private so I could see all her photos. This had not been a good idea once.

Her latest photo was posted on a Friday evening, a picture of homemade sushi. Perfect round rolls, the avocado precisely placed in the middle of the rice. I bet she knew what a daikon was.

I got dressed and went for a walk all the way to central while listening to a podcast on British office culture and how to avoid accountability by never admitting mistakes. It was a warm night, early August and smelled like it. Food gone off and traffic exhaust and antiquated sewage systems. Scattered like a trail of crumbs were gnawed-on chicken bones, someone ahead eating fried chicken and simply dropping the bones on the ground. Like a travelling chicken graveyard. On my right, up a flight of stairs, was a large fox. Not the picturebook red Swedish version. The grey scabious London kind. I figured the chicken bones would be just up her alley.

Later I nearly stepped in vomit. The splash was almost artful. Shoes had walked in it, bikes rolled through it, creating long vomit tracks like entrails out on neighbouring streets. I speculated about the half-life of a street vomit, how long before the shoes and the wheels reduced it to mere silhouette.

And I thought that they existed simultaneously, the good-smelling London and the bad. There could be fresh vomit on a majestic Victorian street. Ghost foxes lived outside bank buildings. When distracting myself with work, I had stumbled on a photo of my ex making sushi with his clean girlfriend. And now I had almost stepped in sick. This was my London life, not the metropolitan romance of my adolescent daydreams. Not the summer with Luc in Diwa's flat, Bruce-Willified and bubble-tead. This was the anticlimactic everyday London, complete with vomit trails and Gabrielles. And I had to ask myself if, maybe, there was someplace else I'd rather be.

•

Cameron and I walk from the Borough Market brewery to Soho. I am relaxed from the beer and the drizzle is cosy, so when Cameron offers me his arm I take it. We still haven't kissed. I am not yet sure whether I want to.

To my left is London Eye and I think of the time Luc and I witnessed the marriage proposal in the next pod over. It had rained that night when we reached Chinatown. I wonder how many walks like this with someone like Cameron it will take to clear Luc off my immediate memory bank. How many mouths I have to taste to not compare them to his.

I ask Cameron's thoughts on some recent twitter drama but he isn't following that particular cluster of pop culture writers. It soon becomes clear that Cameron follows mostly football players, TV presenters, and Hollywood franchise actors. He is not on there much anyway, he says, finds the place demoralising and aggravating. And it displeases me he says this, all the more because I agree with him on principle but don't want him ruining a guilty pleasure.

Now our leisurely pace seems slow. My legs want to speed up and I can't decide what to talk about next. We return to music because it feels like our safest arena. We disagree, but the amiable disagreement itself is where we best harmonise. I like Cameron and I don't want to compare him to Luc so I don't kiss him on this date either.

But of course, Cameron kisses me.

He moves in quick and his lips are on mine and he opens his mouth and his stubble is scratchy. His tongue prods my lips so I have to let him in not to be rude and my mouth responds without me having to ask it. He tastes of beer. Something like kebab. His tongue is smooth at the tip but coarse further in. I don't want my tongue to touch his so I try to fold it back into my mouth without him noticing. He pulls me close and presses against me and it just feels wrong.

So wrong.

Wrong enough for me to slowly pull back and promise my mouth it will never have to do that again.

I resist the urge to wipe my lips with my sleeve, instead I smile and park the thought of his coarse tongue. And when he asks if I want to take him for some vegan food I say next time and skip down the stairs to the tube station.

I get the Northern line to my new home and I use the map in the train to memorise the order of all the stations, to later be able to prove I am a true Northern line resident. Moorgate. Old Street. Angel. Kings Cross. Etcetera. As if anyone would ever ask me to recite the Northern line from start to finish.

At home I continue unpacking. Clothes in the wardrobe, makeup in the bathroom. The Iittala wine glasses in the kitchen with my few other cooking things. They are now the only glasses I own, reminding me of the first night with Luc in our flat, picnic dinner on the floor. I had thought we would just keep living together, upgrading to better flats, one day buying our own. Giving him a kitchen to cook me food in, a bathtub big enough for two. Maybe a balcony, reading short stories aloud on Sunday mornings. I wasn't sure we could handle pets so maybe we'd start with a plant and call it Bruce Willis.

This no longer an option, I feel like an alternative future should have taken its place by now. A job where you travel, rocking on trains, sleeping on planes, eating good food in Mumbai. But no, it hasn't. I still see bathtub and balcony and a plant named Bruce.

Unpacking novels and folders and magazines, I find the second-hand Virginia Woolf book. I open it to read Luc's handwriting. *Thanks for everything, I had a nice time. Luc.* I snicker and smell its pages and put it down.

I take four steps to my bed and lie on my back. It was my first adult purchase, this memory foam mattress. I wonder what the memory in memory foam signifies, if it somehow remembers its sleepers, their imprints forever embedded on a molecular level. If one of those imprints is Luc's. It is pathetic even to me, how little I've moved on. I flip the mattress over and stretch a sheet tight.

Sitting on my new windowsill on a purpose-bought pillow, I stare at the tree outside and then I call him.

'Hey. How's the unpacking?' he says, sounding chatty.

'Yeah it's good.'

'Finished?'

'Almost. Just found your Virginia Woolf book. Remember?'

'That was a bad day,' he says but I can tell he is smiling.

'Yeah, sad. Are you at home?' We only really talk when we are both alone, though this is not something we have openly discussed because it makes our phonecalls seem clandestine. I always ask are you at home. Never are you alone.

'Yeah, at home.' He yawns and moans as if stretching.

'I went on a date today.'

'Oh.'

'Do you prefer not talking about it?' My street is getting dusky but I don't turn on the lights. The dark is soothing to my eyes.

'No it's okay we can talk. It went alright did it?'

'Yeah it was mostly nice.'

'So you will see him again?'

'Maybe. Undecided,' I say although it is very much decided I will not. And I leaf lazily through a magazine and I think that no matter how many mouths I taste I will never not compare them to Luc's. 'Sixty-forty chance,' I say.

'In which way?'

'Not in his favour.' And then after a pause, 'Hey, do you want to come over?'

9 DAYS UNTIL

Lucas

She is waiting outside the food shop with two cotton tote bags as I go through the tube station turnstiles. I haven't seen her since the hospital and the juxtaposition of her sad state that day only makes her summer skin and messy hair all the more gratifying. She hangs a bag on her shoulder and waves. She is bouncy.

When she invited me over I had wanted to hang up the phone and put on shoes and go straight to her flat that exact moment. But I realised I would look overeager which in fairness I was. I said it would be good to see her place and asked if Friday after work was okay.

'That's in five days. I might have moved again by then.'

Now it's Friday after work. We hug almost without touching.

She takes a step back to assess me. 'Gained a few?'

'Hey now. A bit rude.'

I take one of her shopping bags and we start walking up the slope. She is wearing a white short-sleeved shirt, her sunglasses hooked on the collar.

'No no you look good,' she says. 'Wholesome.'

'Jesus Sam can you imagine if I called you wholesome and asked if you'd gained a few?'

She laughs. 'Fine, you don't look wholesome you look ravishing. I almost recognise you again.'

I respond with something like oh well.

Although our relationship is perfectly smooth in its digital format, I feel on edge, out of breath. I am desperate for this to go well to normalise seeing each other without it turning weird. So far we seem okay.

Her street is the next on the right, she tells me. She looks proud, a new addition to the neighbourhood resolved to sound like a local. From the historical titbits she is feeding me, it is obvious she has researched. I humour her, pleased just to walk beside her listening to her impromptu lecture on old pubs and prominent residents. It is a warm day but the sun is on the decline.

Her flat is tiny. Her bed in a corner, her sofa in another, big straw cushions on the floor. A tiny kitchen, a tinier bathroom. Two large windows. The last sun of the day scoots in sideways, and it all looks kind of golden.

She says have a seat and carries the groceries to the kitchen, humming as she opens and closes fridge and pantry. I unlatch a window before sitting on the sofa. She reappears with a bowl of chilli nuts and a bottle of sparkling wine and two of the Iittala wine glasses we bought a long time ago.

'Sorry, these are the only glasses I have so far,' she says.

'No this is great.'

We drink without toasting. She stays standing up. The wine foams in my nose and tastes faintly of yeast. My breath is still short.

'Give me a second. I'm all tube sweaty.' She puts her glass on the table and turns around and unbuttons her shirt, stepping towards the wardrobe in only her bra.

'That's quite naked there,' I say, stupid.

'Oh relax. Nothing you haven't seen before.'

She is right of course but my reaction is far from habitual. I can't tell if she's just at ease being naked around me or if she is provocative on purpose. I really hope it's the first alternative because this nakedness is alarming, unpredictable. It feels like a sort of test. I stare at the chilli nuts. Put one in my mouth. I don't want to chew because the crunch would make a weird soundtrack to her striptease across the room. The chilli stings my tongue so I have to chew. And yes it is a weird soundtrack.

I don't look until she is back by the sofa, now in a dark blue dress I haven't seen before. The material is matte and she looks elegant. Her shoulders are bare, bones and muscle move under the skin. I can see the mark, the mouche thing, above her breast and my blood doesn't find it necessary to oxygenate any other part of me than the part I am desperate to ignore.

She curls her legs up and leans an elbow on the sofa backrest. 'So what's new?' she asks.

'Nothing really. I'm going on this conference thing next week. Which feels a bit weird since my company is paying

and it's pretty expensive and I'm really only going to network and look for a new job.'

'I like it. Crafty.'

'Glad you approve.' I relax my shoulders. I like this work
talk, it's neutral. 'Also I'm having coffee with someone at that
agriculture consultancy firm next week. Just to chat, but still.'

'And you wouldn't consider an internship or something,
since it's a company you really like?'

'Money though.'

'So sleep on someone's sofa for a while. Rent free.'

I chuckle. 'That's a nice thought.'

'This sofa right here is quite comfortable, don't you
think?' She pats the cushion, fishing for a cheeky grin.

'Gabrielle would love that,' I say, feeling the need to voice
her name out loud. I am warm, the sun hot on my neck.
'What about you, work horrible as usual?'

'Yes, no change there.'

'Why don't you just quit?'

She stands up and goes to fluff the pillow on the windowsill. 'So I'm trying not to do the running away thing. Like
stay and deal instead with my problems.'

'That's sad to hear.'

'Sad?' She moves around the table as if curious to see my
face. 'I thought you'd be pleased.'

'No, are you joking? I think you should have quit a long
time ago, like why would I want you to stay in a workplace
where you're basically bullied?' It seems like I am using my
hands a lot so I fold them behind my head.

Her brows draw together and her arms hang limp as if indecisive. Then she says, 'To prove I can handle it, I guess. I don't know.'

'Sam, it's like a talent you have, the running thing. Okay sometimes you do too much of it but that doesn't mean you should stop completely.'

'Huh, that's new.' She sits down again. 'You're saying it's about identifying when to run and when to stay.'

'Maybe.'

'I think we both have that problem, mister pneumonia,' she says and smirks and stretches back, leaning against the armrest.

'You look happy,' I say because she does. At peace. Her fingernails unusually healed, a little messed up but not recently so.

'You know, I basically am.'

'Good,' I say. And it is. Still, a selfish part of me is hurt by this. Seeing her stretched and relaxed in a cramped flat with a bad job, I feel like a failure. I had tried relentlessly to make her happy and it had not been enough, yet now she manages happiness all by herself. It is a warm feeling but with sadness intermingled, like melancholy. She is beautiful like this and I want to touch her.

Even though I don't, I consider the thought itself a kind of infidelity.

There's a sharp noise and I jolt as if caught in the act and she laughs and says, it's just the buzzer, delivery guy, my god, relax. She has her own buzzer sound, that she knows and I don't. I let this sink in.

She stands up and lets the delivery guy in.

•

Last weekend Gabrielle and I were walking through Hyde Park on our way to Notting Hill. There was a market or festival in the park, and she wanted to take a look. Inside the gate it was noisy and packed with people, many different food smells mixing into an amalgam of fried garlic sugar. She had a small bag slung across her shoulder that knocked into me rhythmically as we walked. The sensory stimuli were overwhelming, I had trouble staying with the conversation.

'I don't consider it a big deal to be honest,' I said. 'Even with a pay cut I would manage fine.'

'Yes of course but it's not just about managing,' she said and took my hand. I wished she hadn't, constricted enough by the crowd already. 'It's about valuing yourself and your time. You deserve that payslip.'

'Okay thank you. But it's not the point I am trying to make here.'

Suddenly leaving my side, she veered left towards an ice cream stand. She bought soft-serve frozen yoghurt in a cup with a bright green spoon sticking out of it. She didn't ask if I wanted one since I don't eat yoghurt, but still. Spoon in mouth, she started walking again.

'You can't live with random flatmates in some overripe bachelordom your whole life right. I think we should make some plans, about the future, moving in together.'

I stopped and I was shocked but that seemed unreasonable because surely we had been together long enough to have this discussion. She scooped up yoghurt and sucked on the bright green spoon and there were carousel sounds and it felt like the least suitable place for this conversation.

'Can we go?' I asked. 'Let's not talk here okay.'

'I just think it's great that your ambition and hard work is finally reflected in your salary. We could get like a really nice flat.'

And I thought, she's got me wrong, I'm not ambitious. Not as in promotions and real estate and restaurant reservations. I liked having nice clothes, and one day I wanted to own a decent London flat, which was a holy grail in itself I guess. But when I pictured living with Gabrielle, my mind went white. I couldn't see it, the flat, our furniture, what type of building. I didn't know what our kitchen would be like or which movies we'd watch. Our bookshelf was empty.

'And recently it's been a bit off, hasn't it.' She bit her lip. 'Like we don't work out or do things as much, and now you're talking about quitting your job and that would obviously postpone us moving in together.'

'I'm sorry I can't train for a marathon with you, I had pneumonia. Sorry if that's a nuisance.'

She started walking again, fast. 'Don't be unfair. I'm just saying that we need to work on it. And sometimes it's like you're fluctuating, one second you want a stable life with some money and a nice home, but the next you're talking about taking a pay cut and living like a bohemian in a shitty flat with two other men.'

She stopped in front of a carousel, one of those with horses. She stared at the kids, screaming and laughing and high on sugar. If I stayed on these tracks, I could have this one day. Gabrielle. A daughter of my own on that carousel, frilly dress, sticky with sugar. I could have dinner at the kitchen table, talk about your day, kids past twelve with a mother still alive. I knew Gabrielle was in love with me, that she would do her utmost to be a good partner, make me happy. And motherhood would suit her, I was convinced, after her tireless attention in the hospital and ever since really.

I placed my arm around her waist, both of us facing the carousel. She sighed and leaned her head on me and said, 'I don't know, I think it's time you make up your mind. Grow up a bit.'

'Yeah,' I said, looking at the kids. 'Yeah you're probably right.'

•

I am sitting on the floor when Sam puts a salad bowl and a hot garlic baguette on the living room table. She sits down on the other straw cushion and breaks off a chunk of bread and hands it to me. It is steaming, my saliva glands sting. I am starving. She serves the salad, careful not to spill. She manages and smiles as if a small victory.

We discuss random ideas for a while, changing our positions until we no longer know what we truly think and what are just arguments made for the joy of judgement-free conversation.

'But if it's about identifying when to stay and when to leave,' she says, 'what about the pigeon.' The bread is finished and our plates near empty.

'What about it?'

'Remember at the vet clinic when the woman told us they had to put it down, and she looked at us as if we had expected them to save it, even though it was obvious they couldn't.'

'Oh. Right.' I don't know where she is going but I am feeling awkward because honestly I had thought they would save it.

'And then I looked over at you and it seemed like you were surprised, as if you actually thought they could.'

I lift my head. 'To be honest, yeah, I did.'

'I figured as much. And I thought you were so naive. But now I'm not so sure, maybe you were right.'

'Well obviously I wasn't. The bird died.'

'It didn't die. We killed it.' She starts clearing the table. I stand to help her, stack our plates, and follow her to the kitchen.

'When we were fiddling with the box, trying to trap the bird, I knew I was hurting it,' she says. 'I was trying really hard not to, but it didn't matter. I still hurt it.'

'That's not your fault.'

We go back and forth to the kitchen and this is giving a hectic energy to the conversation. 'And on our way to the vet, the motion of the bus made it bump around in there. I couldn't hold it still enough, so I hurt it even more and the only way to stand it was to think it would soon be dead anyway. It wouldn't feel pain anymore.'

It is dusky outside now but she hasn't turned on any lights. We sit on the sofa, and not seeing her face clearly gives her words a fairy-tale quality. I don't interrupt her, she is working something out.

'Then the pigeon died, so I could stay convinced that you know, I was right, it was beyond saving, it was meant to die. But what if we hadn't killed it, what if we'd tried saving it even if it meant more pain first before it got better. If we had tried and succeeded then you would have been right. You wouldn't have been naive. Instead I would have been cynical. And we'd have a live pigeon right now.' She looks straight at me and slows down. 'The only reason I was right to give up on the pigeon, is because I never got proven wrong.'

'No. You were right. It was beyond saving, way too damaged.' I swallow. 'We did the right thing.'

'Well,' she says, 'now we'll never know, will we.' She shrugs and blows a strand of hair off her face.

Part of me thinks this is the moment to leave. I have seen the flat, we've had dinner, we are a bit tipsy but not drunk. There is no real reason to stay.

She stretches her legs out across my lap, wriggles her toes and smiles, pleased with herself. I think of Sunday mornings, reading Chekhov stories aloud. Slow, almost lazy sex.

And I close my eyes and I feel heavy. I just want to stay like this, my hands on her ankles, not saying anything.

Objectively it is innocent, the weight of her legs on mine, but my emotional reaction is not. My physical reaction neither. I am glad to be wearing jeans. And it is shocking to me how hard it is to stop.

'Sam,' I say. 'Let's not.'

'It's strange,' she says, not removing her legs. 'Although you have a girlfriend, in a way it doesn't matter. I know you so well, I mean, physically. I know what your skin smells like and how your arms feel and when I see you I still think of your body as mine.'

'But it's not.' I sit up straight. 'And if you say things like this you're kind of forcing me into disloyal behaviour.' I take her legs and place them on the floor. 'I'm not that person.'

'I know that.'

But I don't believe she truly cares.

'It's just, I can't bring myself to feel any obligation towards Gabrielle,' she says. 'I've kept quiet out of respect for you, but honestly Luc I don't want you with her.'

The atmosphere has changed so abruptly we seem thrown, both of us.

'You don't know her.'

'I had to see you in a hospital bed. She's wrong, the two of you don't fit, it's obvious.'

'You know, even if we don't fit, even if I break up with her, it won't be because of you.'

'What does that mean?'

I stand up. I am very upset now with this situation. 'It means I'm not going to leave my girlfriend of six months because my ex had a few glasses of wine and wants sex.'

'You think that's it, sex?' She is still seated, radiating this intenseness. As if settled in her tracks, relentlessly moving forward. 'Why are you here Luc. What did you think would happen?'

I wish I could mute her. I wish I could rewind her.

'I'm here because you're my best friend.' I want to sound calm but I really don't. 'And you are scaring me now because this is not how we should be with each other.' I'm out of breath like after a run and I back away further. 'I thought this was important to you too.'

'I can't help that I love you.' She stands up. 'And I always will and it will never go away and you have to tell me if you don't because I deserve to know.'

'You can't ask me that. I don't know, I can't answer that.' And my eyes fill up from the unfairness of once again hearing her say this and once again I cannot say it back.

She comes closer and takes my head in her hands and forces me to look at her. 'Just tell me if you don't love me.'

'Stop.'

'Just tell me!'

'Samanta, stop!' I push her hands off. We stare at each other, out of breath. 'It doesn't matter, we tried, it didn't work.'

'We didn't try hard enough.'

'You don't want kids!'

'Do you?'

I close my eyes. Lean against the wall behind me, focus on calming my voice. 'Not right now, I don't. But maybe I will, one day.'

'Maybe I will too, one day.'

'You won't.'

'No. I won't.' She takes my hand in hers.

I am quiet for a moment, trying to accept that this has happened, that she has picked us up and shaken us this way. I had thought I could have her in my life, that I wouldn't have to choose. 'I do know that we can't do this, whatever it is.' I drop her hand. 'I have to go. Will call you tomorrow and please, please let this not be weird okay.' But of course, it will.

'Yeah, sure, if that's what you want.' She backs away and runs a hand through her tangled hair and I get my phone from the table. 'I'll walk you to the station,' she says.

It is dark outside and this is a blessing. We walk down the same short slope. I try to talk about normal things but almost nothing comes out and she is quiet, her arms folded. By the stairs at the station we stop.

'I'll call you tomorrow,' I say.

'Yeah talk tomorrow.'

'I'm sorry Sam.'

'No no we're good.'

I move in to kiss her on the cheek but she doesn't meet me so I pause. 'Bye,' I say instead and go through the turnstiles and walk down the stairs. I turn around halfway but she is already gone. And it feels like my chest is imploding.

6 DAYS UNTIL

Sam

The tube is Monday morning tight. Today will be one of the hottest days of the year, thirty-four degrees, and the air down here is recycled to an inch of its life. I feel crushed, so I focus on breathing slowly which is hard because the man in front of me is pressing his gym bag into my abdomen. The next stop is Charing Cross. I decide to get off and walk even though this will make me late.

It is better on the street, the heat not truly hitting yet. Jubilee Bridge smells of sun-warm pollution and fetid river water and people's deodorants which is normal. I am wearing trainers so I make good speed, but I have to force my legs forward, my body telling me to cancel today, go get drunk. My black office shoes are in my bag and it seems like an uncertain sort of humiliation changing into them crouched in a doorway somewhere a street away from the agency.

Exhausted by this weekend's emotional avalanche, I can think of few things less appetising than the office. Long hours at the desk, hot outside, difficult inside. Pretending to care about clients like everything is normal, even though Luc and I haven't talked. I don't know where we stand but my behaviour on Friday is sure to have ruined things. I know he wants nothing more than for us to be friends, talk in person. But it is obvious I can't give that to him. I will never not want him. This is out of my control and it is wrecking me. Yet I am hurrying to work to minimise my tardiness. I don't stop in a doorway and I don't change my shoes.

Reaching the building, I enter through the dramatic glass doors. The elevator pings open and I sit down at my usual desk, my pulse high and sweaty. I find my water bottle and I drink and click the desktop, but understanding today's schedule is difficult because I can't seem to concentrate. I am fidgety. My cuticles are in peril.

Although my trainers are jarring in this environment, with their bright white shine and rubbery sounds, I can't change shoes. Baring my feet feels like a vulnerability, as if sock-clad toes is the office equivalent of an exposed throat.

Preya stays in her office all morning. Her voice sieves through the thin walls, monotone and strained. Around eleven, I get an email from Vicki.

You've done it now haven't you.

I stare at the screen. I blink.

•

On Saturday morning I had woken with my stomach pressing up my chest. Luc's visit the night before came back in full resolution and I couldn't turn it off. Me flirting, undressing in front of him, my legs on his knees. The fight. I had pushed away my closest friend. Nauseous as if whiskey hungover, I knew I had to cry but if I started maybe I wouldn't stop. After showering and drinking two glasses of water, I got on the bus to Tabatha.

Luc had said he'd call today. I knew he would but also I knew no one wanted that conversation, so on the bus I intercepted him by texting that I was with Tabatha which I almost was.

Sorry it got weird last night. At Taba's so let's talk later okay x

Before sending I deleted the x. Thought it might come off as suggestive which was the last thing I wanted after yesterday's humiliation. I experimented with emojis for a while but they seemed too frilly. With neither x nor emoji it looked too strict, serious, so I stole from Pappa, always ending our calls with two goodbyes for instant warmth. Hej då hej då.

Sorry it got weird last night. At Taba's so let's talk later okay bye bye bye.

I was mainly pleased with the tone so I clicked send.

He replied four minutes later.

Yeah that was intense. But anyway good to see your new place. You seem happy. Tell Tabatha to put on our nice time playlist. I've added a song (breaking the rules I know).

I was impressed with his text, it was expertly balanced. I could see why it had taken him four minutes. Still devastating, this texting instead of talking. Like always we regressed to our safe mode of concise revisable communication. My stomach contracted, thinking that our relationship would stay here now, witty texts and forwarded tweets. Like two AIs trapped by code, forgetting we had ever communicated without letters. Forgetting we had ever talked, slept, touched, showered.

No matter how many times I read his balanced text, I got nothing more from it than him wanting us to sound normal, be okay. After last night, he wouldn't risk seeing me in person again, risk being disloyal to Gabrielle. I had pushed him out. My stomach was so tight I feared I would retch. Or cry. I held on to the bus seat in front of me and looked at the dirty street outside the window.

I got off at Taba's stop and lit a cigarette and held the smoke in my lungs, smothering the sob building in my chest. It would come eventually, I realised this. And yet before last night, I had been doing well. A new flat, a couple of decent dates, a career with opportunities. But this Saturday I was back to craving Vicki and her bag of pills.

It was pathetic, my behaviour. Submitting to the stuff at work, pursuing a boy who did not want me. He had said so last night, that even if breaking up with Gabrielle it would have nothing to do with me. Appallingly, until that moment, I had believed it would. Hidden deep in some brain fold I had kept a conviction that he would one day be with me. But now I had tested that theory and been proven wrong. Crushingly so.

I suddenly felt I couldn't face Tabatha. I got hot shame flashes thinking of last night's dialogue and did not want a recital so I started walking back towards home. Then Pappa called. Almost immediately he asked what was wrong.

'I'm not sure anymore if living here is the best idea,' I said.

He hummed three times as if thinking. 'You know I was at first a little overwhelmed when I moved to Stockholm.'

'Before you met Mamma?'

'Maybe I have not told you that she broke up with me once.'

'No. You haven't.' I felt like a child, not knowing this.

'It was still very early stages and I was in love, but she had some doubts. Back then she thought marriage was the death of women. Who knows, maybe it was. Anyway, that's not the point, the point is I was dumped.'

This was such a strange word coming from Pappa, dumped. I snorted involuntarily.

'And I thought of leaving Stockholm then because what reason to stay without her. But there was a reason. Turns out even when you're sad Stockholm is beautiful.'

I mumbled a half-assent, like okay whatever.

'But that's not the point either.'

'Just spit it out.' I laughed but it sounded more tragic than anything.

'Alright yes fine, so with Mamma not around I noticed other things. I had made connections to people and I had many nice memories in different parts of the city and I didn't want to give it up. So I stayed.'

'You never regretted it?' I took in the dirty grey city street. Decidedly less pretty than Stockholm.

'I remember when I saw you in Stockholm, last autumn when you came back, you looked wrong. If you ask me, I think London is your gravity, the place you are drawn back to. Lucas must be a wonderful person to have you this sad but I don't think you need him to feel at home in London. Mamma didn't make me a Stockholmare, I did it myself.'

I refused the sob and said, 'But you got Mamma back in the end.'

'Ah. Touché.'

Still, Pappa's words festered. This spring I had lived in real everyday London, not London the escape. And honestly even in misty morning greylight, London was the love of my life. The vastness, the speed, the smell of Chinatown dim sum. My family was here. Diwa, Tabatha. Luc. But after the devastation last night, and the punching where it hurts at work, I was now at a point where I had to ask myself if London really wanted me back.

I woke late the next morning with a hot sun in my face. My heart felt brittle, like the slightest pressure would crack it, so I decided to go out and not think about difficult things. I got ready slowly, applying my makeup with care. I ironed a t-shirt and shorts, toasted two slices of bread and chewed each bite the recommended thirty-two times. The ritualism of these tasks calmed me and when I left the flat, my breath reached all the way down to my stomach. This Sunday would just be me and London. I needed to separate the two, London wasn't Luc.

I walked south, in Camden lighting a cigarette which I enjoyed more than I should. Recently I had almost quit.

I saw many happy dogs in Regent's Park because it was Sunday. I strolled, too hot for anything faster. There were birds everywhere and some people were feeding them bread. The baby birds had almost grown out of their fluffy birthsuits. An old lady with an eyepatch. Kids with bluetooth speakers blasting scratchy music I didn't know. A thirty-something man in trainers and denim skirt. For every Londoner, three tourists in clothes too warm.

Mayfair looked beautiful and clean. My feet barely touched the pavement and I felt I could walk like this the whole day without getting tired. I lit another cigarette and decided I could smoke however many I wanted today because today was an exception.

On Piccadilly, I went into a bookshop. The old one with the wooden staircase. It was cool inside and smelled of printed paper and glue. I went upstairs and looked at the modern classics, then leafed through a beautiful copy of *The Mandarins*.

'One of my favourites,' a woman said behind me, a mouse-like member of staff with short hair.

'Oh is it. Yeah I haven't read it.'

'Then you must, trust me, Beauvoir is a god.' She said it was a roman à clef and spoke literature words at me for a few minutes that I didn't understand fully but her passion was infectious and I felt like we clicked, which there was no way of expressing without being weird except buying the book so I did. She put my book in one of the good bags, the paper one with twinned handles. She slid a bookmark in with the receipt.

'Enjoy,' she said.

'You too,' I said which was not it. Didn't matter, my mood too insouciant to upset. I gave five pounds to a homeless man who called me poppet and then I felt guilty for feeling good about giving the homeless man five pounds. Also I gave myself a forty-pound limit for the day because when I was in this mood receipts tended to pile up.

I smelled waffles as I walked past an ice cream parlour and the scent took me back to last summer. For the first time in months, I got London nostalgia. London acting his escapist self, a deviation from the mundane treadmill of worklife and laundry. Then I saw a pigeon investigating the edibility of a leftover Saturday night vomit. I kind of wanted to tell it to stop but who was I to judge.

In Covent Garden I called Diwa and asked her to come meet me and sat down outside a café to wait for her, a grape-fruit juice and a slice of chocolate cake in front of me on the table. Eight pounds left of my budget. It was hot, over thirty degrees, and my feet were thumping in my canvas shoes. Tourists everywhere, sweating but unswerving in their sight-seeing, patting themselves with paper napkins before each photo. Pitiable waiters running hot in their uniforms, the bouquets outside the florists melting.

When Diwa arrived she ordered a glass of white wine. She looked cool in her half-buttoned linen shirt, and I admired her matte forehead for a while. Then I told her what had happened with Luc that Friday. I was glad to be wearing sun-glasses because I directed my gaze at the building behind her.

It sounded even worse out loud than expected and I knew she would disapprove because I very much did so myself. Especially the part about me still counting his body as mine. 'Like how arrogant am I even.'

'That's hubris to be sure,' Diwa said, and she snickered which made me feel a little better.

'Shouldn't I be over him yet?'

'Yeah. You should.' Her words were soft, but I wanted her back to humorous because compassion made my throat feel like a bunch of guitar strings trying to untangle themselves. 'You will meet someone. If not Cameron, then someone else.'

'Yes I am sure I will eventually and I will fall in love and I will think that it was all for the best because if I was still with Luc I wouldn't have met so-and-so. But the thing is I don't want to.'

'Why?'

'Because it would mean that so-and-so is the real story. That Luc was just the lead-up, the backstory. Told in flashbacks not present tense.'

She took a long drink of wine. 'There's something wrong with you, you do know that?'

'Blame social media.' I waved an impatient hand. 'Owning your narrative and that. Excessive self-awareness.' I lit another cigarette to tranquillise the guitar strings and offered one to Diwa. She declined but I told her no don't worry today doesn't count it's an exception day. She said she'd never met me on an unexception day but still accepted the cigarette.

'Can I test a theory on you?' I said.

'Go ahead.'

I told her then how when Luc and I lived together, I had been unprepared for the kitchen sink aspect. That when moving to London I hadn't expected to become habituated to the city, desensitised to its charms.

'You only thought of that today?' She exhaled smoke through her nose in a superbly smug fashion. I would remember to try this myself when opportunity arose. 'I mean, you always had this London illusion. Ever since you were a kid.'

'You were my daydream sister.'

'Hah, flattery.'

'And Luc has been, I mean ever since I was eighteen and met him that one time, he's been like my image of, ah sorry, but romance.'

She slid her finger through the leftover chocolate frosting on my plate. 'That's a lot to live up to,' she said and put the frosted finger in her mouth.

'Yeah poor Luc.'

Diwa ordered two more glasses of wine and for a while we laughed at some of Luc's less romantic hero traits. His total lack of bravado. His inability to joke about sexism, like even a little. His way of sticking out his tongue when he concentrates.

'I think I'm getting better at realism though,' I said. 'So okay, London isn't an escape anymore but it's my home. And you're not my sister but you are family. And maybe Luc isn't the romantic hero but he could've been a decent fucking boyfriend.'

'You know what you need?'

'Don't say sex.'

'No Sami, you need a new escape city. If London is home now, you need a new London. Go for a cheap weekend somewhere, make some memories. Close by. Undamaged by you know mundanity.'

'Any suggestions?'

'Warsaw? Milan. Berlin. Madrid? Not Paris.'

'Definitely not Paris.'

•

You've done it now haven't you. I stare at the screen, no inkling what I have done wrong. Vicki is not in the office so I ask her to explain in an email. *Please tell me what you mean*, I ask. She doesn't reply.

I hear Preya's strained voice and I pray I'm not somehow the cause. I want someone to talk to, someone friendly, but the five colleagues currently in the room are not fans.

And I consider just leaving. Get in the elevator. Never come back. My legs tremble at the thought, ready for it. I want a cigarette. I bite the skin on my thumb and then I sit on my hands.

I can't work so I just wait. After twenty-two minutes of staring at my inbox, I text Luc.

Hey how are you doing over there. Busy day?

What's wrong? Something happen?

Um no, why?

Don't know you sound anxious.

I don't sound anything. This is a text. It doesn't vocalise.

Are you at work? Should I ring up?

No. But thank you.

I don't know what to do so I wait. Another hour I wait. With my pulse in my ears, I google dry things about the agency's code of conduct.

And then I am summoned.

Preya is behind her desk in un-ironed clothes and a braid coming lose. The room is efficient, grey folders, oak desk, framed photographs facing her. She says nothing but signals for me to close the door and sit down which I do. It seems unreasonable that I am made to do this, like I should object, although nothing has happened really. I wonder what she would say if I just walked out.

'Did you talk to Thom last week?' she asks simply, her voice normal now. Thom has Preya's role but in another team, floor eleven.

'Yes, I did.'

'For what reason?' Her voice is actually not normal at all. It's devoid, set for anti-communication. The voice version of a poker face.

'I had an idea for their campaign, a commercial idea not concerning our team really, I was just trying to help.' I speak fast and sound pleading and I am not proud of this.

The truth is I'm afraid of the woman in front of me. She has no shame and therefore she is unpredictable, in total power of the team because the rest of us abide by the societal shame guidelines. As a form of group dynamic auto-regulation. But Preya doesn't care.

'It sounds like self-interest to me, to get ahead at the expense of your colleagues.' She leans back in her ergonomic chair. 'I consider this undermining my leadership.'

I swallow. I wish I had some water. 'I am sorry you feel that way, though I'm honestly not invested enough in office politics to undermine anyone's leadership.'

'Oh yes that's right, you didn't have to get involved in office politics to get here.'

I say nothing.

'Are you telling me that speaking to Thom was an innocent act of altruism?'

'No. It wasn't.'

She is pleased now, enjoying the crescendo. 'So you did talk to him to undermine me.'

'No. It was self-preservation. To get out.' I hold on to my wrist. 'I really can't stand working for you Preya.'

She is taken aback but attacks on the rebound. 'Why bother then. If you want a promotion you can just nepotist-fuck that Tabatha girl again, can't you.'

'Wow,' I say. And I actually start to laugh, which is shocking, and loud. 'You're not allowed to say things like that I don't think.' And it is like a release. I don't want this job, there is no reason to be intimidated by this person. I have just been proving some kind of masochistic endurance point. And, sometimes, instinctual flight is just the thing.

323

'I'm sure you don't think it's your place to dictate what's allowed,' she says.

'No you're right. That would be HR? They're on the seventh?' I stand up and walk towards the door.

'Wait,' she says.

I don't turn around.

I get my bag and make my way to the elevator and I don't press seven, I press zero. I fix my hair in the mirror while humming some song and when the elevator doors slide open, I walk out the building to the sound of my trainers squeaking on the marble floor.

The sun beats me sweaty on Jubilee Bridge and the breeze is invigorating. In this glorious moment, I refuse to think about paying rent. Instead I consider throwing my office-appropriate shoes in the Thames as a symbol of liberation but that would not be responsible from an environmental standpoint so I don't.

I make it across the whole bridge before I pick up my phone, which is a decent show of restraint in my opinion.

I just up and left the office.

At once, Luc replies.

Wow. And then, *As in you ran out, for good?*

No I walked. But at a brisk pace I would say.

It takes two eternal minutes of me standing on the street staring at the screen before he replies.

I have to tell you something.

0 DAYS UNTIL

Lucas

I go straight to the kitchen and put six bottles of beer in Tabatha's fridge. I look around but there are only four people in the room, two of them staring at their phones. I don't know any of them. Hyena laughs spill out from the living room and it is humid and smells of warm bodies. I go to the window and open it and inhale deeply to calm my lungs and tell myself to slow down and when I turn around, Finn and Tabatha are in the room. They are standing by the kitchen counter, talking so low I can't hear them. Tabatha's shoulders are high.

'Hey,' I say and touch her elbow.

She slips a small jump. 'Oh, hi.'

'Been a while since I was here, hasn't it.'

'Well happy to have you now.' She gives me a short hug.

'Something wrong?' I ask.

'No no, course not,' Tabatha says.

'Taba's annoyed I brought Cameron,' says Finn and waves a hand towards the balcony. I turn to look and there she is.

I knew Sam would be here but that is not the same as actually seeing it. I zone in on her, a magnetic black hole for my senses.

I take a step forward but stop when I register the whole scene. She is on the balcony talking to a man, her back turned so I can only see his face. He looks concerned, eyebrows drawn tight, maybe a bit defensive with his arms crossed. I want to delete him.

Sam must be smoking because grey puffs of mist float between them. Although warm outside she looks cold in her dress with her naked arms. I haven't seen her since our fall-out in her flat last week.

'Cameron?' I say. And it is so unexpected he is here I consider just abandoning the apartment.

'Giulia's friend. They've been on a few dates,' Finn says in his usual unflustered manner. 'Sorry I thought you knew this?'

'Yeah I knew she saw someone a couple of times. Just not that he would be here.'

'Does it bother you?'

'A bit awkward I'd say.' I clear my throat and wish I had something in my hands. I thought Sam had ended things with Cameron but apparently not since he is now here on this balcony.

Tabatha tells me not to worry and squeezes my shoulder.

'Well personally I'm rooting for them. They're good together, like simple fun,' Finn says and just this once I want to tell him to please shut up.

'Finn. Can you not share Sam's personal things with everyone mate,' Tabatha says.

'Oh calm down. Just making an observation.'

'Why would you bring him here though. It's kind of insensitive? To everyone?' A minute nod towards me which I am not supposed to see but I do.

Finn says, 'He's Giulia's best friend, we're all in the same crowd aren't we. We should get used to seeing him around.'

'Still.' She sighs. 'I'm slightly livid.'

'Oh what else is new.'

Not even Tabatha can argue with that and Finn affectionately pats her hair, which does not seem to make her any less livid. I am dying to change the subject. Talking about Sam's love life while seeing it unfold in real time, albeit on mute, is like trying to keep a straight face while being repeatedly stabbed with many small knives. I had charged into this flat with such all-consuming energy, only to be stopped dead. Now the energy is trapped in there, pressurising. I shift my weight from heel to heel. This is all wrong.

Tabatha asks Finn about some girl I don't know, someone they both find annoying, and I hope they can't tell I am agitated. I go to the fridge and grab one of the beers I just put in. Tabatha hands me an opener. I want to put the cold damp bottle to my face but that would be dramatic. Instead I take a swig and hold the bottle so tight my hand goes numb. I turn my back on the balcony.

•

On Monday when Sam texted me about quitting her job, I had replied that there was something I should tell her. This something happened when I showed up unannounced at Dad's the day before. He opened the door looking surprised, as if expecting a delivery and there I was instead.

'Oh, hey, Luke. I didn't, I mean did we have plans today?' He was wearing a dark green sweater and he looked well, durable.

'No, don't worry we didn't have plans, just wanted to see you. Are you busy?' I should have called because I'd be crushed if he turned me away now, still shaken after the incident in Sam's flat, and in need of something stable to hold on to. Dad might be lacking in certain areas but stability was not it.

'No no, come in.' He led me through the hallway. 'So how are you? Any news?' He gestured to sit at the kitchen island before going over to the sink.

'Dad, what do you think of Gabrielle?'

'Oh.' He turned to me and grabbed his chin and froze like that. 'Well. I only ever met her at the hospital. We didn't talk very much.'

'Still. I'd like to know.' This insistence was new terrain for us and the tension came like a clap.

'Fair enough,' he said and filled the kettle, not looking at me, his motions slow and deliberate. 'I thought she was polite. And caring. And she appears to be very capable.'

'She is that.'

'She seems fine to me. Why, are you two thinking of moving in together?' He switched the kettle on and leaned stiff against the counter. 'I don't have anything bad to say, if that's what you're asking?' He swayed from foot to foot. 'Unless you want me to say something bad?'

'God no, of course not,' I said and his face looked so puzzled, so eager to please I both ached and wanted to laugh which would be insanely inappropriate. 'I'm glad you like her. And yes she has asked me to move in, but we haven't decided on anything yet.'

'So?'

'So I guess I wanted your advice.'

He placed two ceramic mugs on the counter and dropped an Earl Grey tea bag in each. 'Alright. But Luke I am not very good at this type of thing, you know that.'

'Well you're the one parent I got so you'll have to do.'

He nodded. 'Go ahead then.'

'So lately I've been thinking about what you said at Christmas.'

'What, you mean about Mum?'

'Yeah.'

He sighed and said, 'Hang on,' and went to the living room, coming back with a bottle of whiskey. He poured us a large serving each, then drank.

I was not at all in the mood for whiskey but I tasted a small mouthful and the burn was somehow comforting in its pure physicality. 'Remember we talked about where you picture her being, you know, since she died,' I said.

'Yes.'

'You said she's not a hundred percent dead because you still know her opinion on things and you let her kind of decide stuff for you.'

'It's silly I know.' He moved back against the counter again, whiskey in hand, tea abandoned.

'No it's not that silly. I mean it is, but I like the idea still. So I thought about Gabrielle.'

'And?'

'And I don't think that I want her to do that. Make decisions for me. Like when I'm old and my wife dies, ah sorry don't mean that you're old,' I interrupted myself but he just waved to continue, 'okay so when I'm old and my wife dies I don't want the person I know best in the world, the person I keep alive by knowing her so well, I don't want that to be Gabrielle.'

'Oh. I see.' He laughed, a bit shocked, and I was glad to amuse him.

'I think my decision-making is already suffering. With her.'

'Sounds like you don't need my advice then.' He brought his whiskey to the kitchen island and leaned forward on his elbows. I mimicked his posture. It was nice. Just talking, drinking, the tension slowly ebbing. And now sharing this with him he actually seemed okay with it. Keen even.

'Well the thing is, there's another person.'

'Samanta?' he asked.

'Sam yes.' And I told him that although she was difficult to be sure, and actually fairly exhausting a lot of the time, I still felt my decision-making was better with her. He hmmed and asked why we had broken up in that case.

'There were many reasons really. The main one that she doesn't want kids.'

'As in, not ever?'

I nodded.

'That's a tough one. Because you do?'

'I don't know, I think so.' The fridge started humming and I got pleasure out of recognising the sound. Small things like that, every time I visited. I told him I had always pictured having a family one day. All the standard things, a house, a wife, children, a car. 'But now when I picture my life I see Sam. Not the wife with the house and the car.'

What I did picture was a flat in London on a street with trees. A big kitchen, Sam jumped up on the counter with a glass of wine talking about nothing while I cooked. Maybe a dog, that I would walk and Sam would wrestle. As if she had pushed the wife and car image out.

Dad lifted the whiskey bottle and said, 'Should we sit down?' He chose the living room armchair and I sat on the sofa while he refilled our glasses. Then he nodded. 'I'm going to be honest with you Luke.' He placed his hands on his knees. 'You are the most important thing to me and it's absolutely true what they say about the love for a child.' He waved his hand, 'Now before you get embarrassed and tell me to stop I want to say this so please humour me.'

I stayed silent, no idea where this was going.

'I couldn't feel luckier to have you, especially now that Mum is gone,' he said. 'But in complete honesty, back before we had you, if your mother had said to choose between her and children, I would've chosen her in a heart-beat. No question.'

'Jesus, cheers Dad,' I said and laughed a little, my feelings not one bit hurt.

When I left Dad's, I went straight to Gabrielle's flat. We talked a while in the kitchen before I said, 'I think moving in together isn't such a good idea.' She went to the bedroom then and I followed and she started making the bed with clean sheets, me standing by the door. With her back to me she ferociously stuffed the duvet into its cover and said some-thing about not seeing the point of dating without a plan for the future and I said, yes I agree, and at that moment she knew I was breaking up with her. She had just flapped the duvet like a cape across the bed. She froze and the fabric floated slowly downwards through air. It was beautiful to look at and my heart ached for her. I wanted to put my arms around her but I didn't.

'So you are saying that you don't want to move in together, and that you agree there's no point in dating if we won't.'

'Yes.'

And I listened to her talk. Her back still towards me, still making the bed, she somehow reasoned until this con-versation turned from being my decision to a mutual deci-sion to really actually her decision. It was only decent to let her have this breakup if she wanted it. To later tell the story as she wished. She was a proud person and I didn't want to injure her.

By the time I left her flat, she had adopted a pitying tone of voice which I thought was a bit much but didn't have any real reason to object to. We were over after all.

The next day, Sam texted saying she had quit her job.

I have to tell you something, I replied. *Gabrielle and I broke up.*

Quiet for a minute or two but I saw the dots indicating she was typing, deleting, typing, deleting.

Are you okay? she asked finally.

I feel bad for saying it but I'm very okay.

Savage.

When I came home that night I kept a close eye on spotify searching for clues to her mood through her song choices. I didn't play a single song, just to make sure. She didn't either. Spotify stalemate.

•

That was six days ago and now it is almost midnight and I still haven't spoken to Sam. I was in the living room when she and Cameron came in from the balcony and I saw her go with Tabatha to a bedroom. They are still talking I think. I don't want to slow my brain with alcohol but I sure could do with the fortitude.

This is a large flat by London standards and yet it is crowded, shrill laughs dropping like offkey piano notes over the constant hum of voices. Everyone appears to be just slightly on edge. I find Henry on the balcony.

'So, singledom. Any regrets?' he asks.

'Zero.'

'Good. It was the right decision.'

'I think so.'

He smokes and we talk about pointless things and juvenile memories and it is a much-needed distraction from the fact that I still haven't spoken to Sam, not since the fight in her flat. I am dying to talk and my nerves are unreasonable because I know her better than Henry even. Better than Dad even. She, more than anyone, is my next of kin.

After three cigarettes back to back, Henry ushers me inside. I peer into the living room and Sam is now on the sofa talking to four people while looking at her phone. Cameron is in the kitchen, I can hear him laughing with Giulia and Finn. This is the opposite of how I had pictured tonight going. Intimately talking to Sam in low voices in a quiet room, heads almost touching, small laughs. Instead there are hysterical people and loud music and I have no way to gauge what she wants, how she feels. I want her to come over, say something. But she already has, in her flat, her legs across my knees. If I want something to happen, I have to do the something.

She doesn't notice me until I stand right in front of her.

'Hello you,' I say.

She scans my face for a second. 'If you're here to ask me to dance, the answer is no.' She grins and I am flying.

'A bit presumptuous,' I say and clear my throat.

'It's like your party trick at this point.'

'So. That was Cameron.'

'That was Cameron.' She folds her arms and raises her eyebrow. The other four people are likely listening but I extremely don't care.

'Are you seeing him?'

'No.'

'Good.'

'Why?'

'Well for one have you seen the size of him. Would worry he'd permanently deform you.'

She clicks her tongue. 'Kind of farfetched. Humans don't deform.'

'Stranger things,' I say. And I think that this right here is my natural state, scoundrel smiling with Sam about nothing really. 'So it looked a bit intense there, out on the balcony.'

'Yeah,' she says, 'maybe a bit. You know me I tend to blurt things and then there's a lot of cleanup.'

'What was the blurt part?'

'The reason I won't date him.'

'Which is?'

'That I am in love with someone else.'

I die.

'Poor Cameron,' I say.

'Very poor.'

'Sam?'

'Yeah.'

I hold out my hand. 'Do you want to get out of here?'

•

She tells the taxi driver to go towards central. I click on my seatbelt and she puts an earbud in my ear, the movement smooth and natural. She plays Lou Reed. 'Perfect Day'. I relax against the seat and turn towards her and although we are not touching it is like we are linked. Particles sticking together by no other bond than vibrating on the same frequency.

'I'm a bad influence, having you run from unpleasant parties,' she says.

'I don't mind the running, as long as I can come with.'

'But, we wouldn't want you catching pneumonia.'

'Funny.' I consider touching her but instead I ask, 'So, where do you want to go?'

'Anywhere?'

'Sure.'

'Italy even?'

'Sure.'

She leans forward to tell the driver she has changed her mind, and gives him her home address.

'This right here, is a bad idea,' she says to me but she's smirking.

'I don't think so.'

'We know so. We've already tried it.' Her naked legs look translucent in the blue lit car.

'We had our good moments,' I say.

'Yes true. But that was before the no kids policy.' Her hands are motionless on her thighs. I wonder if the driver is listening.

'I have kind of decided that children aren't a requirement right now.' I shrug in a way I hope conveys certainty.

'Yeah but one day maybe.'

'Maybe. Though I mean, by that time you could be dead already.'

'Huh. And you would yourself have kids at that ripe old age?'

'You know, I'm actually a man. None of that pregnancy deadline stuff you women stress about.'

'Another bad deal for womanhood.' She holds up her hands despairingly.

We are quiet for a moment and I look at the cars going by. It is dark outside and the lights blur to neon fuzz. Although late it's still warm, humid. And I am overwhelmed by how surreal it is that none of this feels surreal.

'So,' she says. 'You sure about this, mister?'

'Yes. I think so. Are you?'

'It's just, I'm very scared of hurting you again.'

'Yeah me as well.'

'This could be a big mistake,' she says. 'I mean it probably is. We could wake up in two years' time all miserable, and regret spending another two miserable years together even though history had warned us about the certain misery ahead.' She looks at me, a little wild. Searching for reassurance I can't give her because of course she is right.

'But even if certain misery ahead,' I say, 'I'd rather have two miserable years with you than two okay years without.'

She nods. 'Ditto.'

And she clicks off her seatbelt and gets on top of me and when she kisses me she tastes like Sam and I am finally allowed to admit how much I want her.

DAY 1

Sam

'Charlie Chaplin,' I say. We are sitting on my windowsill and I open the window so we can dangle a foot in the cooling night air. It is 2am and I am wide awake.

'What about him?' Luc asks. I stretch a leg across his knee. He strokes my calf absentmindedly and my scalp goosebumps.

'He had a kid when he was seventy-three,' I say.

'Seriously?'

'Yes.'

He seems to mull this over and then he says, 'Did you google old fathers?'

'I did yeah.'

'Jesus Sam.' The wind rustles in the tree outside and there is a pigeon cooing somewhere in the distance. 'I'm fairly sure I don't share that many similarities with Charlie Chaplin though. Likely I take more after my dad in that sense.'

'How so?' I ask because he's lost me.

'Know what he said to me the other day? That if Mum had asked to choose between her and having children he would've picked her, no questions asked.'

I look at him. He is fixed on me, with a face free from care, a smile on half his mouth.

'That's sweet,' I say. 'Hadn't pegged him as a romantic.'

'Me neither.' A car goes by outside, playing bedroom RnB through rolled-down windows. 'I'm sort of excited for you to meet. He wouldn't say it but I can tell he's quite curious by now.'

'Let's have him over,' I say and Luc nods. His hand is warm on my leg. So heavy it seems unlikely to ever move. And in this specific moment, I am convinced it never will.

'Speaking of seniors,' I say and yawn. 'I wanted to send you a Bruce Willis text the other night but I couldn't come up with a movie so I cheated and googled it and seems like he hasn't made any more.'

'Oh really.'

'I think we've officially run out.'

He squints and says, 'Start over? Julia Roberts?'

'Sure okay, I'll go first.' I pause and then I say, 'Runaway Bride,' and he grins and says, 'Closer.'

Acknowledgements

Thank you to my brilliantly sharp (and funny) agent Peter Straus for believing in my work, as well as everyone at RCW Literary Agency, not least Lena Mistry, Stephen Edwards, Katharina Volckmer, and Tristan Kendrick.

Thank you to my editor Jo Dingley. Not only have her thoughtful suggestions shaped this novel into a much stronger version of itself, but her kindness has made the publishing process a joy. I have valued our conversations immensely. Thank you to everyone at Sceptre for their hard work and enthusiasm, especially Kim Nyamhondera, Helen Flood, Fede Andornino, Nico Parfitt, and the wonderful Sarah Christie.

Thank you to my foreign publishers, editors, and translators for early support and for making my work shine in their languages.

Thank you to Bronagh Monahan, not just for being a smashing manager, but a great friend.

I owe thanks to my mentor Rowan Hisayo Buchanan for her high-calibre observations and friendship. I owe apologies for showing her the very first newborn draft of this novel, it must have been rough on the eyes.

The book industry has proven to be a very welcoming place. Thank you to every author, editor, and agent who has given me advice. Especially Molly Aitken who has read, and reread, this novel with such honesty and generosity. I thank Molly for telling me when it sings, but equally for pointing out when she's bored, as a true friend should. Thank you to Elaine Feeney for championing this novel, and for reassurance whenever I've needed to vent (my apologies for excessive use of caps). I also thank Will Dean for reading this novel when it was still just a young short story, and for building my confidence by telling me I have what it takes to 'write whatever the hell you like'. For other words of advice I thank Darley Anderson, Kimberley Atkins, Sam Copeland, and Ailah Ahmed (thanks to the PublisHer mentorship scheme).

Thank you to brilliant Faye Orlove for the ridiculously hot cover illustration, and to everyone who has produced, distributed, recommended, or sold this novel. For research assistance I thank Jas Tang and Art Gower, as well as my Lebanese and Romanian followers.

To all my followers, subscribers, and readers, my heartfelt gratitude for the confidence and practical means to pursue a creative life.

Thank you to friends, relatives, and in-laws for much-needed breaks from the writing bubble. And as always, I am thankful to my family: my siblings and grandmother, and especially my parents, for telling me I can do whatever I damn well please with my life, and for somehow making me believe them.

Finally, I thank you David. There is no way to condense your importance to my work and my life on this page, so I won't try. Whatever I write, I write for you.